Wiijiwaaganag

Makwa Enewed is an imprint of the American Indian Studies Series, at Michigan State University Press.

Gordon Henry, *Series Editor*

Makwa Enewed stands dedicated to books that encompass the varied views and perspectives of people working in American Indian communities. In that light, books published under the Makwa Enewed imprint rely less on formal academic critique, argument, methodology, and research conventions and more on experientially grounded views and perspectives on issues, activities, and developments in Indian Country.

While work published in Makwa Enewed may resound with certain personal, speculative, conversational, political, and/or social concerns of individuals and groups of individual American Indian people, in a larger sense such concerns and their delivery reflect the import, strength, uniqueness, and potential viability of the imprint.

The imprint will gather its strength from the voices of tribal leaders, community activists, and socially engaged Native people. Thus, each publication under the Makwa Enewed imprint will call forth from tribally based people and places, reminding readers of the varied beliefs and pressing interests of American Indian tribal people and communities.

Wiijiwaaganag

More Than Brothers

Peter Razor

Makwa Enewed

East Lansing, MI

The publisher gratefully acknowledges Margaret O'Donnell Noodin's developmental editing of the manuscript and her work, with Michael Zimmerman Jr., to ensure the accuracy of the Ojibwemowin.

⊚ The paper used in this publication meets the minimum requirements of ANSI/NISO Z39.48-1992 (R 1997) (Permanence of Paper).

Makwa Enewed
Michigan State University Press
East Lansing, Michigan 48823-5245

LIBRARY OF CONGRESS CATALOGING-IN-PUBLICATION DATA
Names: Razor, Peter, author.
Title: Wiijiwaaganag : more than brothers / Peter Razor.
Description: First edition. | East Lansing, Michigan : Makwa Enewed, [2023]
Identifiers: LCCN 2022017734 | ISBN 978-1-93806-522-4 (paperback) |
ISBN 978-1-93806-523-1 (pdf) | ISBN 978-1-93806-524-8 (epub) | ISBN 978-1-93806-525-5 (kindle)
Subjects: CYAC: Off-reservation boarding schools—Fiction. | Schools—Fiction. |
Ojibwa Indians—Fiction. | Indians of North America—Fiction. |
Minnesota—History—19th century—Fiction. | LCGFT: Historical fiction. | Novels.
Classification: LCC PZ7.1.R3955 Wi 2023 | DDC [Fic]—dc23
LC record available at https://lccn.loc.gov/2022017734

Cover art and design by Erin Kirk

Visit Michigan State University Press at *www.msupress.org*

James "Peter" Razor, who was also known as Gashkibaajiganinini Aazhegiiwe-Ogichidaa, left this world May 30, 2022, at the age of ninety-three. This is his story of the way things might have been. It was completed with the love and support of his entire family.

Preface

Abuse of students at American Indian boarding schools is widely known but not easily documented. In these schools, Indigenous students were forced to learn English and prevented from speaking their own languages. Students were often given Christian names or names that were English versions of their Indigenous names. Corporal punishment took place in various forms from whipping to isolation according to the imagination of staff. Some abuse undoubtedly occurred beneath the awareness or even concern of staff at headmaster level. Younger students often endured more physical punishments because they were less able to defend themselves; older students were restricted from pleasant events or given additional tasks as punishment. In 1891, the United States mandated that Indigenous children attend school. The government regulated the minimum years of school attendance, but qualified students, most likely with parental influence, could study beyond the required age.

In this story, one small school grapples with problems facing the headmaster's family and the surrounding communities. The Anishinaabe, who speak Ojibwemowin, are witnessing changes that threaten their way of life and their children's future. Immigrants, settlers, traders, and government agents are all trying to survive, not always realizing, or caring, about the impact they have on others. After several brutal incidents, the headmaster is forced to rethink disciplinary codes for his school and eventually re-examine many aspects of life in the woodlands of the Great Lakes and the new United States.

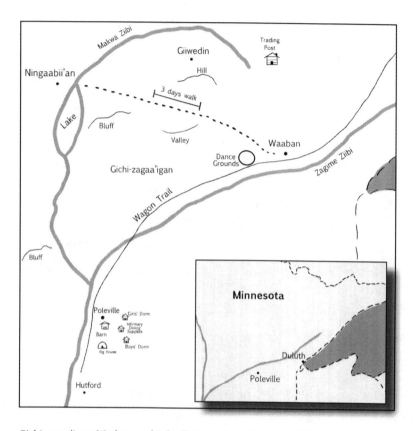

Gichi-zagaa'igan, Waaban, and Poleville in northern Minnesota (Shannon Noori).

Chapter One

Niizh Eshkanag outgrew his childhood name when he used two deer horn tines, one per hand, to defend himself against a threatening dog during rice celebration at the end of last summer. After that his full name was Niizh Eshkanag, which means "two horns" in Ojibwemowin, but most people called him Niizh.

Niizh Eshkanag lived with his family on Gichi-zaaga'igan in northern Minnesota. On US maps, the reservation was called Big Lake. Born in 1878, Niizh Eshkanag was part of the first generation of Anishinaabe required to attend boarding school. It wasn't a family choice, Congress made it the law in 1891—go willingly to school or be taken to school. Whether or not parents considered school beneficial for their children varied according to family perspective, but, for many families, the months of forced separation left them feeling empty amid an already fading culture. This was definitely the case for Niizh Eshkanag and his parents.

Born in Iskigamizige-giizis, the month of maple sap gathering, Niizh Eshkanag counted his thirteenth winter during his third year attending Yardley Indian Boarding School, 120 miles west of Gichi-zaaga'igan. Slender, neither tall nor short, and quietly thoughtful, he joined his peers in conversation or activities that piqued his interest. He excelled academically despite occasional friction with staff and the stress of being deprived contact with his family during long winters.

Yardley Indian Boarding School was far enough west of Gichi-zaaga'igan that Niizh Eshkanag's father, Migizi, and mother, Bizaan, found it impossible to visit him during the school term. Midspring with the school term winding down, the family planned to change that circumstance in advance of fall enrollment. It wasn't only their son's long isolation from home and the forced suppression of Indian language and religion, they were worried about the stories Niizh Eshkanag brought home from Yardley describing verbal abuse and unreasonable physical punishment.

The future of their traditional Anishinaabe ways seemed in jeopardy at Yardley, and Niizh Eshkanag agreed with his parents that what they heard was taught in the classroom at the day school closer to home—about the rights and duties of all people—seemed to leave a door partially open to self-expression and to preservation of the general culture. Bizaan felt it would be better to live in Waaban, the village on the east side of the reservation near the day school where parents could bring students themselves and meet school staff.

Niizh Eshkanag knew his parents considered a move carefully. Migizi was a tribal elder, and he assisted Ogimaa Niigaan in dealings with Indian agents who came to Ningaabii'an, the western village where they currently spent most of the year. When necessary, Migizi met with deputies from Poleville, the closest immigrant settlement. In those meetings, he was a moderating voice, placating anger and supporting what tribal benefits could be achieved within government regulation.

Bizaan also had an important role in the community. She was a tall sturdy no-nonsense woman, but on occasion, she shared her humor at council meetings. She might look up at the smoke hole, corner her eyes at a council member, and chastise him with a tongue-in-cheek smile. Members of the village council never admitted whether they sought more her humor or advice. When she strode about the village, youth gave way to her, if only to hear her soft voice sharing wisdom. They were careful not to offend her.

About the time Bizaan and Migizi began formulating plans to move, another family four hundred miles south and east of Ningaabii'an, was also thinking about the future of one of their own who would soon be in need of a new home.

Roger Poznanski, age thirteen, attended school on Jones Island in the Bay of Milwaukee, where his father was one of the many fishermen who caught; cleaned; and sold trout, sturgeon, and cisco while his mother wove fishing nets and hammocks to sell on the island and in the city growing along the coastline of Lake Michigan. Roger was slender, neither short nor tall, and quietly thoughtful. He heard the adults laugh and say, "many fish to make the purse heavy, and many children to make the purse light," which seemed true to Roger as he came home after school to work alongside his father. But lately his father had been too tired to work, coughing with what his mother called "the consumption." As they grew paler, he worried about his parents and his own future. Despite the dark cloud surrounding him, he excelled in school and dreamed of finding part-time work to help his family.

Listening often at the fringes of adult conversation, Roger would focus intently when his future was discussed, often in connection to some faraway place in a boundless forest teeming with Indians. With side-glances and some fidgeting, Roger tried to shield his own anxiety, but he couldn't avoid thinking: *Indians live in endless forests way up there so far away. Not much good about Indians in the papers.*

When students left Yardley Indian Boarding School for the summer, many would miss the regular meals and some of the other comforts, but most including Niizh Eshkanag and his cousin Giigoo, who was also from Gichi-zaaga'igan, wholeheartedly welcomed school vacation. They were part of the chaos flaunted amid admonishing staff—the shackles of regimen were slipping off!

"Nigiiwemin," Niizh Eshkanag whispered as they watched wagons and stagecoaches assembling near the administration building as the sun was just beginning to rise. He looked at Giigoo to confirm he had heard him say "we're going home" in Ojibwemowin. Giigoo's face reflected uncertainty as he glanced about to see if staff heard their conversation, then crossed an index finger on his lips, and told Niizh Eshkanag to whisper so the staff would not get angry, "Gaaskanazon. Gego nishki'aaken."

"Nahaaw." Niizh Eshkanag replied and looked down to shield his comment about how most of the workers didn't care for Ojibwemowin and simply wanted no talking at all. "Gaawiin obamendanziinaawaa aanind enokiijig miinawaa gaawiin waa-bizindoosinowangwaa."

Giigoo nodded and told Niizh Eshkanag one of the men standing near the wagons was holding the number showing he was headed to Big Lake. "A'aw inini ayaan nindasigibii'iganaan, wii-izhaad Gichi-zagaa'igan."

As he ran to the wagon, Niizh Eshkanag looked back at the administration building and thought with a pang of doubt—*we are really going home, but after months without our families, will we be strangers in our own homes? Endaso-biboon naasaab mii dash bebakaan.... It's the same every year, yet different.*

Niizh Eshkanag had a natural curiosity, found the written word exciting, and he read beyond his studies, exposing mysteries hidden in books.

Giigoo, had seen twelve winters and was playful, but when challenged could turn serious. He did not find school overly interesting, but seeing government agents move in and out of his village and at school provided him insight to the future.

Niizh Eshkanag and Giigoo were in the wagon with other students as it rumbled off the school grounds, and the day began. They were quiet and pensive until the wagon cleared all aspects of Yardley including crop acreage. Their conversation was in English with occasional hushed whispers in Ojibwemowin.

"Some parents move while we're in school." Niizh Eshkanag said in English, frowning at the teamster's back.

"Aangodinong ogitiziiman nibobaniin miinawaa gaawiin gikendanzinig." Giigoo blurted Ojibwemowin because this was also true—sometimes a parent died and no one told the students while they were away.

"I heard that!" the teamster yelled over his shoulder. "That's enough Injun talk. You're supposed to get civilized." He reined the horses to a stop, and spun around in his seat, glaring. "You all know English. Use it!" Nearest the teamster, Giigoo leaned away from him in fright and jumped out of the wagon uncertain what to do.

Niizh Eshkanag reached out to help Giigoo back into the wagon, assuring his cousin the driver wouldn't hurt him, "Boozin. Gaawiin giwii-wiisagibizhigosii."

"Okay," the teamster said. "No more Injun talk. When you get home, use English. Try to sound intelligent." All of the students were quiet, but the two boys had dark thoughts racing through their minds in Ojibwemowin.

The wagon went to a stage connection then to a settlement where it changed direction after dropping Niizh Eshkanag, Giigoo, and another boy off. The three boys then traveled by tribal wagon to Ningaabii'an, the western village of the Gichi-zaaga'igan reservation on the Makwa River.

With little comment, three students headed home, sighing with relief, exchanging lethargic parting waves.

It was long after noon when Niizh Eshkanag reached the entrance of his family lodge and called softly to his mother and "Ninga, Noos, I'm home. Ind'ayaa." The flap over the low entrance moved, and Niizh Eshkanag had time for a short greeting before being engulfed in a warm embrace. "Oomph! Ninga! Geyaabi gimashkawiz." Commenting on her strength, he tried to smile, but he struggled against the conflict of school and home—his home at school and his home in Ningaabii'an. He faced his father, Migizi, and was immediately and silently drawn into another warm embrace.

Bizaan gently tapped Niizh Eshkanag's shoulder and asked if he was tired after travelling, "Ishkwa bimi-ayaayan, gid'ayekoz ina?"

"Enh." Niizh Eshkanag whispered through a fading smile. He glanced down on his sleep place, which seemed untouched since before school. With a sigh-laden murmur, he thought—*indayaa omaa gegapii, home at last.* He lay facing the wall and slept.

After a time, Bizaan touched Niizh Eshkanag's head to announce they would eat and then go visiting, "Niizh, wiisinidaa mii dash mawidishiweyang."

After a quick meal of rabbit stew made by his mother, Niizh Eshkanag and his parents visited Giigoo's family: his father, Zhaabiiwose and mother Boonikiiyaashikwe who was Bizaan's sister. While the elders talked, Niizh and Giigoo walked briefly outside getting reacquainted with neighbors and other youth.

When they returned home that night, school seemed a distant memory. Niizh Eshkanag doffed his school clothes, handed them to his mother and watched her bundle them to be sent back to Yardley.

"Gaawiin gida-biizikaanziinan onowe," Bizaan said, knowing they would not fit him in the fall. She pointed at a tag inside the shirt and asked if the letters "T-o-m" written there were his English name, "Zhaaganaash-izhinikaazowin ina?"

Niizh Eshkanag smiled as he looked where his mother pointed, then up toward his father, joking that it was of course his name because if the tag read M-i-g-i-z-i, the shirt would be twice his size. "Enh, giishpin Migizi ozhibii'igaadeg miidash awashime michaamigag." All three chuckled, Niizh Eshkanag's ending with a yawn.

Niizh Eshkanag lay between ration-issued blankets, and looked up at his smiling mother. Attempting to initiate conversation, he murmured unintelligibly and slept.

On the same day in Milwaukee, David Poznanski succumbed to tuberculosis and was interred in the late afternoon, with the surviving family departing the cemetery under darkening skies and a threat of rain.

Appearing pale beyond the funeral ordeal, occasionally turning aside to cough, his widow, Susan, sobbed while leaning on her son Roger's shoulder. Susan's sister, Beth, and her brother-in-law, Steve Demski, stood beside her.

"Come," Beth said, motioning toward a carriage. She gripped Susan's arm while shielding them both with an umbrella against the sudden drizzle.

Silently contemplating death, Roger frowned as he watched his mother being helped into the carriage.

Steve gently nudged Roger toward the carriage. "You'll both have supper and stay at our place tonight. Bill Stacy, remember him? He'll be coming for supper too."

Susan moaned as a blanket was adjusted over her lap, "Roger needs me now more than ever, but I'm more burden than help. She fiddled with her robe while gazing askance.

Beth shook her head. "Everything will be just fine, you'll see. For the present, Steve and I will take care of everything." Steve reined the horse into a side street.

Susan glanced at Roger while addressing Beth, "Have you received word from Uncle Elias?"

"Not yet, but I know it'll be all right. In the meantime, you're staying with us until you're better."

Guests for supper that night at Steve and Beth Demski's home were Roger, his mother, Grandmother Demski, and Bill Stacy. Roger was quiet, courteous and ate little, but listened to conversation, often with a lowered head and shifting feet.

"I hope Roger enjoys living with Uncle Elias," Beth said. Roger stiffened, stared at his shoes.

"If Elias and Helen agree, that is," Grandma Demski declared nodding toward Roger.

"Do I hafta live with Uncle Elias?" Roger said, sitting erect, frowning. Glancing quickly at Beth then at Grandma Demski, he muttered, "It's so far, and I haven't ever met him."

Steve smiled at Roger. "I hope you use better English than that in school." He faced the others. "Though they haven't answered our letter yet, I know they will."

"My biggest worry is Helen," Beth continued. "I know she still grieves for Donald."

"Sad," Susan added. "Been two years nearly to the week."

"They'd be the same age, Donald and Roger," Grandma Demski said. "Elias would gladly take Roger, but Helen will be the one to turn him out or keep him. Roger could take Donald's place, be more son than nephew . . . or a constant reminder of death."

"Disease also killed many Indians in the region; some were Elias's students," Beth added. "Unfortunately, Helen blames the Indians for Donald's death."

"White man's disease killed the Indians, Donald, too," Steve declared. "And who can say how this epidemic started. It could become as bad as the the Black Plague in Europe that killed so many people during the fourteenth century!"

Later, in the parlor, sipping tea, Beth leaned forward on her chair and motioned with an upturned palm toward Susan. "You're in no condition to care for Roger, even if he is maturing." Susan clasped her hands and twisted the wedding ring on her finger. "It wouldn't be proper holding him back when he does so well in school."

Roger spoke up, "I can do odd jobs. Do I have to go so far away? Besides, who knows what the Indians might do to me when I'm not looking." He waved an arm over his head.

Steve shrugged. "Oh, I don't know. There's bad apples in any basket. You must have troublesome students in school."

"They're not Injuns," Roger mumbled.

"My point exactly!" Steve said. "You have a name for a bad white person, but Indians are bad simply because they're Indian." Roger snapped his head to stare out the window and did not respond.

Beth patted Roger's shoulder. "You could have a home with us, but we can't give you the opportunities available with Elias. And me with child too." She looked about the room with a deep sigh then faced Roger. "If worse happens, and you have no home, the county might take you with no good to come of that!" Roger frowned biting at his lower lip.

"Sounds ominous," Steve said. "If he doesn't go to Elias, I mean." He faced Roger. "Anyway, we have the summer to think about it. If it seems not to work out, come back and live with us. Otherwise," Steve gazed pleasantly at Roger, "you will begin the fall term in the north woods, and likely have very exciting experiences." He smiled broadly and sharply pointed northwest.

"Don't know about that," Roger said, but a failed smile tugged at his lips.

After a brief silence, Roger glanced out the window, then straightened in his chair facing the others. "It wouldn't be fair taking food from your baby," he said. "I'll go." He sagged lower in his chair gazing at his lap.

The morning after arriving home in Ningaabii'an, Niizh Eshkanag woke up to the smell of stew cooking over an outside fire. Beside him lay a fresh breechcloth of trade wool, deerskin leggings, doeskin shirt, and new buckskin moccasins. He dressed and crawled out the low door to stand near the fire with his mother.

She commented on his deep sleep which had helped him forget the winter, "Onizhishin gii-minogwaam ji-waniikenindaman gaa-biboong." Then she scanned her son's clothes, happy to see the old Niizh Eshkanag. "Gete-Niizh niwaabamaa ge-biizikaman oshki-biizikiganan."

Niizh Eshkanag knew his mother was also learning English so he told her in the language from school, "It feels strange . . . good, I mean, without matrons waking us, sometimes yelling. Warm wash water at school was good, but I like home better. This is my real home . . . omaa endaayang."

Bizaan smoothed Niizh Eshkanag's disheveled hair and tended the fire where the stew warmed over the coals.

Niizh Eshkanag motioned he was leaving and said, "Inga-maajaa. I'll be back to eat after I see if cousin Giigoo is awake." He disappeared around the lodge and seeing Giigoo, waved to get his attention. Ginoozhe, an older boy, approached Niizh Eshkanag from another direction, and Niizh retreated, waving goodbye to Giigoo, who also turned away when seeing Ginoozhe.

In the past, Ginoozhe had not been violent, but recently had become more sarcastic to younger boys causing them much discomfort.

One evening, a few days later, Bizaan and Migizi quietly discussed the pros and cons of boarding school. Niizh listened from where he sat on his bed space near the outside wall.

"Gaawiin indandawendaan wii-wiisagendami'aawaad," Bizaan insisted her son should not be hurt. Switching to English, she said, "We should move to Waaban, on the other side of reservation, so he can attend school in the settler town. Some say Poleville Indian School is not bad like we hear about Yardley."

Migizi thought for a time while toying with leather scraps. He glanced at the wall then at the smoke hole. "That could work; Poleville Indian

School is close enough to Waaban for visits, and with new teachers, a different superintendent . . ." He trailed off.

"Geget, debwemigad. Anything would be better than Yardley School," Bizaan added, her voice heavy with meaning.

Days later the family agreed to move to Waaban, which was close enough to Poleville Indian School for East Villagers to bring students themselves. Within days, after discussing their plan with the village council, Migizi sent a letter written by Niizh Eshkanag to the Indian agency noting the family's plan to move to Waaban in September, and pick rations from their new home."

After maple sugar time and forest greening, summer arrived. The forest teemed with the young of animals from the winged to the four-legged to the crawlers. Hides from winterkill were tanned, firewood collected, and some families prepared to move farther into the forest to gather dry roots and berries.

Midsummer, two government agents rode into Ningaabii'an meeting with Ogimaa Niigaan and elders in the meetinghouse. After business was concluded, the men exited, and as though inspecting the village, walked about leading their horses.

Niizh Eshkanag and Giigoo with another boy suddenly appeared running from around a lodge, and unintentionally dashed in front of the men, causing the horses to balk short of rearing.

"You there," one man shouted, pointing at Niizh Eshkanag, his arm extended supporting a fist with a rigidly pointed index finger. "What's your name?"

"Me?" Niizh Eshkanag asked, stopping in front of the man.

"Yes, you!"

"Niizh Eshkanag."

The man studied the boys. "You're supposed to have English names."

"Oh?"

"And wear proper clothes."

"Are you *hot* in those clothes?" Niizh Eshkanag asked.

"Don't be smart with me," the man rasped.

"I not being smart," Niizh Eshkanag said, speaking softly. He motioned to his friends, "Aambe maajaayaang." The boys ran away, their breechcloths flapping on their behinds.

"Brats. I see we haven't made much progress," one man said. He fumed watching the boys disappear.

The other man added, "And it never pays to complain to the chief or their parents."

Over summer, Migizi and Niizh Eshkanag traveled twice to Waaban to build a winter lodge and store firewood. Each trek over Zhiibaa'igan, the trail that led between the villages, took father and son three leisurely days, though the trip would take a runner but one day.

When the leaves began to change color, the next full moon signaled it was time to move, and the family loaded their belongings into a buckboard and headed east on the longer north wagon trail, which coursed north, then east past a trading post near where they camped for the night. Continuing on at dawn, the family camped twice more before reaching a shallow crossing on the Zagime Ziibi, the river named after the little insects who lived in swarms beside it.

During the three-day trip, Niizh Eshkanag lay in the wagon box staring into the treetops or sat scanning the passing forest. He wore an everyday breechcloth and his bearclaw necklace during the day, a plain cotton shirt and leggings during the cold night. Cut short at school, his hair grew over summer, splashing short of his shoulders, needing a leather tie to keep it clear of his eyes. A pair of puckered moccasins was always nearby.

For the trip, Migizi wore tanned buckskin clothes; his braided hair hung past his shoulders as he drove the horse. Bizaan wore a dress of calico, a shawl of trade cloth, high-top moccasins, and several strings of red and blue glass beads.

While traveling, the elders gazed quietly about, discussing anything to pass the time. And Niizh Eshkanag stared at the passing forest looking for anything interesting or unusual.

"Niwii-minobimaadizimin iwedi ina? Will Waaban be a good village for us?" Niizh Eshkanag wondered aloud in both languages.

Bizaan turned half around, looked at her son, and as though reaching for ideas, opened a hand near her brow. "Nimbagosendaamin ina? We hope so, don't we?"

Niizh Eshkanag stared into the forest as though talking to trees, "You said we need to change and learn new things, but there must be a better way than how they treat us at school."

"They don't hurt you, do they, Niizh?" asked Bizaan.

"Not me, but some students. School is not good for some." Niizh Eshkanag frowned. "I don't mind learning new things, but some students there are so sad being away from home all winter they don't even study." He paused as he considered all of the contradictions. "Others just try to stay out of trouble, learn English, and avoid the mean workers because they like the meals, heated rooms, and other comforts."

"Understandable," Bizaan said. She added with an arched eyebrow, "Students who misbehave could make teachers stricter than they would like to be."

Niizh Eshkanag smiled with a mischievous air while gazing over the side of the buckboard. "I'm a good student, well-behaved, the mirror told me. Ingii-aawenaan waabamojichaagwaaning."

"Mm. Inda-waabandaan ge-niin i'iw waabamojichaagwaan," Bizaan said she would need to see that mirror herself.

Migizi chuckled aloud and gestured toward a clearing where they could stop. "Noogishkaadaa mii dash wiisinidaa waa-nibaayaang."

Bizaan said she would cook something, "Niwii-jiibaakwe."

"Bebezhigooganzhiig niwii-ashamaag, I'll feed and water the horses," Niizh Eshkanag added.

Perpetual twilight of the deep forest faded into dusk as the buckboard approached the shallow area along the Zagime Ziibi, and lodges were visible across the water.

The Zagime Ziibi flowed southwest through the Anishinaabe reservation, past East Village, and continued south past Poleville. The Makwa Ziibi flowed southeast past West Village, and, a four-day walk farther southeast, it joined Zagime. The meeting of rivers was a full day hike north of Poleville, and the triangular area between the two rivers was known as the Makwa Zagime Baketigweyaa.

"Indoshkiwiigiwaaminaan," Migizi said. He pointed at their new lodge visible under the tall forest.

"Gegapii!" Bizaan was pleased to finally arrive. The horses splashed through water, carefully feeling their way through shallows knee-high to a man.

Migizi reined the horses near a recently built lodge. Bizaan bustled to the lodge, walked around feeling its bark exterior, and peered through the low entrance before straightening with a smile.

"Ginitaa-ozhitoon." Bizaan told her husband he had done well and chuckled when she added that she may have more to say about that on cold winter nights, "Gonemaa gida-miigwechiwi'in apii gisinaag biboong."

"Anooj da-ozhichigaade," Migizi humbly replied that it could be better, but the Winter Maker would certainly not find comfort inside, "Beebooniked gawiin wii-nayendaagozisii biinjaya'iing."

"Nigii-wiidookaagoo epiichi ozhitooyaan ishkodekaan." Niizh Eshkanag told his mother he had some help making the fire pit but found the clay to top the rocks on his own.

"Gegaa debwe," Migizi said he almost had that right, chuckling low, pointed out that it was Niizh Eshkanag who helped Bizhiw and his son Esiban make the pit. "Niizh ogii-wiidookawaan Bizhiwan miinawaa Esibanan."

Niizh Eshkanag smiled and admitted that many of the villagers had helped. "Enh, debwemigad gaye baatayiinowag bi-endaajig gii-wiidookoonangwaa."

Bizaan stood inside the lodge and then examined the rocks that would be used to warm their sleeping spaces. "Gi-gichimiigwechiwi'in. Nimbagosendaan Niizh wii-minwendang oshki-gikinoo'amaadiiwigamig." She thanked her husband and hoped her son would like his new school.

Everyone went outside, and Migizi waved at an approaching family: Bizhiw, his wife, Ziigwan, and their son, Esiban. As they conversed, the time since their last meeting dissolved.

Barefoot, shirtless, wearing tattered trade pants, Esiban was thin but had been listening and learning for twelve winters now. He looked about, curiosity crinkling his forehead.

Migizi smiled and told Esiban to look for Niizh Eshkanag holding a horse. "Nandawaabam Niizh bebezhigooganzhiin dakonaad."

Niizh Eshkanag stooped to look under the horse's neck and greet Esiban. "Ho, Esiban."

"Bebezhigooganzhii niwii-dakonaa," Bizhiw said, reaching for the reins because he knew his son wanted to run with Niizh Eshkanag.

The contents of the wagon were scattered inside the lodge, to remain so until Bizaan had time to fashion a home from them. As an offering of asemaa was dropped into the fire pit, the flames danced and cedar twigs were dispersed about the floor. Then everyone went to the home of Ziigwan and Bizhiw for a meal around an outside fire.

For Niizh Eshkanag and Esiban, it was a relaxing time—firelight flickering about treetops, the crackle of logs and smoke curling skyward.

The meal finished, and Bizaan leaned toward Ziigwan to whisper her worries about Niizh Eshkanag, who did well at his old school but hated it, and moved like an old man when he first came home. The summer was half gone before he seemed his usual self, and then it was time to think about school again.

"Gekinoo'amaagejig aakwaadiziwag Poleville-ing," Ziigwan warned that the teachers at Poleville Indian School were also strict.

"Ogiichigonaawaan ina abinoojiinyan?" Bizaan asked if they took the children by force from the village.

"Moozhag ogaagwezegiaawan," Ziigwan explained that they mostly used threats and did not take those older than fifteen, but once came after a girl who refused to go. She told Bizaan that might not be the same with all reservations or schools. Most importantly, she confirmed the school was near enough for them to visit and bring the students themselves.

"Gekinoo'amaagejig miinawaa anokiijig owiisagendamaan ina abinoojiinyan?" Bizaan pressed for information about teachers or school workers hurting the children.

According to Ziigwan, the school in Poleville was not as bad as the school in Yardley, but she pointed out they follow the same laws, "Naasaab dibaakonigewinan odebwe'endaanaawaa." She thought for a moment then added that Esiban told her some of the workers are mean, but others are decent "Esiban ingi-wiindamaag aanind aakwaadiziwaad miinawaa aanind minwaadiziwaad."

"Chimewinzha gaawiin abinoojiiyan obakite'aasiiwaan Anishinaabeg." Bizaan pointed out that in the old days, Anishinaabe seldom struck their children, but now they learn that children must be beaten instead of encouraged.

Niizh Eshkanag agreed with Bizaan and told them at school he heard them say "spare the rod, spoil the child."

Migizi nodded with the talk, looked up at treetops swaying in the light of a dozen campfires. He seemed to stare through his son, as he said, "Niizh chigikendaaso miinawaa daa-nandagikendang ingodwaaso-biboonan giishpin andawendang." *Niizh is quick to understand beyond our world; I wish him to study longer than six seasons, but it will be his choice.*

Ziigwan pointed to a pouch on the wall, and said the boys would be leaving for school in three days taking with them only what the school allows, not enough to remember their Anishinaabe ways. "Gaawiin bagidinigosiiwag wii-biidoowaad gegoon ji-mikwendamowaad Anishinaabe izhitwaawinan."

Bizaan glanced at the boys, saying they can learn the lessons in white man's books, but will not forget the lessons of the first Grandfather. "Owii-agindaanaawaa Gichi-mookomaan-mazina'iganan aanwi gaawiin wiikaa wanendanzigwaa gaa-gikinoo'amaagoziwaad wayeshkag Gichi-mishomis maadaajimod." Her manner was gentle, and when she spoke, youth listened in silence.

Niizh Eshkanag's family settled into the village of thirty-five lodges, widely scattered beneath tall jackpines and sugar maples, each within sight of neighbors but not of the entire village. A small opening in the forest hovered directly over a large central building, the round meetinghouse.

One day before leaving for school, Niizh Eshkanag and Esiban walked near the dance circle, izhi-niimi'iding, the hub of seasonal rites and celebrations. Two girls were near one's home.

Niizh Eshkanag motioned toward two girls and asked if Esiban remembered them from school, "Gimikwenimaag ina Ajijaak miinawaa Nagamokwe?" He frowned and complained they called him a child, while they were only one year older than him. "Bezhig eta biboon awashme biboonigiziwaad aanawi izhinikazhiwaad 'abinoojiiyens.'"

Niizh Eshkanag smiled and wondered if they would call him a child. "Abinoojiiyens ina niwaa-izhinikaazhigoog?"

Esiban called out and told the girls his friend Niizh would like to talk to them, "Ho, Ajijaak! Nagamokwe! Niijikiwenh Niizh gida-gaganoozhigowaa."

Ajijaak turned, smiled sideways toward Niizh Eshkanag, and asked if his tongue was broken, "Biigoshkaa ina gidenaniw?" Both girls waited, faced each other or glanced about until the boys were near.

Ajijaak looked past Niizh Eshkanag's shoulder and complimented him on the home she watched him build with his father over the summer. "Gigii-ganawaabamin wiigiwaam ozhiitooyeg niibinong."

"Gimiigwechiwi'in," Niizh Eshkanag thanked her and told her this was where he would be living now. "Omaa niwii-endaamin noongom."

"Ingii-noondaan wii-izhaayan Poleville Anishinaabe Gikinoo'amaadi-iwigamig." Ajijaak said she had heard he would be attending Poleville Indian School then asked if he liked school. "Giminwendaan ina gikinoo'amaadiiwigamig?"

Niizh Eshkanag nodded halfheartedly and explained he liked to learn but didn't like being away from home. "Niminwendaan ji-nanda-gikendamaan mii gaawiin minwendanziwaan maajaayaan endaayaan."

Ajijaak agreed and added that she also didn't like being treated badly and thought often about how their elders never had to go to a school and couldn't help them with this problem. "Gaawiin niminwendanziin ezhi-majidoodoonangwaa miinwaa gaawiin izhaasiiwaad ningichi-ayaamaanaanig gikinoo'amaadiwigamigong mii noongwa gaawiin bwaa-wiidookoonangwaa."

Niizh Eshkanag nodded and turned to go, but then to make her smile, he explained that his father wanted him to try on a new pair of white-man's pants for school. "Aabdeg maajaayaan nos andawendang wii-gagwekawag Gichi-mookomaan-giboodiyegwaazon."

Standing next to Ajijaak as they both wore tanned hide skirts to their knees, calf-high beaded moccasins, and trade wool capes trimmed with fur, Nagamokwe laughed as they parted and said they might go try on some ugly American dresses. "Gonemaa baanimaa inda-gagwekaamin Gichi-mookomaan-majigoodenh."

Meanwhile, Migizi and Bizhiw attended a meeting of elders to decide which children must go to school and who would take them. He volunteered to accompany Bizhiw, who was selected to cart students to the Poleville School.

Chapter Two

In Milwaukee early in September, friends and relatives of the Poznanski family, including Bill Stacy, met for supper at Steve and Beth Demski's home. After the meal, everyone convened in the parlor.

Smiling toward Roger who appeared troubled, Steve turned to Bill. "About your business trip to Canada, when will you go?"

Bill nodded. "I'm flexible, so in the matter of Roger traveling to northern Minnesota, we can await confirmation from Elias. Of course, I'll be happy to see Roger to Poleville. It's longer than my normal route, but travel is good through there. Be sure to mention that he'll have to be picked up in town."

"Elias will have the stage schedule," Steve said.

Roger raised his hand, "Doesn't the train go there?"

Bill explained, "They're working on railroads all over the place, but I think we're stuck with a stage after we get off the train. We travel west by train to St. Paul then transfer to a train going north to Duluth. South of Duluth, we take the stage northwest to Poleville."

Roger faced Steve. "I know Uncle Elias works with Indians, but what exactly does he do?"

"He's headmaster of the Indian boarding school in Poleville," Steve explained.

Roger frowned. "Isn't that dangerous? Anyway, newspapers describe trouble with Injuns."

Bill nodded to Steve and faced Roger. "I suppose we could call them Indians.

"Elias works with the Anishinaabe where you're going, but south of them; when I was about the age you are now, there was a serious

Dakota conflict, something to do with treaty violations. I'm not sure of the particulars, but it's settled down now. Gossip suggests bad things are still ongoing against Indians in California—ranchers being paid by the state government to destroy Indian villages, that sort of thing."

Steve nodded. "Your Uncle Elias has never spoken of trouble outside normal discipline at the school. Newspapers could make a thing seem worse than it really is—have to sell papers, you know. Where you're going, it's a small school, should be easy to get along. If you treat other students decent, more'n likely, they'll reciprocate."

Roger paused, slouching, hands on his lap. "Yeah, I guess." He looked up with sharpened eyes. "Could you tell me more about the school? Is it government run?"

"I'm not sure how it's structured," Steve replied. "Some are run by churches but funded by the government. It's basically a boarding school, and besides a regular curriculum, it teaches the Indians our ways."

Beth nodded, adding, "I think Elias lives too far from a regular school, so you'd go to school with natives. There are children of employees to be friends with; in case you've forgotten, your cousin, Karen has been going to school with natives since Elias took the job some four years ago."

Roger stiffened as though sensing the reality of his near future, then he spoke with an extended sigh, "So . . . Indians had nothing to do with cousin Donald dying?"

"It was the same illness we face here," Beth said. "Helen's letters tell of farm activities. I'm not sure what, but they raise crops, have cows and horses—we all need horses, you know. It could be interesting!"

"Uh huh," Roger fussed. There was a long silence.

Beth motioned northwest as she explained, "We should have prepared you better after a sad summer, but school begins soon and Uncle Elias would not want you to miss studies. We're fortunate Mr. Stacy can see you safely there."

A letter from Milwaukee arrived at the general store in Poleville. The store included the post office and stage stop.

Early morning in Poleville, the postmaster handed a pack to a young man on horseback. "There's a letter from Milwaukee for the Indian school, and some mail for Ogimaa Negadenimad in Waaban. You may have to wait for an Indian student to read and interpret it for him. Your route will keep you busy, so I won't expect you 'til evening. Be sure to feed and rest the horse."

Days later, Susan Poznanski received a telegram.

> Dear Susan and family . . .
> We are pleased to confirm our commitment to have Roger stay with us.
> Will collect Roger at the stage office in Poleville per schedule . . .
> Loving regards,
> Elias and Helen Poznanski.

On the day of departure, the train rumbled slowly westward out of Milwaukee. Roger felt alone, but Bill's pleasant easy conversation somewhat eased Roger's discomfort. Gloom still lined his face as he stared out the window at the receding city. *Those relatives up north are strangers. According to some, Indians are savages, and not trustworthy.* A sandwich appeared under his nose.

"Beth sent food," Bill said. "What'll you drink, beer or mineral water?"

"If Mom knew I drank beer, she'd have a fit." Roger broke into a smile. "Yeah, I'll have beer if you please."

"That-a-boy!" Bill said chuckling. "I thought you'd forgotten how to smile. He poured beer into a glass and handed it to Roger. "Half a glass won't hurt." He motioned toward the window with his own beer glass. "Seems you're worrying too much about your new home. There's adventure there, you'll see. It could very well find you first."

Roger shot a glance into Bill's face. "Adventure? Danger, probably." But he managed a wan smile.

"Oh, not danger," Bill said. "No more than in Milwaukee. Learning about Indians, I mean, about the north, animals, and people. It's big country, a man could walk miles and miles without seeing a soul."

"That's what I figured." Roger shielded a frown as he sipped beer and bit into his sandwich. "They say *redskins* do terrible things." He winced while facing the window.

"Might be you read too many stories written for the wrong reasons," Bill said. "Look at it this way; you'd be part of real change—historic change, and northern Minnesota might just be the first chapter of your book. Not many boys have such an opportunity."

"I'm only thirteen. Oh, and five months."

"I know. Just the right age for new experiences."

"Yeah?"

Roger and Bill waited hours in St. Paul to board a train heading north toward Duluth. And as the train rumbled north, Roger slept on a vacant seat across the aisle from Bill. He stirred when the train stopped at small towns, but Bill showed no sign of moving, and the train rumbled on luring him back to asleep.

Bill shook Roger's shoulders as the train slowed again. "Come, here's where we get off. We have time to eat before the stage arrives."

Roger sat up, stretched with a gasping yawn, and followed Bill and a young woman off the train. They entered a small café convenient to the station and were met with the aroma of breakfast in the making.

"Welcome folks," the cook said. He was a burly man with an apron covering much of his shabby clothes. "Business is slow this early, but I like to be open for the stage. Venison and eggs with flapjacks are my specialty this morning." He chuckled. "And most every morning." Looking at Roger, he smiled warmly while placing both hands on the counter. "Looks like you'll have the works."

"I *am* hungry," Roger said. He glanced at Bill. "I didn't bring money."

Bill nodded. "Your relatives gave me money for expenses." He turned to the cook. "Give him the works; he needs more meat on his bones."

More relaxed after eating, Roger followed Bill to the stage office where the clerk and the young woman were the only ones there. Bill nodded to the woman and sat with Roger on a bench.

Sleepy, short of befuddled, Roger looked out the window noticing horses being hooked to a stagecoach.

"Guess that's us," Bill said, grinning. "It's a four-horse stagecoach, just right for northern Minnesota." He exchanged nods with the woman and followed her and Roger outside and onto the stage.

The stagecoach departed heading northwest, and Bill tipped his hat to the young lady. "G'morning, miss. Not much traffic on this road, which probably explains why we're the only ones aboard."

"I agree," the young woman replied. "Saw you and your son on the train from St. Paul. Where might you be going?"

"Sorry. This here's Roger Poznanski. I'm Bill Stacy, friend of the family. Just seeing the young-un to Poleville."

"Pleased to meet you," the woman said. She extended her hand. "Emma Pierce. I'm going to Poleville, too, so we'll be together until tomorrow." She glanced curiously at Roger and faced Bill. "I've accepted a position as school nurse at the Indian boarding school."

Bill glanced into Roger's brightening face. He chuckled with his comment, "well, I'll be, Roger's going there, too. Small world, I'd say."

Emma looked pleasantly at Roger. "You have straight black hair, but you don't look Indian to me. Did you say, Poznanski? That name sounds familiar."

Bill lit his pipe. "Roger's uncle is the school headmaster." He motioned toward Roger and blew a cloud of smoke at the roof. "Roger's father died this past year, and with his mother ill now too, he's to live with the Elias Poznanski family."

"I see," Emma said leaning toward Roger. "Sorry about your father." She paused to look out the window. "I may have to see you for checkups."

Roger nodded. *If a woman doesn't worry, must be safe enough. Even so, I don't have to like being in school with them.*

Roger stared out the window and talked softly as though thinking aloud, "I don't remember Uncle Elias, though Mother said I met him years back. He must be the tall man who visited us." He looked down and leaned forward, elbows on his knees, his face and manner reflecting curiosity. "Are they, Indians, I mean, the same as us? Does an Indian boy my age have the same body, and brain and all that? I know they look different, but you read stories about them being forest people, not sociable at all."

Appearing overly thoughtful, Emma glanced to Bill before replying, and then whispered almost too low, "Yes, they have sharp teeth that glow in the dark. You mustn't touch them either or you might have bad luck." She leaned back as though contemplating a triumph. Bill looked out the window, a grin working his face.

Roger's eyes widened at first then he looked sheepishly toward Emma, his eyes glinting through slits. "You say, they're the same as us except, maybe, color and face?"

"Certainly," Emma replied. "They breathe and eat the same; can think as well or as poorly as we do, and are just as lazy or ambitious." She paused, seeming to have exhausted the possible comparisons. "I think, Mr. Poznanski, if you take an Indian baby and raise him in England, he will speak with an English accent and fit very nicely into a group with skills and interests similar to his. They do have weaknesses; many die from diseases that only make white folk sick." She hesitated. "I worked at another Indian school in the south after graduating from the university, now I'll try the north. I suspect Indians here will have the same differences and similarities as other Indians and the rest of humanity. My experience with Indians is that they are highly educated in their culture and many become wise elders."

"Oh." Roger settled back more relaxed and stared out the window.

The remainder of the day was spent in either silence or casual conversation related to passing scenery. The road surface varied from hard gravel or short wet stretches underlaid with logs, called a corduroy road. Where the logs were mired deeper, the horses slowed to a grind. The stage stopped at a waystation with no café, and the stage company included room and board with the caretaker. Anticipation, wonderment, and worry had depleted Roger, and he fell asleep, fitfully, fending concerns about his new home. Departing early the next morning, the stagecoach traveled alongside a river for miles and by midafternoon crossed another river and pulled into a small town.

"Poleville," Roger breathed aloud when he saw the sign. The stage pulled up to a store at the town center, and all three riders stepped down and stretched.

Bill warmly embraced Roger. "I'll see you down the trail," he said. "Take care of yourself, and Miss Pierce, too." He shook hands with

Emma and climbed back into the stage followed by a young couple also going to Canada. The stage changed teams, picked up mail and packages, and then continued north.

Roger studied a paper Bill had given him. "We're to find a carriage or wait for it," he said.

"Right!" Emma nudged Roger, flagged a paper she held while motioning at a carriage a dozen paces up the street. "C'mon. Bet that's our ride." A man, pipe in mouth, stepped out to face them.

Emma waved to the man, "Are you from the Indian school, sir?"

The man withdrew the pipe, slowly knocked the ashes out before replying, "I am. You must be Miss Pierce, and the young-un must be Roger, I'd say. I'm Mike Murphy." He pointed behind his seat. "Hop in. We'll be there in half of an hour and supper will be waitin' fer ya. By the way, I'm grounds and maintenance; Mrs. Murphy is head cook." He smiled. "Any complaints about the food, tell her."

"Glad to meet you, Mr. Murphy," Emma said. She looked about, adjusted her shawl against a breeze and cast an expectant glance at Roger.

"Uh, yes, glad to meet you, Mr. Murphy," Roger said, his manner distant.

Mike climbed onto his seat, slapped the reins and the carriage lurched forward heading out of town. The carriage rode well in spite of a road with sections of hard ruts. Still flushing with apprehension, Roger stared at passing farms and an occasional cabin the first mile from town. His anxiety heightened as they passed towering trees shading a narrowing of the lane. "Are Indians in there?" He asked trying to appear casual while carefully studying the thickening forest.

"It's nigh dusk," Mike said, "Indians, no less than you 'n' me, turn in for the night. Far as there being Indians here, not likely. They are north, inside the reservation."

As Roger began his last day of stage travel to Poleville, Niizh Eshkanag was in Waaban exchanging his clout for baggy pants and a shirt. Lacking white man's shoes, he wore moccasins and reluctantly handed his necklace to his mother.

With heavy hearts, the parents of seven Waaban children waved goodbye as the wagon rumbled off. Children, including Nagamokwe and Ajijaak, waved with barely moving fingers.

They traveled all day with a brief lunch and rest stop near a stream, and by late afternoon, the wagon lumbered through a thinned forest past small farms.

Entering the school grounds, Bizhiw reined the team near a hitching rail in front of a large building. Older children gazed about with little expression, and those arriving for the first time scanned the grounds with a mix of curiosity and apprehension.

Nagamokwe raised her arm past Niizh Eshkanag's face pointing at a sign. "Administration." She read the sign aloud. The administration building housed the infirmary, dining hall, and supplies. Boys' and girls' dormitories were on opposite sides of the Administration Building, the boys' dorm to the south.

Called Big House by students, the superintendent's residence was near the southwest reaches of the campus, gazing officiously down from a low rise.

The Poleville School raised much of its own food, and during the school term, used student labor under adult supervision. The barn was near the west reaches of the campus, and the fields farthest northwest. A wagon road crossed the river at a shallow on the Zagime River and continued on to Poleville a half-hour carriage ride away.

Everyone in the wagon watched a man and woman approach from the administration building. Migizi and Bizhiw stepped down, and Bizhiw motioned youths to do likewise, all assembling near the wagon.

Niizh Eshkanag nudged Esiban and asked if that was the man who gave orders. "A'aw inini ina ogimaakaadaage?"

Esiban nodded and whispered that the man was honest but the woman stung. "Enh mii a'aw. Gwayakwaadizid. A'aw ikwe ojaka'aan."

Bizhiw motioned for the youths to stay put, and he moved with Migizi to meet the couple.

"Aaniin, hello," Bizhiw greeted the couple.

"Hello," the man and woman replied almost together.

"I'm Joe," the man said. He motioned to the woman with him. "This is Miss Purge. Mike Murphy usually meets new arrivals, but he's in town on another errand." He scanned the group, "This all you have?"

"Enh, yes," Bizhiw replied. He held up seven fingers.

"Seven, then," Joe said. "We expected more."

"Do they all speak English?" Miss Purge asked. She sighed audibly, "It'll be a blessing when they assign English names."

"Speak English? Yes," Bizhiw replied. He opened and closed a hand near his mouth. "Maybe not all good." He looked into Joe's eyes. "You learn Ojibwemowin, and it will go better."

"Ah, yes," Joe said. He stepped back. "I don't think I could learn Indian."

"Ojibwemowin," Migizi corrected. "The language of other tribes is not the same." A chill permeating the meeting seemed exacerbated after the exchange, and Bizhiw motioned toward the wagon. "Come, meet students."

As she approached the students, Miss Purge coughed, overdid an icy scrutiny of the group then scanned her clipboard. "I'm a boys' dormitory matron. I'll get your names, but the agency plans to give English names to everyone." And she added in undertone, "so we can pronounce them and know who's who. Go with Joe for a late supper in the student's dining room, then with him for uniforms and registration." She sighed while staring over the students' heads.

Students from other villages were either in the dorms, the school building, or being processed elsewhere, one step ahead of those from Waaban.

As the group went to be registered, Niizh Eshkanag looked back to see the wagon trundle away and the elders glance once back at them. Looking in another direction, he noticed a carriage entering the grounds with a white boy and woman sitting behind the driver.

Roger shifted on the seat, staring at buildings as the carriage entered school grounds and pulled up to a hitching rail near the Administration Building.

Mike stepped down and motioned at the building. "Indians came today, and it looks like they're still processing. We'll go here, and I'll get the boss. I'm sure he'll want to see his nephew right quick."

Roger followed Emma, and as they gathered luggage, he scanned the grounds. Trying not to, he stared at brown-skinned boys and girls. *Some wear uniforms. Others are poorly dressed. That boy wears rag pants and shirt. Just coming from the reservation, maybe.* A hand touched his shoulder from behind. Startled, Roger spun around to face a tall, thin man in casual dress.

"Roger, I'm your Uncle Elias," the man said. "Welcome to your new home." Roger opened his arms to be embraced, but Elias firmly extended one arm while his other arm remained limp at his side.

Roger shook hands. "How do you do, Uncle Elias?" he said.

"Fine. Let's get you something to eat." Elias turned to face Emma. "Glad you chose to work here, and I hope you like it. You can eat a late lunch and get acquainted with other staff."

The dimly lit dining hall smelled of oil lanterns mixed with the aroma of food. The meal was a simple lunch for latecomers. Roger ate a sandwich and drank milk near Emma and a teacher.

Elias gazed at Roger as he ate. "You've grown these past years. I'm sorry I couldn't get to the funeral. Your father was such a good man." He motioned toward Emma. "You know Miss Pierce." He motioned to another woman. "Miss Jacob, seventh-grade teacher."

"How do you do, Miss Jacob," Roger said. "I'll be in your class, then."

"And she'll have no favorites," Elias said. He chuckled while glancing at his watch. "After eating, we can go to the school building; staff is still registering students, so we might as well sign you in."

After eating, Roger followed Elias to the school assembly hall. The principal and a teacher were registering seven students who still carried their clothing issue. Elias approached the principal while Roger was in a line of students waiting to register. *Some look my age. Dressed worse than street kids in Milwaukee. We're really helping them by giving them an education, good clothes, and food.*

Elias stopped near the principal and nodded toward Roger. "My nephew, Roger, there, will register, too. I'm going to the nurse's office and will be back when you're through signing in." He motioned for Roger to join the line of registrants.

After Elias departed, two boys ahead in line turned and glanced at Roger. One spoke Ojibwe to the other and asked if Roger belonged at the school. "Awenen aawid Gichi-mookomaan? Omaa ina dibendaagozi?

"Ganabaj naasaab biboonigizi ge-giin," the younger replied.

Roger heard without understanding. *They must be talking about me.*

The principal stood and spoke sharply. "I will overlook it now, but after today, only English will be spoken. It's the rules."

"I only spoke to Niizh Eshkanag," Esiban said.

"I spoke first," Niizh Eshkanag said quickly. "We don't all know English."

"There will be no excuse. If you do not understand, ask the teachers. On work details, ask those employees. You will be punished if you speak Indian." Niizh Eshkanag shot an angry glance into Roger's face, and both boys glared at each other, neither giving way.

Roger hissed, "Were you talking about me?"

"Make no matter," Niizh Eshkanag retorted, "Principal hears only you."

"I'm not talking about the principal. I'm talking about you and him and me." Roger said. He tried not to, but frowned as he pointed at Niizh Eshkanag and Esiban.

"Niizh asked if you go school here." Esiban explained.

"Oh," Roger said. "Yes, I'll go to school here." Then he smirked, "Niizh is a funny name."

"What is your name?" Niizh Eshkanag asked.

"Roger."

"Roger is a funny name." Niizh Eshkanag snapped, turning away. Roger blushed, and looked off shifting a step away.

Elias walked Roger through the darkness to Big House and into a spacious kitchen. A bright lantern glowed on the table and another lantern glowed through a doorway from the parlor. In the kitchen, a thin woman turned, and unsmiling, looked at Roger.

"So this is Roger," she said."I don't see he'll be happy with savages, but I suppose, if no one else will have him."

"That's unfair, Helen," Elias said. He spoke softly without looking at Helen. "It's not Roger's doing that David died and Susan took sick." He turned to Roger and motioned toward his wife. "Here is your Aunt Helen."

Roger extending his hand. "How do you do?"

Helen ignored the hand. "Wash up, boy, and we'll have tea before bed. There's church tomorrow in Poleville, and we must be up early."

Distraught at Helen's coldness and Elias's stiff formality, Roger suddenly felt tired, and sagged onto a chair staring down at slowly twisting fingers on his lap.

The door suddenly burst open, and a girl rushed in. Roger sat erect, surprised.

"I stopped to help the new nurse at the infirmary," the girl said. "Sorry I'm late." She looked at Roger with feigned surprise bending over with exaggerated moves to look into his face. "Looks like you know about the end of the world or something." She gently punched his shoulder. "Hey, I'm your cousin, Karen, who's glad to meet you." Karen gripped his shoulders and pulled him to standing.

"Oh?" Roger brightened. "Forgot. Yeah, Karen," he mumbled then smiled. "Just tired, I guess."

"Something tells me you were not properly welcomed." Karen pulled Roger into a warm embrace, whispering into his ear. "You'll get along just fine. I'll see to it."

Confusion of leaving the only home he knew in a bustling city stressed Roger. After days of travel and exposure to unfamiliar circumstances, he had retreated into melancholy, but with Karen came hope, and he brightened into a cautious smile.

Karen was a strong girl of sixteen years, athletic and taller than Roger. An honor student with the academic skills of her father, she was above the frailty of her mother, who would not accept the death of her son.

Chapter Three

"Everyone up, make your beds, tidy the dorm!" Miss Purge said louder than needed from the doorway of the boys' dorm. "After breakfast, it's campus chores then everyone to chapel—to help you become good Christian citizens," she gazed around the room then spun about and departed, her shoes clacking on the wood floor. Boys slowly lifted themselves up on their elbows with raised heads.

While dressing, an older boy sat on his bed and complained about having to pray the teachers' way, "gaawiin gida-biskinikezhigosiinaanig ji-anami'aayang dibishkoo anami'aawaad."

Niizh Eshkanag glanced to the door. "Niminwendaan Gizhemanidoo gaye Shkaakamigokwe anami'etawagwaa," he quietly asked Esiban about Roger as he laced his shoes. "Aaniin enendaman gii-idang odoozhiman?"

"Obagwanawizi." Esiban said Roger seemd like a snob. "Ingoding inda-inaajimo'aa Zhaaganaashimong." Then he heard Miss Purge's footsteps returning and said, "Let's talk English now, Jaka'ikwe, the one with the stinging tongue is coming."

Niizh Eshkanag was distant as he straightened his bed. *That boy, Roger, seems out of place here—like us. I hope he's not in my class.* He faced Esiban, "An older student said he heard the cook tell another worker that Roger's father died, which is why relatives sent him here to his uncle, the headmaster. Maybe, same as us, he had no choice. He did not look happy."

"He seems different than gwiiwizensag of other workers," Esiban said. "Like he's lost or something."

Later, in the chapel, Niizh Eshkanag gazed about paying little heed to the sermon. *Will it really be better than the old school? For now, I must stay with school–my family would not approve if I quit or even wanted to quit.*

Roger awoke from a deep sleep but was still tired from days of travel and the strangeness of beginning a new life. The sun glinted orange near the horizon, but it did not yet shine in his brightening window. He was about to get out of bed when there came a gentle rapping at the door.

"Come," Roger garbled. He cleared his throat. "Come in!"

Karen burst into the room. "Hey, Cuz!" Her face glowed with enthusiasm. "Up and at 'em! It's off to church in the big city. After breakfast, that is."

"Yeah?" Roger looked at Karen from behind a blanket but couldn't hide a grin as she pulled the covers off him. *Wonder what she's so happy about?*

"Five minutes to the dining room," Karen sang as she breezed out of the room.

On the way to Poleville, Roger and Karen sat behind the elder Poznanskis. Helen was reserved and proper beside Elias.

Roger gazed at the passing forest, musing afar, elsewhere. *Seems they don't really want me, especially Aunt Helen. I'll try it, but if Aunt Helen still seems to not like my being here, I'll write a letter to Milwaukee, tell them it won't work. If not Milwaukee, I'll live on my own, someplace, somehow.* Deep in thought, he became oblivious to farms and cabins outside Poleville and only became alert when the carriage entered town.

Elias hitched the horse to a rail beside the church and met Dr. Norton and his wife as they walked toward the entrance. Elias nodded to the couple, "Good morning."

"It's a fine day," Dr. Norton replied, pausing. He looked at Roger. "I don't believe I know this young man."

Elias motioned toward Roger. "Roger Poznanski, my nephew from Milwaukee. He's to live with us."

Mrs. Norton smiled at Roger. "Quite a change, I'd say, coming from Milwaukee."

"Yes, Ma'am."

"His father died."

"Sorry to hear that," Dr. Norton said. He extended his hand to Roger. "I hope you like the north country."

"Me, too." Roger shook hands with Dr. and Mrs. Norton, and everyone entered the church.

Still mulling his circumstances, Roger gave little heed to the service. *Karen is nice and seems friendly to everyone, but I'm out of place here. I'm glad Indian students don't seem exactly like I thought. Bill was right—"bad apples in any basket."*

Back home by early afternoon, the Poznanski family ate a late dinner, made tolerable by Karen's enthusiasm about almost everything.

"Hey, is Milwaukee growing?" Karen asked from across the table.

"Think so. People rushing around anyway."

"Miss it much?"

"Kind of, but I guess I have to get used to the wild animals, Indians and all."

"Don't talk with a full mouth," Helen snapped. Roger frowned, clasped both hands tightly on his lap and turned to look at the floor near his chair.

Karen forced a bright smile, leaned toward Roger, pointing at her head. "Anyway, the Anishinaabeg will like you if they know you like them."

"Seems a waste of money educating natives," Helen said. "Roger would be well advised to stay away from them."

"Working with natives gives us our living," Elias rejoined. "Let's drop it. Shall we?"

Karen ignored her parents, leaned closer to Roger, talking soft. "You're my brother, now, and you don't even need to change your last name. By spring, you won't want to return to Milwaukee."

"Don't know about that."

Elias cleared his throat. "Let's not confuse Roger about preferring one place over another. But you're right, he'll see for himself."

Monday morning, wearing uniforms identical to the Indian students, Roger and Karen walked across campus to school. Karen went to a special class for college prep. Roger entered the seventh-grade room and was assigned a seat. He watched past lowered eyebrows as students entered and sat. When a student paused just inside the doorway and stared at him, two pairs of eyes met, blinked, and glanced away. The only white student there, Roger felt isolated.

Morning was spent in class orientation, assigning seats and writing names on the blackboard. After lunch, Miss Jacob questioned students to determine academic standing, addressing Niizh Eshkanag in turn, "Did you study Africa at Yardley?"

Niizh Eshkanag stood. "Yes. Africa has big deserts; Sahara is one. They have Negro tribes with tall people and short people. The pyramids and the Nile River are in Africa."

"Very good," Miss Jacob said. "You may sit."

Roger sat erect, surprised. *He has an accent but speaks well.* He glanced in another direction. *That girl stares at me!* At noon, he waited near the door as other students exited. About to leave the room, a girl, Nagamokwe, was ahead of him, and Roger was about to follow her out, but Ajijaak suddenly stepped ahead of him.

"Pardon me," Roger mumbled as Ajijaak passed through the door.

"Uh huh," Ajijaak whispered. Roger followed the girl out, careful to keep his distance. Suddenly he was more thoughtful about Indian students than before—the mist was clearing somewhat.

During gym classes, as days passed, Roger occasionally drifted to be near a white student from eighth grade. Still detached from Indians, he had become more curious than distrustful.

Running contests by age were held outside during one gym class.

"Niizh Eshkanag and Roger are about the same size and age," the teacher said. He pointed to the ground beside him, then a bush some distance away. "Start here. When I blow the whistle, run to that bush and back."

Roger started quickly and took the lead to beat Niizh Eshkanag by inches in a short race. Later, a longer race began with Roger ahead at first, but by the second lap, Niizh Eshkanag took the lead, putting with each long stride more distance between himself and Roger to easily win. Indian students chided Niizh when he lost the short race and teased Roger for losing the second race.

The teacher went inside motioning students to follow, and Roger rudely nudged Niizh Eshkanag with his shoulder. "You were lucky!"

Niizh Eshkanag faced Roger. "I let you win first race—Gichi-mookomaan!"

"Don't swear at me, Injun," Roger snapped. He shoved Niizh Eshkanag who stumbled and fell. Before he could walk away, Roger was grabbed by other students and held firmly by both arms. Niizh Eshkanag stood facing him, glowering, and other students formed a circle around Niizh Eshkanag and Roger.

"Bakite', Niizh, wii-dakonangid!" one of the boys urged Niizh Eshkanag to hit Roger while they held him.

"Teach the white boy lesson," another said in English then called him a snake in Ojibwemowin, "Wa'aw dibishkoo ginebig aawi."

Roger struggled but was held by too many hands, and he squirmed trying to avoid a face or stomach blow. An older boy spit on Roger's face.

"Gego bakite'aaken abinoojiiyens," Niizh Eshkanag hissed, saying they should not hit a baby. Roger listened to the sharp conversation in Ojibwemowin. Then Niizh Eshkanag spoke English. "I will not hit a baby or spit on a captive." Roger was released as the teacher returned, and students grouped away from him.

"Is there a problem?" the teacher asked, scrutinizing Roger's disheveled appearance.

With pursed lips, Roger looked aside, wiped his face with a sleeve, brushed a hand through his hair and adjusted his pants. "No problem," he said softly. Glancing at Niizh Eshkanag and the other students who stared his way, he faced the teacher, tossed his head back and spoke clearly, "A misunderstanding. My fault."

"All right. Everyone inside," the teacher said. "Things will go better when you get to know each other."

Weeks passed with Roger and Niizh Eshkanag generally competing in sports, but when they vied with each other, earlier gloats or frowns, as time passed, gave way to cautious grins.

Students were issued winter clothes. The pine and hardwood forest became dark leafless claws amid spires of green.

Although Niizh Eshkanag remained aloof to Roger, he would not avoid meeting him and was focused on things other than race and culture. Attending boarding school and his future were more important to him than the relatives of the staff.

Ajijaak was taller than Roger and displayed neither hate nor interest in the white boy who sat an aisle away from her in class. The two had not yet spoken to each other, but when their eyes met it revealed to each, something other than dislike.

Snow fell, and ice formed at the edge of the rivers in early November, or Gashkadino-giizis, A friendly snowball fight began during school recess one day.

"Want to join, Ajijaak?" an older boy asked.

"I would slide and run on snow, not throw it," Ajijaak replied. "This snow seems icy and is too dangerous."

"Nagamokwe plays," the boy chided. Sides developed, and Roger joined the smaller group. Suddenly, an older boy threw an icy snowball that hit Ajijaak painfully in the face. Ajijaak moaned and bent over to clear her eyes.

"Damn! You hit her on purpose!" Roger yelled confronting the older boy who threw it. "She wasn't even playing!" Without a word, the older boy hit Roger hard in the face, and the two fell grappling and punching.

Standing nearby, Niizh Eshkanag stepped in front of Ajijaak peering into her eyes and asked if she was in pain. "Giwiisagine ina?"

"Niwii-mino-ayaa," Ajijaak let him know she would be fine. Then she pointed at the older boy. "Wewiib Niizh! You need to help Roger that boy is too big for him." Uncertain, Niizh Eshkanag watched as Roger was subdued, and the older boy sat on him punching his face and chest. Blood oozed from Roger's nose and lips.

Niizh Eshkanag turned to Aijaaak, "It is good lesson, not to fight bear larger than him."

"Niizh Eshkanag!" Ajijaak shouted. "Roger helped one from your village, and you watch him get beaten!"

"Others will laugh, but I will help the weak pale one," Niizh Eshkanag sighed. He jumped on the larger boy knocking him off Roger, then both boys immediately jumped on the larger boy.

Two older boys pulled Niizh Eshkanag and Roger off and separated all three boys. "Gekinoo'amaaged dagoshin," one of them hissed. "She should not see who fights the headmaster's nephew." Roger stood as Miss Jacob arrived hands on hips appearing dismayed.

"I won't ask how this started," Miss Jacob said, "I think we should all try to get along." She looked at Ajijaak's red eye then at Roger's, bruised eye and bloody face. "The pair of you, to the nurse. When it comes to eyes, we can't be too careful."

Niizh Eshkanag watched Roger and Ajijaak walk side by side to the infirmary, frowning as neither flinched apart when their elbows touched.

Roger and Ajijaak were present for the final hour of school, and lingered outside after school with Niizh Eshkanag and Nagamokwe.

Ajijaak thanked Niizh Eshkanag for helping Roger, "Gimiigwechiwi'in gii-wiidokawad."

"The pale boy needed help," Niizh Eshkanag said, tossing his head back and to one side.

"Niizh Eshkanag means more than one horn or something, right?" Roger said. "Instead, you should be called Many Tongues. Miigwech aanawi."

"I have never heard you speak a lie," Niizh Eshkanag said. "One day, maybe, we are friends, wiijiwaaganag."

Ajijaak stepped aside, nudging Roger.

"Okay. Sure," Roger said grinning. He extended his hand. "Yeah, someday wiijiwaaganag." The boys firmly shook hands.

"I will talk to you again," Niizh Eshkanag said. "We are going to change into work clothes now."

"Or they'll have Knitter punish you, I suppose." Roger said. "I think he could be mean with half an excuse. But Uncle says his supervision keeps the barns going."

"With slaves," Esiban retorted.

Ajijaak spoke, "Our matron slaps us if we do not mend clothes just right." She gazed at Niizh Eshkanag, "That careless boys tear." Nagamokwe smiled with a nod.

"Girls mend clothes; boys fix tables and things that girls break," Niizh Eshkanag retorted. With backward waves, two boys and two girls headed for their dorms; one boy headed for Big House.

Roger entered Big House through the kitchen entrance, passed his aunt and Karen with his head turned aside and went to his room to wash his face, but Helen noticed his bruised face at supper.

"It was a running exercise," Roger explained. "I tripped and fell, bumping my face on dirt."

"I see," she said, but Karen knew.

As time passed, Roger and Niizh Eshkanag spent more time together outside of class. In Big House, Helen did everything for Roger that a mother should, except love him. To make that lack obvious, although Roger had his own room and three meals right on time, she remained aloof and cold to him.

Karen was brightness for Roger, and the two spent long evenings playing cards and other games. And Roger began to visit the barns when Niizh Eshkanag had that duty.

One evening Helen was pleasant at supper. "Roger should have a hobby or pet," she said. "Perhaps a dog to keep his mind off Indians."

"Great idea," Elias said. "Not necessarily to keep his mind off Indians, which it might do, but as a companion." He turned to Roger. "How about it?"

Roger looked up, surprised. "A dog? Yeah."

Elias went to Poleville on business that week and returned with a large dog with Labrador features. The dog had been called Sniffer, and Roger continued to call it that. Within weeks, Roger and Sniffer became companions, going everywhere together except inside buildings. Nevertheless, Roger continued to visit his Indian friends in school and after school.

In December, Manidoo-giizisoons, the month of the Little Moon, Helen sat stiff and staring straight at Elias's plate at the opposite end of the table. "Some take more interest in Indians than their own kin," she muttered. "And one would think a dog could occupy a boy's spare time." Roger shifted uneasily and continued eating. Roger and Karen sat at opposite sides of the table between the elders.

Elias coughed. "Our work is with Indians. One cannot avoid talking to them, and it's reasonable that Karen and Roger make friends with well-behaved students."

"*Your* work is with Indians," Helen snapped.

Elias shook his head. "I see no need restricting a young woman who has shown she wisely chooses friends, and has been among Indians for some time." He gazed at Roger. "On the other hand, Roger is young, should exercise more care with whom he spends leisure."

Facing Roger directly, Elias cleared his throat. "There is something you can do for the school. The student who carries notes or packages between the office and buildings also has other chores and should have time off. You can relieve him Friday after school, and Saturday after the noon meal. On those days, report to the office to see if they have a message or even a package to be delivered elsewhere on grounds."

"Yes, sir. May I be excused?" Still flushed from ridicule, Roger spoke quietly, almost in a whisper.

Helen stared at her plate and the table near it. "Yes," she said stiffly. Roger stood without looking at either his uncle or aunt, and went to his room.

"I'll excuse myself," Karen said, her voice and manner edged with ice. She stood and followed Roger out of the dining room.

Chapter Four

The stars watched over all the children who were away from home, and the full moon called Gichi-manidoo-giizis rose and set over Poleville Indian School. It was January, and Miss Purge seemed more irritable than usual as she hung a lantern inside the boy's dorm complaining about a light dusting of snow. "Everyone up! Aandeg will scrape snow from the stairs, and shovel the walkway between the boys' dorm and dining hall." She paused and scanned a paper she held. "Wait! It seems you didn't tell us your English names from last year, but the Yardley office sent a name change. So now we will give all of you English names. Aandeg is now Allen Crow. Esiban is Billy Coon. Ajijaak is Sally Crane, and Nagamokwe is Mary Song.

Mrs. Murphy expects Bine for kitchen duty in fifteen minutes. He will be known as Max Partridge. Niizh Eshkanag will now be called Tom Horns, and he is also due for kitchen duty." She lingered in the doorway, haughty, gazing about the room.

Propped on elbows, Bine stared at the doorway until Miss Purge was out of sight, then in Ojibwemowin he said softly that he thought she was all talk and no work, "Jaka'ikwe gaagiigido eta mii dash gaawiin anokiisiid."

"Ayaangwaamizin," Esiban warned him to be careful because the matron seemed to know even when they thought in Ojibwemowin. "Gikendaan ojibwe'inendamang."

Miss Purge approached Aandeg as he finished scraping snow off the stairway. "Allen, you must do the steps better. Someone could slip and get hurt."

"Looks good to me," Aandeg muttered without looking up.

"My word! We'll see about that," Miss Purge said looking down from the platform with a taut face and extended index finger. She clacked off without another word.

Aandeg cleaned the steps better then headed for the lavatory to wash for breakfast.

Days later, Miss Purge visited the dorm as usual. "Everyone up." After hanging the lantern, she stopped at Aandeg's bed, and coldly motioned to the door. "Allen, dress and report immediately to the day room."

"Nishkaadizi. Giwii-bashanzhe'ig?" Bine noticed how angry she looked and asked if Aandeg thought he would be punished.

"Owiidigemaan wiindigoon," Aandeg grumbled and said Miss Purge must be in love with an evil one in the woods. He dressed and headed for the day room where he found Miss Purge and Mr. Knitter waiting.

"You made good time, Allen," Miss Purge declared. "I believe you know why Mr. Knitter is here."

"No," Aandeg mumbled. He stared at the floor.

Miss Purge turned to Mr. Knitter. "Refresh his memory. He gets three swats for sassing. Be sure he feels them."

"He'll remember," Knitter spat. He was of medium height with a strong square build, graying and in his forties. He held a stout hardwood paddle, which he flourished between Aandeg and the table. "Bend over the table."

His eyes watering, Aandeg nevertheless endured the punishment with low moans, and his gait reflected pain as he left the day room. He was quiet and sullen the remainder of the day.

Friday night, Aandeg lay in bed staring at the ceiling until after bed check. He then silently dressed in fall clothing, stole past the matron's room, out of the dorm into a calm mild night. Snow had melted throughout the day leaving scattered patches.

Traveling first on a trail bearing northwest, Aandeg veered to intercept a wagon road that led to Giiwedin, the northern village on Gichi-zaaga'igan reservation, his home. Reaching the narrow wagon road in the early hours before dawn, he plodded steadily following Giiwedinanang, the North Star. Even as the forest slowly brightened, the dark sky remained ominous in the northwest. Aandeg moved off the trail into a grove of pines, crawled under low branches, covered himself with shrubs and slept fitfully until midmorning.

Awakening cold, stiff, and hungry, Aandeg doggedly pressed on. The air had cooled while he slept, snow was falling, and the wind moaned tediously through treetops. Gusts whined amid leafless bushes near the road. Aandeg shrank deeper into his coat and pulled his stocking cap lower.

Later, numb from hunger and chill, Aandeg moved into a dense balsam grove, and made a shelter of shrubs and fir branches. Facing heavier snowfall, and increasing winds, he curled into a ball shivering himself to sleep.

Saturday morning in the dorm, Niizh Eshkanag sleepily dressed and pulled the covers off Esiban warning him to get up or get paddled. "Onishkaan jibwaa Jaka'ikwe waabamig mii dash bakite'igaazoyan."

"Enh. Howah, must speak English. Yes."

Niizh Eshkanag pointed. "Where is Aandeg?"

"I have not seen him."

When Aandeg did not show for breakfast, and after questioning students, Miss Purge went to Big House, knocking at the kitchen side entrance.

Karen opened the door. "Come in, Miss Purge. Would you like to speak to father?"

"If I may, please." Miss Purge stepped inside and closed the door as Karen called for her father. Karen remained in the kitchen after Elias came.

"Yes? Miss Purge." Elias said.

"I believe a boy, Allen, has run away."

"When?"

"During the night."

"Any apparent reason?"

"None that I know of." Miss Purge shook her head and glanced at the floor.

Elias thought a moment. "Is he one of the younger boys?"

"He is one of the twelve-year-olds, from the north village."

Elias stepped into the yard and scanned the horizon. "I believe we're in for some weather." Still outside, he looked back through the open door. "Karen, have you heard anything unusual about Allen?"

"No." Karen moved closer to her father. "He's a small boy, quiet, seems to be thinking a lot though not about school, I'd say." She brightened. "Roger talks to the Anishinaabe students; he might know something."

Called from his room, Roger frowned when he was told Aandeg had run away. "He probably ran away because . . ." he hesitated, glancing at Miss Purge.

"Whatever," Miss Purge interrupted. "Homesick, more'n likely."

"He was paddled." Roger looked straight at Miss Purge.

"Normal discipline," Miss Purge explained. "They have to be taught respect for authority."

"Of course," Elias agreed. "Thank you, Miss Purge. Meet us at the school in thirty minutes?"

At the school, Elias and Karen met with Principal Joe Losset, Knitter, and Miss Purge. Soon Mike Murphy entered and all studied a map of the area.

Elias faced the principal, "Joe, do you have students familiar with the area between here and Giiwedin?"

The principal scratched his jaw. "Perhaps a number of them. Most are too young to be of help." He brightened and nodded.

"What is it?"

"A transfer from Yardley Indian Boarding School. The family used to live in Ningaabii'an, which is close to the lane going to Giiwedin. He's only thirteen, but he'd know the country thereabouts."

"Who is it?" Elias scanned the map as he talked.

"Niizh Eshkanag." The principal held his hand up as he paused. "I believe he's now called Tom Horns."

"What does the name mean?" Elias said.

"Don't know." The principal said, shaking his head.

Karen raised her hand. "He's Roger's friend, very bright, way beyond his age, and a strong runner if you need one."

"Mm, yes." Elias turned to Miss Purge. "Find this boy right away." Facing Knitter, he spoke while motioning north. "Hitch the carriage to the fast horse." He turned to Mike. "I'll ask Mrs. Murphy to send hot tea and blankets with you in the event you find the boy."

The principal arrived with Niizh Eshkanag who stood fidgeting until informed of the problem then he eagerly explained, "My father and I have used that trail before. It is an easy trail in summer, but snow could be this deep now." He held a palm high over his ankle. "Aandeg, uh, Allen does not plan good and could have trouble."

"Could he be home now?"

"No. It is a three-day fast walk in good weather."

"A life is worth more than a guess," Elias muttered.

Niizh Eshkanag pointed to the map. "Carriage is slow, go long way around where, uh, Allen could be. It is hard to see walking signs from a carriage, but I could go through the forest, maybe find him quick, and the carriage can bring us back."

Mulling options with a hand on his chin, Elias gazed thoughtfully at Niizh Eshkanag. "You could not go alone."

"I could, but there is one who is a strong walker. This one has dog to help find Allen."

"Who might that be?"

"Your Roger," Niizh Eshkanag firmly stated.

"Well . . ." Elias looked hard at the principal then at Niizh Eshkanag. "I don't condone children getting involved in solving school problems, but I'm obligated to explore reasonable solutions." *If even one death can be prevented, the school would fare better at spring audit.* Elias faced Mike. "How dangerous do you think it would be for two thirteen-year-old boys traveling in this weather?"

Mike gazed at Niizh Eshkanag, the floor, and finally squarely at Elias. "It's not bitter cold; these two could travel twice as fast as Allen. They would be dressed warm, and would carry food and equipment. Exhaustion is less possible when the carriage brings them back." He paused. "The down side; weather is unpredictable, could turn colder, snow harder."

"My sense as well." Elias faced Miss Purge. "Ask Mrs. Murphy to pack three flasks of broth and fire starters as soon as possible." Facing Mike, he pointed to the map. "Take the light carriage this far on the west trail near where it meets the north road, but use your own judgment after that. I'll return with Roger if he agrees to join young Niizh. . . uh, Tom Horns."

Elias entered Big House and went into the living room where Roger and Karen played cards on a corner table. Helen looked up from baking bread in the kitchen, talking through the door into the living room. "What's the rush? Looks to snow harder, and we'll just have to ride it out."

"Right, dear." Elias faced Roger, "It will be your choice. Could you take a vigorous hike, possibly into night? You would go with Tom Horns to find a runaway boy."

"It's Aandeg, I mean, Allen, isn't it? Sure, I'll go! Will an employee go with us?"

"That's just it. You, Tom, and Sniffer too would take a short cut and search for Allen. Mr. Murphy will follow the road. If you find Allen, Mr. Murphy will bring you all back in the carriage."

"If we don't find him?" Roger asked. He fiddled with his coat buttons as he spoke.

Elias almost murmured in response, "We must think positive."

Roger shielded a pang of dread at the thought of trudging into a blizzard, but he nodded and disappeared into his room to dress for winter hiking.

"That's what young Tom suggested," Elias said, as though to himself. He turned facing Helen who now stood in the living room doorway. "I have an errand that can't wait."

Helen looked off. "Humph. Traipsing all over creation looking for runaways is no simple errand." Elias ignored Helen and headed back to the school building.

Roger was fully dressed for winter weather as he met with staff in the school office.

Elias faced Niizh Eshkanag. "You say you can get past the large valley even with no trails, through fresh snow?" Elias asked.

"Yes." Niizh Eshkanag pointed to the map. "Allen could be near here."

"Seems reasonable!" Elias said, "I would not risk either of you. Mr. Losset is not worried about your endurance, and I concur."

"What is con-cur?" Niizh Eshkanag asked aside to Roger.

Roger glanced at Elias and then explained, "I think Anishinaabe say, debwetaw, something like that."

Niizh Eshkanag smiled in thanks. "Nahaaw dash, giishpin idaman."

Elias turned away as the boys spoke Ojibwemowin. "The wagon should meet you, hopefully after you have found Allen." He reached for knapsacks and handed one to each boy. "Mike says there are fire starters, broth, sandwiches, and blankets in these." He handed Roger a compass. "This might help until you reach the wagon road."

Niizh Eshkanag looked up and frowned as Knitter entered, but he turned to Roger. "Ready?"

"Sure!" Roger bent and petted Sniffer. "Come on boy, let's find Aandeg . . . I mean, Allen. The boys headed for the door with Sniffer beside them.

Niizh Eshkanag paused in the doorway and glared back at Mr. Knitter. "You beat Allen very hard. That why he ran away!" He missed Knitter's black scowl as he followed Roger out the door.

Elias faced Mike. "Better get going. The way they're moving, I'd say they'd be waiting for you on the carriage road. It's going to be long and trying for everybody. Good luck! I'll alert Miss Pierce to two possible cases of exhaustion and one of exposure."

In an hour, Niizh Eshkanag and Roger were on the foot trail heading to the ridge. They moved swiftly, Niizh Eshkanag leading, with Sniffer leashed to Roger. They studied a sketch, and chose a route, which would take them over the ridge across Zhiibaa'igan, the trail that ran between the west and east villages, saving about two miles. Early in the afternoon, the storm abated, and the boys topped the ridge stopping to snack and rest.

Hiking west off the ridge under darkening skies and heavier snowfall reminiscent of approaching night, the boys trudged into a huge sheltering valley.

On advice from Niizh Eshkanag, Roger now used the map and compass to set a course straight west. Walking was better in the tall forest, though the wind whined through treetops. Heavy flakes of snow pelted their faces and whitened their clothes. Niizh Eshkanag maintained a steady pace with Roger and Sniffer close behind. Snow outlined trees as the forest darkened.

"Must be wild in the open," Roger said.

"We cannot outsmart Bebooniked, the one who makes winter," said Niizh Eshkanag. He waved his arm at the surrounding forest. "We thank Gizhemanidoo, the Creator, for trees that shelter us. Creator could be the same one you call God."

"It's hard to see the compass," Roger complained.

After walking into the blizzard for a time, with Roger pacing beside him, Niizh Eshkanag asked, "How long are we in the valley?" raising his voice to be heard over the wind.

Roger squinted at his watch. "If this were summer, the sun would be way over there." He pointed west toward an invisible horizon, and both boys leaned over to see the watch.

"We have been two hours without a trail," Niizh Eshkanag said.

"Hey, I didn't know Injuns could tell time!" Roger said with a one-note giggle.

"You have compass; can you find Aandeg better than Anishinaabe?"

"Maybe not," Roger muttered. "When we have traveled two hours in the valley, we should be on the trail in half an hour."

"White boy is learning. But we can find the trail quicker than that."

"Are you sure?" They approached a long opening in the forest.

"It is under the snow where we stand," Niizh Eshkanag said. "Now Sniffer can work." Unleashed, Sniffer zigzagged around thickets and bounded through pine groves. The boys trudged against wind that occasionally coursed in gusts along the carriage road.

Niizh Eshkanag yelled in Anishinaabe listening for response. "Aandeg, gidayaa ina?" Dusk approached, then night swallowed the forest.

"We could rest until the wagon comes," Roger mused aloud, "but Aandeg could be bad off if we wait."

"Geyaabi nandawaabamaadaa giiwedinong." Niizh Eshkanag motioned for them to continue searching in the north. The boys walked another half hour and rested. Moonlight above the clouds and fresh snowfall made for tolerable visibility.

"We could make a big circle in woods. If Aandeg is near, Sniffer will smell or hear him," Niizh Eshkanag offered.

When the storm abated to a dull murmur, Niizh Eshkanag yelled in all directions listening for response. To enlarge their search, Roger followed Sniffer off the trail, but finding no clues, returned to the road farther north where they sat to rest. Frustrated, Roger anxiously rubbed Sniffer's neck. Sniffer suddenly yipped and squirmed free, bounding off the trail.

"Ogii-noodnaan gegoo," Niizh Eshkanag gazed into the dark forest to find out what Sniffer heard. With Roger behind, he followed Sniffer toward a balsam swamp from where a faint cry wafted.

Niizh Eshkanag pointed, cried out, "Iwedi! There!"

"Nahaaw! Right!" Both boys stumbled toward the sound. Sniffer disappeared into the evergreens, revealing his whereabouts through whines and yips.

"Enh! I would go there if I was tired and cold!" Niizh Eshkanag yelled. Sniffer watched with whines as Roger and Niizh Eshkanag dug first through a layer of snow, then leaves and branches. Soon they had uncovered Aandeg shivering and incoherent.

"Quick Roger! Make a fire so Mike can see us," Niizh Eshkanag yelled, his voice quivering as he wrapped Aandeg in a blanket.

"OK! Nahaaw!" Roger responded.

"Wewiib! Hurry! He shivers, maybe like one who might soon die."
Niizhi Eshkanag held Aandeg who was too numb to talk while Roger
slowly fed him broth. Touching Aandeg's face from time to time, Niizh
Eshkanag suddenly blurted, "His face warms! Onizhishin!" Roger
rushed to the trail to wave down the approaching carriage.

Mike stepped down from the carriage. "Ah, thank God, you found
him alive." He squatted near the fire for a moment then stood. "He will
get sick from this, so we better get him back to Miss Pierce right quick."
He reached down and scooped Aandeg in his arms and walked to the
carriage. "Put snow on the fire, and we'll get going. Good work!"

When they returned, Aandeg was put to bed in the infirmary. Knitter put
the horses in the barn; Joe Losset walked with Mike and two exhausted
boys to Big House.

"You go. Helen does not like Anishinaabe to be with you," Niizh
Eshkanag said while motioning Roger to go in.

"You two were together," Principal Lossett said emphatically.
"Certainly Niizh Eshkanag should go with you. I doubt either of you
could have done it alone."

The door opened as Roger reached for the doorknob.

"Two brave boys!" Karen said as she reached out, grabbed both boys
by a wrist and pulled them into the house. "Is Allen all right? But he is.
It's in your eyes."

"He is maybe sick but should be good," Niizh Eshkanag said between
gasping yawns.

"Exposure," Roger mumbled through a yawn.

"Good!" Karen smiled. "That he's alive, I mean." She took a step
toward Niizh Eshkanag reaching for him, even as Niizh Eshkanag
retreated against the wall. Karen gave the shaking Niizh Eshkanag a
warm hug then turned to Roger. "Your turn."

"Come on, Cuz, do you hafta?" Roger pretended to complain as
Karen gave him a big hug. Meanwhile, Helen coughed uncomfortably
and went to the parlor.

Roger and Niizh Eshkanag sat against the wall while Mike reported to Elias.

"They are very tired and will probably sleep a long time," Mike said. He glanced down at the boys. "They're not waiting, I see." Both boys had sprawled on the floor sound asleep.

"They can sleep as long as they wish," Elias said.

Mike reached down and lifted Niizh Eshkanag. "I'll carry him to the dorm."

"Can I sleep in the dorm with him," Roger slurred, half asleep. "Aandeg, Allen is in the infirmary, he won't need his bed."

Elias nodded approval, "I'll have Emma check them both out." He lifted Roger, and though Roger tried to stand, Elias carried him to the dorm, laid him on Aandeg's bed, and covered him with blankets.

Soon Emma entered the boys' dorm, knocking to alert everyone that she was entering. First she went to Niizh Eshkanag's bed, checking his vitals, then checked Roger. Neither boy woke during the checkup. Emma wore a look of satisfaction as she departed.

Roger and Niizh Eshkanag slept the remainder of the day, awoke for food, returned to bed and were impervious to comments by other students.

"Ho," Esiban asked where Roger came from in Anishinaabe as he and Bine hovered over the sleeping boy. "Aaniindi wenjibaad?"

"Biiwide, onjibaad waasa giiwedinong," Bine replied, calling him a stranger from the far north.

Esiban nodded, reminding Bine the elders say there is no summer that far north. "Gaawiin niibinzinoon giiwedinong."

The older boy who had once given him a bruised eye, scowled and asked why Roger was in the dorm. "Aaniin dash ginebig omaa nibaad?"

Esiban pointed out that Roger should be welcome in the dorm because he had gone out in search of Aandeg. "Ogii-nandawaabamaan Aandegoon mii noongwa gashkichige omaa nibaad." The boy grunted and left.

"Gida-ganawenimaanaan." Esiban suggested they should watch over Roger to keep him safe.

"An older boy pointed out that the bullies wouldn't dare touch him or they would end up ashamed of themselves. "Gaawiin owaa-dookinaasiiwaan Rogeran wenji-agadendaagoziwaad."

Niizh Eshkanag and Roger were in school Monday, stiff and sore, but rested. Aandeg developed a mild fever from exposure and spent two days in the infirmary.

Helen said little but stewed over the incident involving a member of her household.

Chapter Five

After the experience with young Aandeg, known to the school staff as Allen Crow, Elias sent a letter to employees recommending they end harsh corporal punishment for minor infractions. Knitter's services were no longer requested to punish students, and he kept closer to the barn. Dormitory life, recreation, and classes were better in spite of the strict regimen. Younger boys still feared the farmhand's temper, and boys assigned to barn duty did their best to avoid him.

The dreaded pox struck Giiwedin during Namebini-giizis, the Moon of the Sucker Fish, also known as February at the school. Many of the villagers, including Bine's parents and younger sister, died. Bine was told of the deaths during his week of barn chores. At the end of the school year, with no immediate relatives, Bine would be removed from his home in Gichi-zaaga'igan and sent to a church orphanage or state institution where he would finish school without further contact with his Anishinaabe relatives.

During his week of barn duty, Niizh Eshkanag was paired with Bine to work after school and on weekends. Niizh Eshkanag wanted to talk to the animals, pet them, feel their spirit, but Knitter was everywhere and didn't allow the students to tarry.

Bine and Niizh Eshkanag finished their week of barn detail on Saturday evening. After the morning milking chores, they cleaned stalls while the horses were out watering.

Niizh Eshkanag leaned near Bine careful to use English around Knitter. "While you finish here, I will see how much more work we have in the calf pens."

Moments after Niizh Eshkanag departed, Knitter was suddenly in the wide barn door, which swung out. He glared around then said to Bine. "Damn! This all you done so far?" He pointed to the empty feed boxes.

"I forgot," Bine said with the news about the deaths in his family fresh in mind, and suddenly threw his pitchfork on the ground.

Knitter leaped at Bine, shoving him roughly against a wall. "Pick it up! Now!" He pointed at the pitchfork.

Bine glanced into Knitter's sneering face and terrorized, leaped toward the door, but Knitter grabbed him, lifted him almost overhead and tossed him easily against a wall hung with harnesses. Bine cried out as he was flung, grunted as he hit the harness rack, and fell to the floor. After a brief moan—like a sigh of resignation—he lay twisted, motionless. Knitter stared at Bine then stood in the doorway facing out, frowning.

On his way back to the barn, Niizh Eshkanag heard Bine's frightened cry. He quickly headed back to the horse barn, thinking a horse has kicked Bine. Then he remembered Knitter was headed to the barn and saw him standing in the doorway. Niizh Eshkanag stopped when he sensed an omen in Knitter's stance. He saw Bine lying just inside the doorway.

Niizh Eshkanag shouted, "Giwiisagendami'aa! Wiindigoo gid'aaw!" He knew Knitter was evil and had hurt Bine. Niizh Eshkanag made one leap away from the barn, but was grabbed by both arms from behind and pulled off his feet.

"You'll tell no one if you know what's good for you!"

"Gimaazhichige," Niizh Eshkanag told Knitter what he had done was wrong. Squealing from pain, he struggled in the farmhand's vise-like grip. Helpless, he could only grunt as he felt himself hoisted and thrown with an ominous thump onto the doorframe. He fell numb, nearly unconscious, gasping for air, to lay on his back, an arm bent oddly beneath him.

Staring down at two injured boys, Knitter frowned then went to the fence where he stood looking across the field at the forest.

Niizh Eshkanag's ribs hurt, and pain jabbed his arm when he attempted to move. His thoughts began to clear, and he turned his head to see that Bine was not moving. "Bine gaawiin bagidanaamosii." *Bine is not breathing*, he said to himself. He started to move toward Bine, but his chest hurt too much, his entire body ached, and he could use only one arm. He lay back and waited for someone to come, wishing his father and mother could protect him now. "Nimbagosendaan ingitizimag da-ayaawaad omaa ji-ganawaabamiwaad." He trembled and knew this was not the kind of lesson his parents had wanted him to learn.

Minutes earlier, Roger finished carrying wood and shoveling snow. He threw a happy smile to Karen, a cautious nod to Helen and headed for the door. "I'll see who has messages to deliver." He stopped with a grin and looked back at Karen as he spoke. "Since a wage is not offered, I should at the very least charge postage for carrying things."

"Dreamer!" Karen threw at him. "Be careful around workers, especially Mr. Knitter. You know he doesn't like to be bothered."

"Okay, Cousin Sis. I'll walk past the barn to say hello to Niizh . . . uh Tom, only if Knitter isn't there." *Changing names is confusing.* He buttoned his coat and headed toward the barn. On the way, he saw Knitter with his back to the barn, leaning on the fence staring out over fields and distant woods.

Suddenly filled with foreboding, Roger could not greet Knitter. *Something's not right. No sign or sound of Niizh Eshkanag or Bine.* About to leave the barn area, Roger noticed a shoe and ankle protruding beyond the open door. *Why is someone lying on the barn floor?* Alert to movement from Knitter, he quickly walked behind the farmhand and saw Niizh Eshkanag lying inside the door favoring an arm, breathing in shallow puffs. He knelt beside him and looked across him at Bine. "What happened?" He blurted.

Niizh Eshkanag moaned, and talked between gasps. "Bine is bad . . . I think, very bad! Be careful around Knitter!"

"What happened?" Roger exclaimed moving beside Bine. "Damn! He isn't breathing!" He touched the stain near Bine's head then stared at sticky red goo on his hands. Frowning, without thinking, he quickly wiped his hands on his pants and returned beside Niizh Eshkanag. Where are you hurt?"

"Arm, chest," Niizh Eshkanag mumbled. "Quick! Get your uncle and Miss Pierce. Help Bine, uh, Max, whatever his name is!"

"Of course! Yes!" Roger leaped toward the door. "Be right back!" he yelled over his shoulder, and watching Knitter to avoid going near him, he disappeared around the barn.

On the way to Big House, Roger met Mike. Breathless from running and excitement, he managed between gasps to explain what he saw then continued on to Big House.

Mike stopped at the dining hall for his wife, who went to get the nurse, and all hurried to the barn. Mike took one look at Niizh Eshkanag, knelt beside Bine and shook his head. "I fear Bine has passed on."

Niizh Eshkanag closed his eyes and asked the Creator to watch over them both. *Gichi-manidoo daga wiidookawishinaam. Gaawiin geyaabi o'ayaawaasiin inawemaaganag anami'etamaagod.*

Roger burst into Big House. "Uncle! Bine and Niizh, uh, I mean, Max Partridge and Tom Horns are hurt bad. Bine is very bad!"

"What on earth now?" Elias grabbed his coat and followed Roger out the door, both talking on the way to the barn.

"They were beaten in the horse barn! Niizh says it was Mr. Knitter." Roger's words tumbled rapidly out in nervous succession. "Mike said he would get Mrs. Murphy and Miss Pierce. They could be there, now."

Arriving in the barn, Elias looked at Miss Pierce who knelt beside Bine.

"I'll use his real name; Bine . . . has passed away," Miss Pierce said, her voice soft, solemn. She moved to Niizh Eshkanag, and after a quick examination, angrily declared, "Arm broken, injured ribs, bruises—who knows how severe and where." She looked into Niizh Eshkanag's eyes declaring, "You, young man, must go to the Poleville doctor. Now!"

"Right!" Elias addressed Mike. "Harness the trotter to the two-seat carriage with a box. We'll get the boys ready." He faced Mrs. Murphy. "Will you and Roger get the stretcher from the dining hall and fix a soft bed of quilts and pillows in the carriage box when Mike brings it?"

Dr. Norton can decide whether we need to take him to the hospital at Hutford. We'll take Max, too, so the doctor can determine the *exact* cause of death, and make out the death certificate. I'll notify the marshal about Knitter after we get Tom to the doctor." He turned to Miss Pierce. "Get what you think we need for the trip and dress warm. I want you along in case young Tom's injuries complicate."

Mike returned with the carriage, Roger and Mrs. Murphy came with a stretcher and bedding. Niizh Eshkanag was carefully laid in the carriage with Bine who was was wrapped in a blanket beside him.

Elias faced Mike. "I want you and at least one other employee to watch Knitter. Make sure he has no access to weapons, and if possible, get him into the lockup room at the administration building." Elias climbed onto the carriage.

"I'd like to go with you to Poleville," Roger declared.

Elias looked hard at Roger, contemplating what that would mean to Helen, to the school, to government policy. "All right, get on and help Miss Pierce while I drive the horse."

Roger held a blanket over Niizh Eshkanag's face the half hour to Poleville. Though his friend grimaced when the carriage traversed bumps and ruts, he took the trip without complaint.

Dr. Norton fumed while examining Niizh Eshkanag, pointing once at Bine's body, "You say he killed Max Partridge, then threw you against a doorway? So much damage in such a short time!"

"Knitter is big and strong," Elias explained, "and has a temper but never hit like this before."

"Well," Doctor Norton murmured, as he cut Niizh Eshkanag's shirt off, "this boy has a broken upper arm, bad bruises, looks to have cracked ribs and says his legs hurt. I'll probably find more injuries before I'm done."

Elias motioned to Roger. "The deputy sheriff should be home on a weekend. Would you go to his house behind the community center and ask him to come here?"

"Right!" Roger ran out the door.

Dr. Norton and Miss Pierce soon had Niizh Eshkanag undressed to winter underwear bottoms, beneath a blanket and strapped to the table.

"It's goin' to hurt when I set the bone," Doctor Norton warned. "But it's a simple break, and he's thin so it should be easy to set." He gingerly examined Niizh Eshkanag's chest. "Ribs and internal organs could be questionable for days." Miss Pierce gently held Niizh Eshkanag's head with both hands.

About to comment, Elias moved to meet the deputy entering with Roger.

Roger moved alongside the table opposite the doctor and with a stiff smile, laced with concern, he looked down on his friend. Niizh Eshkanag clenched his teeth, squirmed in his restraints with soft moans escaping while his arm was set.

"Well, that's that," the doctor said with a sigh. "Now Miss Pierce and I will splint the break, then we wait a few weeks."

"What is a splint?" Niizh Eshkanag asked.

"Holds the bone until it heals." Roger said.

"Roger can help him get dressed for bed," Dr. Norton said. He faced the deputy and Elias.

"Sad," the deputy said. "Do you have a cause of death, Doctor?"

Dr. Norton motioned to Bine's covered body. "Young Tom Horns says he saw Knitter near the barn but did not actually see him hit Max Partridge. I see a back puncture that could have injured him internally. It was a head injury, though, by something hard and small, that killed him. Almost instantly, I'd say."

"He threw Tom and could have thrown Max," Elias said. "The harnesses hang on large spikes. Could he have hit one of those?"

"That might explain it," Dr. Norton agreed. He faced the sheriff. "Death resulted from a head injury. You'll have to decide how it happened, though hitting his head on a harness spike would match the injury."

The sheriff finished writing. "Thank you, Doctor. That'll do for now." He faced Elias. "I'll go immediately to bring this Knitter fellow in."

"Good. I'll follow you to the school, but first," Elias faced the doctor, "Max, his name was also Bine, recently became an orphan. Would you have the undertaker bring him to the school for services in two days? We'll bury him in the school cemetery. How soon can Tom, uh, Niizh Eshkanag, return?"

"I'm concerned about quickly moving him. The trip to town was certainly hard on the injuries, and he is quite weak. Sometimes these injuries complicate days later, and I would like to be near if suddenly— heaven forbid—he developed fever or internal bleeding. The village helps maintain this small infirmary, and a nurse, Mary Boude, stays overnight when needed."

"Very good! You know the procedure for payment from the school. Would you bill for her expenses and wages as well? When Tom returns to school, you can finish his treatment on your school rounds." Elias turned to Roger, crooked his finger as he started for the door. We best get back to the school."

"May I stay with Niizh?"

"Helen might not approve."

"Apparently these two are very good friends," Dr. Norton said. "It's worth considering; not to ease an injury, but the death of a school mate could hit young Tom harder as he feels better. It could help to have a friend around."

"I could clean and carry firewood," Roger offered.

With a hand on his chin, Elias gazed briefly at Niizh Eshkanag, then at Roger considering the fact that they both helped save another student. "Very good. Send Roger's food and personal expenses directly to me, not the school office." Elias left with Miss Pierce and followed the sheriff to the school.

Roger helped put Niizh Eshkanag to bed then went to contact Nurse Boude. He later helped with food, washed dishes, and cleaned.

The first night was quiet, with Niizh Eshkanag enduring pain in silence. He was more alert the second day, bantering with Roger into late evening.

Roger brought a chamber pot for Niizh Eshkanag. "You could get spoiled real quick here. I'll do everything for you but feed you and pee for you. I could even eat some of your food, if you like." He grinned as he continued, "Tomorrow you are out of bed moving around. Not too much, though. You might have trouble with your ribs. The next day, I want you walking around as much as possible, but not so your ribs hurt. If you're a good boy, you can go back to the school in four days."

"My pale friend's tongue is on a strange journey," Niizh Eshkanag muttered while shifting in bed. He almost smiled but could only grimace. "If you are trying to be doctor, I will never be your patient."

"I heard the doctor talk to Miss Boude."

Nurse Boude entered from her room at the end of the room. "I'm giving Tom medicine for pain," she said, dimming the lamp "Good night, boys. If you must talk, keep it down so I, at least, can sleep."

Feeling better the following morning, Niizh Eshkanag looked about, saw no one, but sounds and smells of cooking came from the small kitchen.

Soon, Roger and Nurse Boude brought breakfast and ate on a small table near Niizh Eshkanag's bed. "Wonder what'll happen to Knitter?" Roger asked of no one in particular.

"Some say another boy died last year," Niizh Eshkanag said. "The man whipped him or something very hard for sassing and he got sick, like something inside him was hurt. Five days they say it took him to die. The man no longer works for your uncle, but I do not know what was done to him."

"And this!" Roger exclaimed without shouting. "Bine is gone and look at you!" He grew angrier as he spoke.

"Knitter is strong," Niizh Eshkanag said. "When he threw me, I was like feather." He winced from the thought.

Miss Boude spoke. "I hope this sort of thing is not an everyday affair at the school."

Niizh Eshkanag grimaced while adjusting himself in bed. "School is strict, but maybe some workers should not have that job. They should not hire ones who hate Indians. Some workers search for reasons to punish us; for them, it is a game they can't lose. Young ones are treated worse, like Bine or younger." He shifted in pain. "They want to teach us white man ways, but they are unkind to us. Roger's uncle is strict, but I do not think he likes to see us hurt."

Nurse Boude listened patiently to Niizh Eshkanag, then glanced at Roger. "So you're the headmaster's nephew! That answers my question. If he lets you stay here with an Indian friend, he must be trying to do the right thing."

"Uncle's all right, just too busy for personal things. Aunt Helen maybe doesn't hate Indians, but she blames them for the epidemic that killed her son, my cousin. She'll really raise the roof now that I'm staying with Tom, uh, Niizh." Roger suddenly looked around. "Just don't tell anyone I said so."

"It's not my place to repeat what I hear during work," Miss Boude said. "But I remember the smallpox epidemic that killed the Poznanski boy. That pox was brought from Europe. If anything, your aunt should blame the government for not vaccinating natives." She pursued that no further and went to fill in her report and prepare for the doctor's visit.

The deputy did not come until the fourth day, and Niizh Eshkanag walked and appeared better, though bent from rib discomfort. He took a statement from both boys, then explained, "Knitter is in jail and might get prison for injuring Niizh Eshkanag."

"Might?" Roger questioned.

"With no witnesses to Max Partridge's death, a lawyer could call it an accident. A jury of white folk could have trouble convicting their own for killing an Indian without witnesses. They'd settle for something beside murder, and give him a short jail term."

After the deputy left, Roger muttered while staring out the window, "Do all Indians have some kind of a bad story they could tell? I mean about something that happened to them?"

Niizh Eshkanag glanced at Roger's back, then at his sheets. "Yeah, the bad stories, like Bine's, can be told only by others who soon forget. There is talk sometimes that the long sleep is maybe better than school."

"That's terrible," Roger said. "Why didn't they build small schools in each village that let you stay home?"

"Don't know," Niizh Eshkanag replied.

"I have a different trouble," Roger said. "My uncle works so hard; he doesn't see some things, doesn't take time to notice how people feel, like students and all. If it weren't for Karen, I think I would do like Aandeg."

"Run away?" Niizh Eshkanag replied sharply. "I think you could easily stay away from your aunt in such a big house."

"I could go to Milwaukee, but my mother is ill and I don't want to burden her. I have another aunt, but she has nothing to spare which is why I was sent to stay with Uncle Elias. When I went with you to find Aandeg, it took Helen forever to stop complaining about it. Now it'll start again because I'm here."

"Gimiigwechiwi'in . . . thank you," Niizh Eshkanag said, "uh, for helping me. Maybe you should not tell your aunt when we talk."

Roger glared at an invisible specter of Helen. "She cannot pick my friends! Indian or white!" Then he softened. "Karen can pick her friends, but it's different with her. She's *their* daughter and older."

"Karen does not make a bad memory for your aunt like the son who . . . Karen told me of your cousin who is in the other world. If I go to the other world, Mother and Father would be sad but glad to take another boy, make him happy. Helen should want to make you happy. She will never get her son back. You could be like her son."

Roger shrugged. "Can't say. Maybe."

"Not all grown-ups are wise. Indian or White."

"I think about that, too," Roger said.

Niizh Eshkanag returned to school with sore ribs, his arm in a cast. Roger returned home and, with Karen's support, endured Helen's tirades in the third person, berating him and calling him ungrateful.

To please Helen, Elias banned Roger from seeing the Anishinaabe students outside of school. Nor could he take part in activities with them.

Though separated in class, Niizh Eshkanag and Roger talked together during recess, and both slipped away at night behind the equipment shed to talk, joke, or simply sit in silence, each feeling the presence of the other.

Niizh Eshkanag's cast came off near the end of March, as the days were getting warm enough to melt the top layer of snow. Onaabani-giizis was also the month of the new year for the Anishinaabe students who knew their return home was growing closer. Niizh Eshkanag's ribs no longer slowed him with disabling pain, and he raced again. Roger beat him in their first races inside, but as days warmed and physical training classes went outside, Niizh Eshkanag again became the strongest runner.

Just before the April holiday of Easter that year, as the sap began to flow in the middle of Iskigamizige-giizis, Roger received a small package from the mail carrier. In it was a letter from Uncle Steve and Aunt Beth saying his beloved mother, Susan, had died of the same illness that had taken his father. The delivery included a small square package with the words "Bòże pòmagôj" written on the outside. Roger recalled some of the Kashub language his parents and relatives used in their small Polish community on the island in Milwaukee and knew these words meant, "God bless you." When he unwrapped the bundle he found the smooth gold wedding ring with the polished red coral center his father had given his mother when they left the Baltic Coast to come to America. Roger felt more alone than ever before.

Chapter Six

Balmy weather before and after cool, drizzly days heralded the coming of summer, and scents of an awakening forest wafted into classrooms refreshing memories of family and friends.

Niizh Eshkanag lay on his bed as other boys dressed, and he stared at an imaginary smoke hole where the stovepipe disappeared into the off-white ceiling. *We're soon home for summer.*

Esiban stood beside Niizh Eshkanag's bed smiling down telling him it was time to get dressed. "Aapideg biizikonayen. I will help straighten your sheets."

"Miigwech." Pleasant, short of smiling, Niizh Eshkanag raised himself, sat on his bed and yawned wide with a gasp. "Soon it is Strawberry Moon. Ode'imini-giizis sounds better than June to me."

Esiban's smile grew brighter, more genuine than it had during winter. "Gaawiin inda-manegiimiisiimin. Gichi-ayaayag neyaab gibiizhigonaanig endaayang," he told Niizh Eshkanag he was happy they would be picked up by their elders soon and would no longer need to run away.

Niizh Eshkanag nodded and thought of how they would let their hair grow and wear deerskin and moccasins. "Niwii-gagaanwaanikwe miinwaa biizikamang waawaashkeshiwegin gaye makizinan."

Esiban shook his head. "Mikwendan ina? Remember? The agent wishes everyone to wear white man's clothes, even in our own villages."

"And use the English names they gave us," Niizh Eshkanag declared. "Like the gym teacher says, Rubbish! Gaawiin sa! Cotton wears good enough in spring and fall, wool rubs the skin and is not warm like fur in winter, and mosquitos feed through cotton easier than deerskin. Nimbiizikaan minwendamaan. I wear what feels best." He contemplated a seam in the wood floor. "Poleville School is better than Yardley, not counting . . . gaa-izhiwebag biboong." He thought of what had happened that winter then stood and pulled his pants on and commented on the difference between Poleville, where Aandeg was told to work extra for running away, and Yardley where students died and the others never knew why. "Omaa Poleville-ing ishkwaa Aandeg ogii-giimii mii dash o'onashamaawaan chi-anokiin miinwaa iwedi Yardley-ing gikinoo'amawaaganag gii-nibowaad mii dash gaawiin wiindamoonangwaa."

Niizh Eshkanag finished dressing and walked with others to the bathroom. "Nayaazh ishkwaaj ingii-noondawaag ingitizimag gaye apikaadizoyaan." He fingered his strands and wished he could hear his parents and braid his hair again.

"Nigiiwemin wayiiba," Esiban whispered they would soon be home.

Niizh Eshkanag pulled his shoes on saying how very difficult it was to wait a very little time. "Chi-zanagad bangii eta ji-baabaabii'oyang."

After breakfast, Roger and Karen sauntered about the woods out of sight of crop fields, feeling the serenity of spring after a difficult winter.

Spring is a time for life to flourish, but Roger's cousin Donald Poznanski died during spring and Helen's melancholy deepened, as though she needed each spring to relive that sadness. Elias tried to reach her through small talk but found it difficult to penetrate her depression.

"It seems we accomplish absolutely nothing with the natives," Helen declared. "Methods other than boarding schools should have been tried; we'd not have this problem today!"

"Now, Dear," Elias soothed, "it takes time to affect change, and we *are* making progress."

"They've influenced Roger so he has less interest in school," Helen countered. "His studies have slipped." She stood. "I have mending to do."

"Yes, dear, I also have work," said Elias heading for his study.

Days later as the family finished eating supper, Helen glanced at Roger and looked at Elias's plate. "Relatives in Milwaukee could certainly have provided a better home for Roger then we in the wilderness." Looking down, Roger shielded a frown, and Karen sat erect looking straight at her mother.

"It's much less a wilderness than five years ago," Elias said. "Are you suggesting we send Roger back to Milwaukee?"

"No, unless he wants a vacation from Indians."

Karen resisted shouting, "Indians are not the problem! If father does not stand up for Roger and you do not want him, he becomes friends with whomever!" She glared at the wall. "If you couldn't make him feel at home, you should've rejected him right off. So he and you could both be happier. I want him to stay, but I'm surprised he hasn't already left."

Elias positioned both hands flat on the table and moved to stand. "Perhaps Roger will become closer friends with the children of other employees this summer."

"If you allow Roger to visit Niizh Eshkanag's village, it would be a big step to getting through to him," Karen said.

"What?" Helen spat. "You've lost your senses!"

Elias shook his head. "I could not expose Roger to the dangers of an Indian village."

"Dangers?" Karen retorted. "An Indian boy here was paddled until he ran away, another killed by an employee, and Niizh Eshkanag was seriously injured. Yes, Indian boys under white care! How do you think Indian parents feel sending their children *here*? Father, have you even asked yourself what Roger sees in Niizh Eshkanag? Seen their faces when they're together? It has nothing to do with one being Indian, the other not."

"Aren't you missing the point?" Elias interrupted.

"I don't think so. You should know that few children of employees are as bright as Roger. Niizh Eshkanag is not only Roger's equal, but they have similar views and fit together hand in glove."

"An Indian equal to a white student? Nonsense!" Helen retorted.

"Niizh Eshkanag is a bright student and does remarkably well with our curriculum," Elias admitted. "If he stays in school, he and other native students could join you in preparing for college."

Niizh Eshkanag and Roger both turned fourteen in April, Niizh Eshkanag one week earlier than Roger. Final exams were over, and school officially ended. Students were off Friday afternoon and allowed to build a bonfire that night after supper to celebrate the end of the school year.

In Big House, Elias read the weekly paper from Hutford, Helen knitted, and Karen read near a lantern.

Roger peered out the window at moving silhouettes about the fire. He felt the excitement and heat from the fire on Niizh Eshkanag's face. When Niizh Eshkanag shielded his eyes, so did Roger, as though standing there himself. *I have to see my friends one more time before they go.*

Roger twisted to look back at Elias, careful to avoid looking at Helen. "Uncle, may I go outside by the fire?"

Helen looked up, her knitting unabated. "With those out there?" she said. Roger frowned from the chill.

"There should be no harm," Elias said, "but perhaps not now; it might interfere with student activity."

Disappointed, Roger sat watching students through a window, their silhouettes seeming to dance with the flames. "Why can't I go for a few minutes, Uncle? I won't see them for a long time."

"All right," Elias said. "Not over fifteen minutes." Helen opened her mouth to speak, but Roger was out the door.

Roger sat beside Niizh Eshkanag, Esiban, and the others, all staring in silence at the fire, as if their thoughts danced together in the flames. Other students simply glanced at Roger as if he was another student.

Roger broke the silence addressing Niizh Eshkanag, "Niizh, what will you do when you're home?"

"Help Father cut and collect wood for winter. And there is always food gathering. The good part will be visits to Uncle Zhaabiiwose, Aunt Boonikiiyaashikwe, and cousin Giigoo at Ningaabii'an, our western village. If somebody goes with me, I can camp on a cliff for days over the Makwa River—where Father took me when I was twelve winters. When it is your August, our Manoominike-giizis, moon of the wild rice," he gazed north, "I will fast four days alone."

"You will eat nothing?" Roger blurted. "Why?"

"To search for a vision. Like my father and mother, and their father and mother." He nudged Roger with a one-puff laugh. "I will also visit girls. What will you do?"

"Some children of employees work for extra money, others work because their parents make them, though I think they get paid. I will probably work for spending money. We have time off, but other white kids and I have different interests. I'll miss all of you this summer."

"Why does your aunt hate so much?" Esiban asked.

"It's maybe not hate," Roger reflected. "I sleep in her son's bed, which is a bad memory for her. Why she doesn't want me to see you, I don't know." Roger paused breaking into a grin, almost giggling. "Remember when I first came here?"

"I dreamt your scalp hung near our home," Niizh Eshkanag said, grinning as he edged the comment with sarcasm, "so I could spit on it every day."

"So now you want me to laugh," Roger retorted, feigning anger. "I thought you, Indians, I mean, really would scalp me or burn me over a fire."

"You learned this in Minowaki newspapers?"

"I suppose." Everyone at the fire laughed.

"I joke about your scalp," Niizh Eshkanag said. "We see newspapers and hear stories, same as you. Some stories begin with truth, others don't, but because most stories are written for whites, Indians are not—as one not-so-bad-teacher says, described in a good light."

"I know."

"Let's change the subject," Niizh Eshkanag continued. "About your aunt; Indian students died, but she blames them for her son's death. Mother says she might not change until something very serious happens to her or a close relative."

"What could that be?"

"Can't say." Niizh Eshkanag thought a moment raising a finger heavenward without pointing directly at Roger. "You are a relative, but her mind has a stronger memory. I do not think her son, your cousin, has finished his journey in the spirit world."

"You think so? . . . Mm. Anyway, I might go to Milwaukee and solve the problem."

Niizh Eshkanag stirred the fire and looked north into the darkness. "I spoke of you to my parents when they visited at Easter, when they came to mark our new year in spring. They would like to meet you. Maybe you could visit this summer, stay with us." He talked slow, measuring thought and word, "If you ran away from a cold heart, you could live in a lodge with warm hearts. I think good spirits visit us in our homes more than at school."

Roger shook his head. "You know my uncle. If something was out of place, if I went on my own, I'd have to be put back." Roger shook his head with a shrug. "If things get too bad, I might just leave anyway—make everyone happy."

Niizh Eshkanag glanced into Roger's face. "When we go home . . . maamakaajichigaade . . . it's what you call wonderful, a celebration."

"I'll talk to you later about summer," Roger said. A glimmer of excitement flashed in his eyes, then faded. "I would like to visit your village, but Uncle would never allow it." Niizh Eshkanag did not respond and stared at the dying fire.

Roger stood and stretched. "You must get to the dorm, and I must get to the house." He brushed dirt and ash from his pants, waved to the others, and headed toward Big House. Esiban yawned while he and Niizh Eshkanag headed with others for their dorm.

Elias rested nodding in a soft chair as Roger entered the house. Karen cleaned in the kitchen with Helen.

"Lo, Cuz," Karen called as Roger entered.

"Hi." Roger said just loud enough for Karen to hear.

Helen scrutinized Roger's ruffled look, then moved to look closer.

"I thought so!" she snapped. "Look at those clothes!" Karen rolled her eyes at her mother's tone, rather than what she said.

"Hard to stay away from blowing ashes," Roger said softly.

Helen turned to Elias. "Aren't you going to say something?"

Elias was now fully awake. "Uh, yes," he began, "your clothes *are* dirty. I see no excuse for that. More of your thoughtlessness, and I'll have to punish you. Is that understood?"

"Yes, sir." Roger went to his bedroom. From bed, he listened to living room chatter, understanding through it all that Helen was working harder to take his Indian friends away. *Does she hate my being here? Is it mostly her hatred of Indians? Is it because Donald is dead and I'm here? Karen says she's with melancholy.* Roger slept amid myriad dilemmas fending off what he could in his dreams.

Niizh Eshkanag excitedly met Roger behind the equipment shed Friday. "About you visiting my village, my parents would let you come, but my father insists that your uncle agrees."

Roger frowned. "Helen will not allow me to visit an Indian village, and I have no right to say I want to live there. When did you talk to your father? I know telegraph doesn't go to Waaban."

"Howah. He came with another last night," Niizh Eshkanag explained. "We only talked for a short time. Father said, if you ran away, an agent might come to the village looking for you, and the village or my family could get in trouble. Father also said that ones our age are old enough to walk our own trail, but white man's law is not the same as Anishinaabe law." He shrugged and headed for the the boys' dorm. "Nimaajaa."

Lying on his bed adjacent to Esiban's bed, Niizh Eshkanag told the younger boy that Roger wanted to visit their village, "Roger o'andawendaan wii-mawidishiwed Waabaning."

Esiban sat facing Niizh Eshkanag, elbows resting on his thighs and warned that Roger's selfish aunt would never allow it. "Onoshenyan mangodaasiwi miinawaa gaawiin wiikaa waa-bagidinanzig."

"Debwemigad," Niizh Eshkanag replied in agreement. "Aaniin dash Roger waabishkiwid miinawaa andawendang Anishinaabewid dash Anishinaabewiyang miinawaa andawendamowaad waabishkiwiyang?" he wondered why Roger, who was white wanted to be like them, while others tried to make them be white like Roger "Aaniin waa-minobimaadiziyang?" Niizh Eshkanag whispered in a low voice that this could not be a good trail for them to all be on.

"Niminwenimaanaan Roger mii gaawiin minwenimaasiwangwaa odinewemaaganiman," Esiban said, pointing out that Roger was liked, but not by his family, adding that he liked Roger too, but wasn't sure why, "Gaawiin ingikendanziin wenji-minwenimag Roger."

Niizh Eshkanag told Esiban he was thinking too hard about why Roger has a good heart, "Gidonzaamendaan. Roger minwaadizi eta." Niizh Eshkanag told Esiban his mother always said it was blindness of thought not to see through color. They both knew Roger had spoken of troubles in Big House, of his parents' sickness and then death. Niizh Eshkanag decided Roger needed the advice of elders but maybe not of his uncle and aunt.

Saturday dawned clear and mild.

Niizh Eshkanag was ecstatic talking with other students about the arrival of his father, Bizhiw, and Gekendaasod, "Nos, Bizhiw miinawaa Gekendaasod ogii-dagoshinog."

"Aaniin dash gichitwaawendaagozid ayaad omaa?" Esiban asked why their spiritual leader had come.

"Gekendaasod giwiidookaagonaan ji-boonendamang biboon," said Niizh Eshakanag, explaining he would help them forget the winter of trouble. "Aanind Anishinaabeg gaawiin geyaabi debweyenimaasigwaa aanawi debweyenimag." Niizh Eshkanag said that some Anishinaabe students no longer trusted him, but his family still did. He asked Esiban if he heard the drum last night, "Dewe'igan ina ginoondaawaa?"

"Ingii-nagamootaadiz ji-nibaayaan," Esiban replied that he sang himself to sleep with the sound of the drum's heartbeat.

In Big House after breakfast, Roger was at the parlor window peering out pensively at activities near the Administration Building where students boarded wagons for the short journey to local villages or to catch stages at Poleville. He felt the excitement, wanted to be part of it.

"I have to say goodbye to Niizh Eshkanag, uh, Tom!" Roger announced staring out the window. He passed Helen on his way to the door.

"Don't you dare go out there, Roger Poznanski!" Helen's voice was low at first, then louder, stinging.

"Roger," Elias interrupted. "Helen is right; don't go out just now. It might disrupt things to have you walking about."

"I won't bother them, just yell farewell to them." Looking straight ahead, Roger went out the door and ten paces away from the house. He shouted, "Niizh Eshkanag! Esiban! Ajijaak! Nagamokwe! Giga-waabamininim! Goodbye. Have a safe trip! See you in school, I hope!"

The four waved, then others from the wagon. The elders looked without expression at Roger. As the wagon trundled away, Roger saw Niizh Eshkanag point to him while an elder looked his way, and he knew Niizh Eshkanag's father saw him. The wagon soon disappeared beyond the pines.

Roger returned into the house, entered the living room where Elias met him whip in hand with Helen rigid behind him.

"Tell me, Mother, Father," Karen demanded. "What has Roger done to earn a whipping?"

"Disobeyed!" Helen retorted, her voice quivering.

"I only went a few steps from the house," Roger declared matter-of-factly.

Karen talked firmly short of hissing, "You have no right to stop friends from saying goodbye and no right to whip." To protect Roger, she stood in front of him. "You'll lose your nephew, my cousin!" Nevertheless, Helen pulled Karen away while Elias gripped Roger's wrist pulling him out the door behind the house. The whipping was light, though it stung, and Roger struggled to understand why friendship needed to be punished. Elias returned to the house, and Roger went behind the equipment shed to sit and think.

Minutes after the last wagon had gone, Roger peered around the corner of the shed at the house then at the dorms. More time passed, and he gazed north into the pines. Suddenly, clarity replaced uncertainty. It wasn't only the whipping, Helen's bitterness, the loss of his own mother, or because he couldn't visit his Indian friends, but all that. I respect Uncle Elias, and I know Aunt Helen is with melancholy, so if I go to Milwaukee, it might be better for everyone. Mm. I should first go to Waaban, ask their advice before traveling southeast. I'd be found in Poleville, and Hutford is too far.

"Roger?" Karen called from the house yard.

Roger emerged from contemplation. "Over here." He waved at Karen.

Karen came and sat beside Roger, laying her hand on his forearm, "Did it hurt?"

"Not really," Roger said. "I've been thinking. Aunt Helen acts like she doesn't want me around. Uncle Elias doesn't help, as though he doesn't care. I want to stay out here for a while. Will you bring a lunch and water? I want to eat alone."

"I see," Karen said. "Father will understand that you want to be alone for a while, but mother will think you ungrateful. If you're sure that's what you want." She stood and amid a sense of uncertainty, went to the house disappearing inside.

Roger sat fidgeting, but his mind focused north along Zagime Ziibi. He was still considering what to do when Karen returned.

"I found what I could." Karen said. "Mother said nothing; Father was busy, so I raided the pantry."

"I love you," Roger said hugging her.

"I love you, too. But we're not parting. Are we?"

"Um."

Puzzled, Karen turned to go. "I'll leave you be for now." With slow steps Karen returned to Big House.

Roger took the food, slowly nibbled some while gazing at the Zagime Ziibi trail. Suddenly resolute, he stood, adjusted his clothes, and looking straight ahead strode north on the wagon trail.

Chapter Seven

Roger stared at wagon ruts as he walked or scanned the forest focusing on suspicious looking trees or bushes. *What's to happen now? They don't really care, except Karen, and she knows what's what.* His thoughts raced short of confusion. *The wagon moved slowly leaving the school but had a lead so I must hurry. . . . I suppose the Anishinaabe could do something bad to me for coming to the village. But they wouldn't, would they?*

Sunny warmth eased Roger's worry of being alone, but anxiety about unknown dangers nagged unabated.

Nearby raven calls seemed different than they would at the school—like immigrant children at play in Milwaukee. Roger perspired, which was exacerbated by worry, and though not faltering, he tired somewhat by high sun. His energy waned giving rise to a new omen—*Holy cow! What if I'm turned out? I've food only for the day. Niizh Eshkanag says that Wiindigoo prowls at night looking for food, that it prefers white boys. I really think he jokes too much. He has an odd sense of humor.*

Nevertheless, Roger maintained steady pace, was alert for sounds and signs of movement ahead and about.

The sun moved westward, and Roger had not seen the wagon, nor heard the chatter of students on the trail ahead of him. Do the horses trot? Wonder if Uncle Elias will miss me. Helen won't, that's for sure. Karen will play with her hair, look puzzled, sad, too, wondering where in creation I went. But she'll figure it out. With luck, I can be on my way to Milwaukee after visiting the village. When I get to Milwaukee, I'll send a letter thanking Elias and Helen—I really think they meant well. Niizh Eshkanag says tribal elders travel by wagon to other villages.

They'll know how I can get to Hutford. I can then take a stage . . . Ooh. Money. Guess I'll have to work at Hutford to earn enough money for stage and train fares.

While resting, sipping from his flask, Roger concluded that he had no idea what the Anishinaabe elders would say. He would have to trust Niizh Eshkanag and his family to not turn him out. *"But I will earn my way, yes siree.*

Not long after Roger left the school grounds, Helen called from the kitchen, "Elias! Have you seen the boy?"

"I've been busy, dear. I'll call him if you like." Elias continued his work in the study.

"I haven't seen him since the Indians left." Helen called.

"Probably around the buildings sulking," Elias said. He sighed as he lay his pen down. "I'll look for him."

Karen entered as her father reached the door. "Hello, Father. Through with books already?"

"No, dear. Oh, have you seen Roger?"

Karen appeared thoughtful. "Come to think, I haven't seen him for hours. Have you checked the barns?"

"Never mind," Elias said. He went outside, first to smaller outbuildings then the dorms where he pressed teachers and Mike Murphy into the search.

Later, convinced that Roger was nowhere on the grounds, Elias returned to the house.

"Now that you're back we'll have lunch," Helen said. She set the table while talking, "Any sign of the boy?"

"I believe he has left the grounds."

"Ungrateful, that's what he is! The very idea!"

"Would he go to an Indian village?" Elias wondered. "He couldn't reach the closest village before night." He turned to Karen. "Did Roger mention anything to you?"

"I had little time to talk with him," Karen said as she poured tea. "He appeared depressed and might have taken a walk in the woods to think. I hope he's not lost or . . . or hurt." She stared out the window.

"There now, we'll do our best," Elias soothed. "He's my brother's son, and we must find him."

"He's my cousin, but more a brother," Karen said.

"What will our relatives think," Helen said, "I suppose we have to find him. I hope he realizes how much trouble he's causing."

"He's not familiar with the forest other than where he went in the blizzard, and the one you call Tom Horns, Niizh Eshkanag, was with him that time," Karen said. "In his frame of mind, depressed and all, he could lose his way."

Elias sipped his cup empty, and after a long silence, left the house. He soon returned. "We have no option other than to notify the authorities. Mike is preparing the carriage, and we'll go to Poleville, notify the sheriff, and send missing posters to nearby towns to watch for Roger. We'll take a picture along for the posters. If Roger doesn't show in a day or so, I'll have the posters distributed to trading posts."

Mike entered the house during the conversation. "Carriage is ready. You might add Waaban to that list," he said.

Elias glanced into Mike's face. "I knew he would've liked to go there. I didn't think he would under these circumstances, but I believe you're right. We must notify the Indian agency for that. And I'll wire the relatives in Milwaukee."

"Heavens! Don't tell the folks in Milwaukee! Not yet!" Helen almost shouted.

"If you don't mind my saying so," Mike said as he and Elias rode the light carriage to Poleville. "I think he's with the Indians. The way he talks to Tom Horns and that girl, Sally Crane. Too young to get downright serious, maybe, but he sure likes to talk to her. Besides, where else would he go around here?"

Elias nodded. "He's too smart to go to Poleville. Here, I thought, was a city boy just needing to get used to the north."

"Employees knew Roger was unhappy," Mike said. "Not that you haven't done your best with him. He's a good boy, which maybe can't be seen right off."

"I guess I knew that all along," Elias said. "But my work kept me too busy to consider what Roger really needed. Like the way he went with Tom, to rescue the runaway, and stayed with Tom when he was injured."

"It ain't my place to say," Mike continued, "but workers know how your wife talks to Roger and looks at him."

"I guess," Elias said. "Perhaps Helen will have time to think and will change when Roger comes back."

"Ah, yes . . . when he comes back," Mike added almost whispering. "Too bad. Everyone likes him."

Karen consoled Helen at Big House, "Now, Mother, Roger is resourceful and can take care of himself. Maybe he isn't lost. If he went to the Indians, can you blame him?"

"He's just ungrateful," Helen stewed. "All I've done for him: cooked and washed and mended."

"And hollered and took his friends away and had him whipped," Karen added. "As though he were truly bad, which we both know he isn't!" She went outside to settle down.

Roger walked doggedly, fatigue slowed his pace, and no longer could he run in spurts. He sat to cool and eat a sandwich then lay on his back staring at treetops. Under better conditions, the gently swaying branches would be mesmerizing, peaceful, but Roger had no energy or will to dwell on the beauty of nature. *Niizh Eshkanag says this trail goes straight to within sight of the village. I'm never going to catch the wagon; I might just as well rest.* While relaxing, he heard rustling in the forest to his left. Sitting erect, he stared into the forest on both sides of the trail but saw nothing. A horse whinnied, and Roger stood into running stance. *A rider? There are no wild horses these parts. Mr. Murphy could be looking for me, but I don't know if he even rides horses.*

Nothing more unusual was heard. *Niizh Eshkanag says a bear can sound a little like a horse. I better keep moving.* Roger was convinced that whatever made the sound had moved on, and he began a fast walk, carefully scrutinizing the ground beside the trail.

Suddenly, a man appeared standing on the trail ahead of him. Instinctively, Roger spun around ready to bolt, but another man was less than ten feet behind him.

Indians! Old newspaper articles flashed in his mind, and Roger sprinted for the woods where he almost ran into two Indians carrying a deer between them. He stopped with a deep sigh of resignation. *Okay, so now what?* The men on the trail were soon around him and those toting the deer had set it down.

"Hello, Boozhoo," Roger said. He nervously raised his arm in greeting. The men spoke rapid Ojibwemowin, which Roger recognized but understood too little to follow.

"Where you going? Why you here?" One man said, speaking broken English. "Your hair Anishinaabe, but you white." Roger flinched as the man fingered his dark hair. The other man gently but firmly held both his arms from behind.

Roger finally collected his wits, squirming one arm free, blurting, "Aaniin! Go to Niizh Eshkanag, his father, Migizi, in the wagon!" He pointed north along the wagon path.

Another man said Roger was too young to be an Indian agent, "Gaawiin o'aawisii Anishinaaben-wegimaad onzaam oshkaya'aawid." He felt Roger's arms and suggested he might be a baby agent. "Gonemaa aawi Abinoojiiyens-wegimaad." The men broke into friendly laughter.

The man holding Roger motioned in the direction of Poleville. "He might be runaway, and we should send him back or we in trouble."

"Waasa Poleville," an older man said that Poleville was too far north and suggested they take Roger to the wagon ahead because he seemed to know them and perhaps they would take care of him. "Gonemaa oganawenimaawaan waabishkiwid." Motioning Roger to follow, the men made their way to a tethered horse, tied the deer on the horse, and lifted Roger behind the deer and led the horse through the forest.

The man leading the horse, looked up at Roger, speaking English, "We see wagon, we will catch for you." The group set off at a fast pace.

"Miigwech!" Roger said aloud so all could hear. The men raised their arms without looking back, and Roger heard soft laughter.

The wagon was soon visible ahead.

In the wagon, Migizi saw the approaching group and decided to stop because they seemed to want to talk. "Noogishkaan, andawendamowaad ji-gaganoozhinangwaa."

As the hunters approached, Niizh Eshkanag raised a hand near his face in a slow, cautious wave to Roger.

"Ginitaagiiwosem," Migizi joked that the men had a good hunt, but asked why they had a fawn. "Aaniin dash gidagaakoons ayaaweg?"

The hunters all laughed and said they found the white fawn wandering the forest. They didn't want him to hurt the bears and wolves so they took him. Then they offered to sell him cheap. "Gida-giishpinazhaawaa wendaginzod."

Roger did not understand the conversation, but realized from fits of laughter that he was the object of their humor.

Niizh Eshkanag looked up and told his father this was Roger. "Wa'aw Roger."

"Ingikenimaa," Migizi recognized the boy. He faced the hunters and asked if he promised not to let the white boy harm the bears or wolves, would they hand him over, "Giishpin waabishkiwid gaawiin maanzhi-doodawaasig makwan gemaa ma'inganan wii-odaapinangid?"

"Ginitaa-adaawe," one man said, chuckling at the trade. He reached up and helped Roger off the horse and gave him to Migizi, "Nimiigiwemin."

Bizhiw laughed and thanked them, suggesting they were happy to be rid of him. "Gimiigwechiwigoom gaye inendamaang minwendaagoziyeg." The hunters laughed and nodded agreement.

Roger moved to sit near Niizh Eshkanag as Bizhiw reined the horses on.

"Are you coming to our village?" Esiban asked Roger.

"May I visit the family of Niizh Eshkanag for the night, at least?" Roger asked. He glanced into Migizi's eyes, which were not aggressive, but flashed intensely and Roger quickly faced Niizh Eshkanag.

"Roger chi-ayekozi noongom miinawaa onoshenyan inigaa'idizod mii wenji-giimiid," Niizh Eshkanag explained that Roger was only escaping his mean aunt and would be too tired to return to school the same day. Then he asked if Roger could stay the night, "Gwii-bagidinaa anwebid endaayang?"

Migizi and Gekendaasod exchanged words, and Migizi motioned for Niizh Eshkanag to interpret for Roger.

"The wise one says that the young of any race should be helped, and the council will hear your story." Niizh Eshkanag wrinkled his brow and asked Roger, "Has something happened? Why do you come now?"

Ajijaak gazed aloof over Roger's head. "I do not remember this one from our village. Black hair does not make him Anishinaabe." In spite of fatigue, Roger was buoyed by a vision of freshness her voice conjured—a waterfall cascading into its own mist.

"I'm glad to see you Ajijaak," Roger said. "But have no energy to argue such mysteries." The elders remained silent, but a smile flickered on Migizi's face. Others watched the meeting of Roger and Ajijaak in silence.

The sun lowered behind trees. Plodding horses and the rumbling of the wagon were the only sounds. Children stared pensively ahead toward an unseen village.

After a long silence, Migizi spoke to Roger in English, "I hear of your trouble at home, that you want learn more about us. Niizh Eshkanag speaks good of you. We will talk after the feast." He turned to face the spiritual leader both talking low.

Roger whispered to Niizh Eshkanag, "There is a feast?"

Niizh Eshkanag noded. "To celebrate our return from school. Every family will have its best food to share, and visitors are welcome. That you share our feast and home is different than why you are here." Niizh Eshkanag and Roger became silent as both watched the forest. Roger stared at a huge pine, which forced the road to curve. Twilight descended, but the trail could still be seen for some distance.

"How many wigwams, homes, in your village?" Roger asked.

"Twenty last fall," Niizh Eshkanag replied. "For summer, some families go deeper into forest to hunt and fish or visit others. We move a lot, like those hunters who helped you." His face flushed with excitement. "They might have a summer home outside a village, probably east of us."

"I thought they might do something to me."

"Minowaki paper, huh?"

"Yeah." Roger smirked. "But unlike what the Minowaki paper might print, they were very helpful and even let me ride the horse."

"Funny," Niizh Eshkanag declared. "You sound bad trying to speak with an Anishinaabe accent."

"You're rubbing off on me."

"Not funny."

The wagon rolled into the village and stopped paces from a large fire near the home of Esiban's family, and the cargo unloaded itself. Roger stepped down but held back as milling youth and kin engulfed each other. His everyday clothes did not appear much different than the students' clothes in the dark but questioning glances were cast at him.

Migizi hugged Bizaan. "I have been surprised," he said to her in English, "it is now your turn to be surprised." He motioned Roger to approach.

"Surprises are not always bad," Bizaan replied in her best English. "If you mean that two-legged yearling, he needs a family." She reached out, gently taking Roger by the upper arm and pulled him close, whispering in his ear, "Niizh Eshkanag speaks of a white boy who helps our students." Roger stiffened, glancing wide-eyed at Niizh Eshkanag, but soon relaxed. "A friend of a son is also a son," Bizaan said as she released Roger.

Satisfied that Biizaan accepted Roger, Migizi smiled and motioned about, "Welcome to our village." He faced Niizh Eshkanag. "Would you stay near Roger in the village tonight?"

"Yes, Father." Niizh Eshkanag said, and whispered aside to Roger, "But I will not be his mother."

"Nor will I be your puppy," Roger retorted, grinning.

Migizi looked at Roger. "The gossip of you was like a tree full of ravens when we visited the school, your spring holiday. We hear good things about you." He faced Bizaan. "Is there room in our home for the pale one?"

"He can share Niizh Eshkanag's side," she said kindly in English so that Roger would know he was welcome.

Niizh Eshkanag stored his school clothes for the summer, dressing now for a feast in his best Anishinaabe clothes, short of dance regalia. Bizaan had estimated how much Niizh Eshkanag might grow over winter and had tailored his clothes accordingly. Esiban also wore ceremonial clothes.

After a short blessing of ten minutes, which included smoking the pipe, a youth collected samples of food, which Gekendaasod offered to Shkaakamigokwe, and the feast began. Elders and grandparents were served first by the young. Niizh Eshkanag motioned for Roger to help, which he did, feeling sharp eyes following his every move.

Two large fires lit the feast, and to avoid stares, Roger ate in Migizi's shadow. He became speechless at the sight of Ajijaak in ceremonial dress, a white feather in her hair. He watched in surprise but was enthralled at her carriage and expression, how proud and light-footed she walked. From trade pants and shirts to Anishinaabe finery, every dress variation could be seen about the village.

More surprises awed Roger, including the variety of food: wild rice, venison, dried berries from the previous summer; fry bread made from ration flour, and chewy roots sweetened with ration sugar and maple syrup.

After eating, the long walk began to tell on Roger. He squelched a yawn, and appeared wan. Missing little, Bizaan motioned Roger and Niizh Eshkanag to follow her and Migizi home.

Seated inside their lodge, speaking only to Migizi, Bizaan told him they should speak to the elders about their guest. "Gida-ganoozhaanaanig gichi-ayaayag."

"Wayiiba giwii-inaajimo'aanaanig," Migizi said Bizhiw would send the village messenger soon, and they would go then to the elders.

Roger studied the interior of the wigwam. *There is more room inside than it seems from outside.* An oil lantern glowed at the far end of the lodge.

"It grows cool. Wrap yourself with these while sitting before the council," Bizaan said, handing blankets to Niizh Eshkanag and Roger.

"He limps and must have blisters from the hard walk," Niizh Eshkanag said, pointing to Roger's feet.

Bizaan motioned for Roger to remove his shoes then applied lotion to raw blisters on one heel. "Your people do not make clothes for the forest." She stretched overhead, took a pouch from the roof framework, removed a pair of moccasins, and handed them to Roger. "They are big, but can be tightened."

Roger mimicked the way Niizh Eshkanag tied his moccasins, and ready for the meeting, suddenly felt anxious. *Maybe they will send me back to Poleville or like Niizh Eshkanag says, put me outside the village for the Wiindigoo. He jokes too much.*

Shortly, a knock sounded at the home of Bizaan and Migizi.

"Biidigen," Bizaan called. A youth of eighteen entered and stood just inside the doorway, waiting. He wore an apron with a beaded floral design, knee-high leggings of black cloth, and carried a staff, the symbol of his duty, with an eagle feather flying from it.

Migizi nodded to the youth. "You look well, Bemised. Is it time?"

"The council waits," Bemised replied, "for Niizh Eshkanag and the one called Roger."

Migizi motioned the boys out the door, Bizaan following.

At the meetinghouse, the group waited outside while Bemised entered and returned moments later to usher them into the center of the lodge. Migizi and Bizaan sat along a wall with Bizhiw's family. Migizi was a council member, but because his family was involved, he would have no voice deciding Roger's immediate future.

Gekendaasod packed and lit a pipe while gazing at Niizh Eshkanag and Roger without expression. He then motioned them to stand, smoked the pipe, and handed it to Bemised who carried it between elders.

The chief then stood. "Gichi-mookomaan izhinikaazo Roger gagwejiminang ajina wii-endaad endazhi-daawaad Bizaan miinawaa Migizi." Niizh Eshkanag translated for Roger as Ogimaa Niigaan explained the situation. Ogimaa Niigaan did not question that Bizaan has agreed to accept Roger but asked what his stay might mean to the village, his white family, his Anishinaabe hosts, and to Roger himself.

"Anishinaabe biboonigizi ashi-niiwin dibenindizod mii geyabi chi-ayaayan bizindawaad." The chief noted that a young Anishinaabe of fourteen winters belongs to himself but still listens to his elders, while an American boy of fourteen belongs to his parents or his government. He breathed deeply then looked straight at Roger, who stared at the ground. The elders asked if Roger had the approval of his family to be on his own. Niizh Eshkanag explained that Roger ran away without asking for approval because he felt he was not wanted. They pondered all angles of this question: why he left, who considered him family, whether he was seeking a new life, and what options would be best for all of them.

When the deliberations ended, Ogimaa Niigaan motioned to Migizi and asked for his thoughts but explained his conflict of interest meant he had no say in the final decision.

Migizi stood and glanced about the lodge and to the boys and began by stating that while he had only first laid eyes on Roger recently, he felt he knew him through the stories of Niizh Eshkanag. "Ingii-waabamaa Roger nitaam noogom aanawi gikenimag ge-dibaajimigod Niizh Eshkanan." He went on to share some of the stories about Roger and how he had helped others at the school. He described the murder of Bine, and Niizh Eshkanag's injuries and the bravery of the search for Aandeg when Bebooniked, the Winter Maker, saw the honesty of both boys and softened his breath. Migizi gazed through the smoke hole, then looked at the elders and said in both languages, "Gaawiin ingikendanziin Bebooniked gaa-azhenaad Aandegoon gIlshpin Rogeran

maji-manidoowaadizinid. I do not think he would have given Aandeg
back if Roger were a bad spirit."

Migizi pointed south and also explained what he knew of Roger's
family, how he lost his parents and was sent to live with an aunt who
did not accept him and spoke harshly to him. Migizi asked the elders
to consider his desire to eventually travel to Milwaukee, seeking
relatives who love him, and asked that they not break his spirit by
turning him back now. He concluded by saying, "Ingii-windamaa
wii-boonigidetawaad onoshenyan gaye omishoomeyan. I have told
him to give his uncle and aunt another chance."

The elders exchanged views with the chief and after the last elder
spoke. Ogimaa Niigaan stood, motioning toward Roger, and announced
their decision. Roger was not to be seen in any village for seven days,
which is when agents search with the sharpest eyes. If he returns to his
home, that means he was not ready to leave. After seven days, he would
be free to come and go as he wishes, and his Anishinaabe friends may
do for him what they can. Migizi and Bizaan were comforted by the final
statement, "Gaawiin awiya anaamimaakaniwid giishpin oshkinawe
dagoshing nazhikewizid. No one can be accused of stealing a boy who
wanders in after days on his own."

After this proclamation, Niizh Eshkanag raised his arm to speak. The
chief nodded to him.

Niizh Eshkanag stood. "Gaawin naasaab giishpin maajaayaan
endaayaan ge-maajaad Roger. It is not the same for me to leave home
as it is for Roger," he said. "Aabawaa miinawaa Shkaakamigokwen
gizhewaadizi gikendamaan miinawaa Roger gaawiin gikendanzig
ezhi-gagwejimaad. It is warm, and Mother Earth is generous to my
family who has shown me how she shares. Roger does not know how
to ask her for food and shelter." Niizh Eshkanag said he would help the
white city boy in the woods as he helpd the Anishinaabe students at his
Uncle's school then sat trembling with surprise at his own boldness.

The chief looked to the other elders who, after a brief discussion,
raised their hands in approval. He then faced Migizi and Bizaan
who nodded assent. Knowing Niizh Eshkanag would soon search
for a vision, the chief said, "Niizh Eshkanag oda-babaamiwizhaan

Rogeran megwayaakong. Miinawaa Rogeran oda-mikwendaan odinewemaganiman wii-metisinigod iidog." Niizh Eshkanag was deeply honored that he would be allowed to guide Roger in the forest and told Roger immediately, adding that Ogimaa Nigaan had also said he should consider that his family may miss him and want him to return.

On their way to the family lodge, Niizh Eshkanag was breathless with excitement.

"Can we really do that?" Roger asked. *Would it be adventure or danger? Ooh, maybe both. . . .* When do we go?

"When the sun rises tomorrow, waaban."

Later that night while two boys slept, Bizaan and Migizi worked into early morning preparing trail packs.

"We must rise at dawn," Migizi said to the boys in English so that Roger would be sure to understand. "An agent could come quick." He gazed at Roger half sleeping and half listening at the far side of the lodge.

"We can watch for the agent. I say let the boys sleep until they are well rested," Bizaan countered.

"Maybe so," Migizi agreed. "For each, there is a knife, fire sticks that must be kept dry, a bow with ten arrows, snares, and fish line. Niizh Eshkanag knows the forest trails for two sleeps in three directions, four sleeps west. He knows which plants to eat, how to fish and hunt small animals. He will need no gun."

"Many days will be warm, some hot," Bizaan added, "but nights could be cool and they must carry warm robes for sleeping.

It was midmorning. "Wake up, sleepy one," Niizh Eshkanag said, shaking Roger.

"Be polite to guests," Bizaan scolded.

"Sorry, Mother," Niizh Eshkanag said. He laughed watching Roger stand, rub his eyes shivering as he stood. "You cold?"

"It's cool. Didn't expect to sleep without clothes, and I'm stiff from walking and all. Where are my clothes?"

"Behind you," Niizh Eshkanag said.

"I see only deerskin clothes," Roger said.

"Father thinks you will return to Big House and saved your clothes in the forest where no one will find them. We have old baggy pants that would be hard to wear in the forest, and Father says you could wear the deerskin clothes. Shirt and leggings are for cold days or walking through thick bushes."

Roger smiled. "Helen would have a fit, but Karen would like to see me dressed in them. I will dress the same as you. Shall I put the clothes on now?"

"Good idea," Niizh Eshkanag said grinning. "When the others see you, they will cover their eyes at the brightness, but Mother says your pelt will darken fast. Uh, for a white boy."

Migizi and Bizaan sat around the outside fire eating the morning meal as Niizh Eshkanag and Roger crawled out the low doorway.

Biizaan twisted to see the boys and pointed to a pot of stew and meat warming on rocks beside the fire. She carefully studied Roger in moccasins, leggings, deerskin shirt and breechcloth. "The clout is plenty big for one who is only bones," she observed. "Moccasins fit, yes?"

"Thank you. Miigwech. For the loan of clothes." Roger smiled as Bizhiw and Nagamokwe joined them.

Migizi bit into fry bread, studied Roger, and asked Bizhiw if he thought Roger would make it seven days with Niizh Eshkanag, "Gidenendaan ina Roger miinawaa Niizh Eshkanag wii-zhaabwiiwaad niizhwaaswi giizhigadoon?"

"Gichi-waabishkizi," Bizhiw pointed out how pale Roger was and added that it might make him weak even if he did walk for a long time after leaving school, "gii-baabimose mii gonemaa niinamizid?"

Roger could not follow the conversation but thought he was discussed, which was confirmed when Niizh Eshkanag raised eyebrows at him. "Do I look that funny?" Roger asked, frowning. "You steal my clothes, then laugh at what I wear."

"If you wear the baggy pants it could bring more laughs," Niizh Eshkanag said. "We do not laugh at you; we only want you to feel good, to not get sick in the forest."

"You know what is in the packs. Go when you are ready," Migizi said in English. "Agents are sly and could come any time."

Niizh Eshkanag and Roger helped each other adjust packs. Niizh Eshkanag took his bow and quiver of arrows then faced his parents. He embraced them and stood aside as they embraced Roger. Bizhiw embraced the pair together.

Niizh Eshkanag and Roger headed to the village outskirts, turned for a final wave, and saw Nagamokwe and Ajijaak watching from near the meetinghouse. After a flurry of waves in two directions, they disappeared into the forest.

Bizaan appeared calm as she waved one more time at an empty trail. *Her only child would need to teach another about that which he knew so little himself: of forest foods, hunting, and the storms of summer.*

Chapter Eight

Hiking west on the trail between Waaban and Ningaabii'an, hands gripping shoulder straps, two boys were soon dwarfed by the tall forest. For some time, they walked in silence, the soft padding of their moccasins almost heard over breezes whispering through treetops, and both seemed to be musing about their personal circumstance, not ready to share fears and hopes in conversation.

Later the boys hiked up a steady though moderate rise through a thinner forest amid narrow beams of sunlight.

"I have been here, but it feels strange without Father," Niizh Eshkanag said, and he slowed shifting his pack as he talked. "We should rest; my shoulder straps hurt, uh, a little."

"I sweat," Roger said, "but my straps don't rub too bad. I think your father gave me the best pack. Wanna trade?"

"No. We will fix our packs at camp." The boys continued up the slope.

A little past midday, the boys rested in a small patch of sunshine below gently swaying trees. Tall pines on a north downslope with little underbrush allowed visibility some distance toward the valley.

Roger sensed adventure but was not aware what dangers might await them or what his role would be in the days ahead. Since leaving Big House, what lay ahead seemed misty and dark to him, but he trusted Migizi who had faith in Niizh Eshkanag.

Both boys worried that an injury to one would impact both.

"Your father says we should camp on the high ridge tonight," Roger reminded Niizh Eshkanag, "where we ate lunch when looking for Aandeg. Remember?"

"Uh huh," Niizh Eshkanag murmured. "There is water below the north slope and small animals to trap. From the school, we went northwest to the ridge; from the village, we travel west to get there."

Roger laughed softly. "Hope it stopped snowing and warmed up." Then soberly, "Come to think, I should have taken the compass from home."

"We do not need a compass," Niizh Eshkanag said, as he studied Roger from head to foot. "Though you and I have almost the same body, we do not look the same." A faint smile twitched the corner of his mouth.

"Yeah, uh huh, I could blind the sun." Roger began untying his shirt. "It's warm, and did not your mother say that the giver of life will darken my pelt?"

"Hide," Niizh Eshkanag corrected. "She did. Because you are sooo white, you must wear the cape when you first take the shirt off." He paused, savoring a thought before adding, "So the agent will not see you from Poleville."

"Har, har. You are almost funny. What she really meant was for me to not get sunburn. Anyway, if you're through joking, I'll get a little sun."

Niizh Eshkanag sobered. "Me, too. Deer skin is warm; I'm taking off my leggings and shirt. If you are hot, you could take your leggings off, too, and no one will see you from Poleville."

"Let's change the subject," said Roger but smiled at their senseless conversation.

The boys packed shirts and leggings and continued west on the trail. They walked a short distance and Niizh Eshkanag noticed Roger's knife hanging loose from his waist thong. "This is no joke, tie the knife to your leg, or it will lose itself when you run."

"I don't plan on running," Roger said. "But if it makes you happy, I'll tie it better."

Niizh Eshkanag snickered once, "your plan will change fast if we see mama bear with her cubs."

The boys walked in silence for hundreds of paces. "Father says," Niizh Eshkanag whispered, watching the ground ahead, "it is easy to empty the mind when walking all day, and one should scatter thoughts carefully along the way." Later, he pointed to a shady spot beneath a tree. "When Father and I first traveled to Waaban, we camped there." He motioned farther up the trail. "Father said, when he was my age, he walked here with his father . . ."

"Your grandfather?" Roger asked, piqued. "Since I came here, to Poleville, I mean, I often wondered about your ancestors and how they lived."

"It would take too long to explain even parts of it." Niizh Eshkanag said.

"Yeah," Roger murmured, "It would take too long to tell the story of you walking with your father, or the stories about your grandfather?"

"Enh. It was on this trail, but more west of the hill where they came upon white ones who had killed an Anishinaabe boy and wounded his sister."

"Then what?" Roger walked close behind Niizh Eshkanag.

"It is a long story, often told around winter fires. Sometimes it changes when the teller is excited, but the killing is the same. One teller said the Anishinaabe boy was a hero. He wounded a white boy with an arrow, and his family carried the white boy to Ningaabii'an, which was not where it is today."

"About the white boy," Roger began, "what happened to him?"

"He was too young to carry a gun and was accidentally wounded by an arrow. After he was made well by a healer, my grandparents adopted him. He was our age, I think. He lived in two worlds after that, Father says, and married Anishinaabe woman named Ziibi-Ikwezens."

Roger shrugged. "Which means?"

"When we speak English, I forget some of the Anishinaabe words, but I know that name means River Girl."

"Webbed feet and all?" Roger said with a one-note giggle.

"Do all white boys talk silly, like that?"

Roger shook his head and moved ahead along the trail.

Niizh Eshkanag nodded. I have relatives in Ningaabii'an: Aunt Boonikiiyaashikwe and Uncle Zhaabiiwose. Oh, and Cousin Giigoo."

"Will we meet them?" Roger asked. He now walked directly behind Niizh Eshkanag on a narrowing of the trail.

"Not now."

"I know. Days, weeks, I mean." Roger puffed a laugh. "Okay, years maybe? When agents get tired."

"Agents are paid to never get tired, but my white friend could first tire of this forest life."

Roger nodded, "I get the idea."

Midafternoon, Niizh Eshkanag and Roger lay back, arms behind their head lulled by breezes whispering through gently swaying branches.

"Walking is hot work," Niizh Eshkanag said. "It was easier before we spent months in school."

"Yeah," Roger mumbled. "Karen would say I was getting soft."

After making their way through a tall forest on level terrain, the boys wearing shirts against the sun, labored up a long gradual slope. After half an hour, they surveyed the east aspect of the ridge.

"We could camp there," Niizh Eshkanag said, pointing to a grove of pines not far off the trail.

"If you think so." Roger dropped his pack and lay beside it. "I'm tired."

"Me, too, but there is work before we sleep."

"It's not the same as home where I would smell Karen's baking." Roger sighed shaking his head. "I've never done this."

"This is not school," Niizh Eshkanag teased. "Or Big House where supper waits."

"Please, I've no time for lectures," Roger grumbled. He paused to watch Niizh Eshkanag face west and sprinkle tobacco to thank the setting sun for a good day.

Niizh Eshkanag motioned in the direction of Poleville. "We are not able to honor the sun at school."

"As I understand it, you could be punished for honoring the sun."

"Maybe."

Roger's face wrinkled as he asked, "Do many use the trail?" He pointed to ashes.

Niizh Eshkanag shook his head. "Maybe a family or trapper, not many. None at night, unless they camp like us." He nodded as he studied the ashes. "Those ashes are not old. We should move farther off the trail."

The boys walked a hundred paces off the trail, and Niizh Eshkanag pointed to thick bushes near a large pine. "How is this?"

"How am I supposed to know?" Roger mumbled. "Better, I guess."

The boys walked about the ridge, inspected the trail to the west and returned to the pine. Satisfied with the location, Niizh Eshkanag began constructing a simple lean-to, and Roger gathered firewood.

After a campsite had been fashioned, including hanging food from trees to foil the four-legged scavengers, Niizh Eshkanag pointed to the ground near the lean-to. "Now we eat and sleep."

"Yeah." Roger yawned audibly, which seemed to echo the haunting cry of a distant wolf. Provisions were heated and mixed with fresh greens, and the boys relaxed to a skimpy meal.

As he ate, Niizh Eshkanag observed Roger. "My parents, maybe others in village, wonder how the white one will like a week in forest with four-legged and flying ones."

Roger raised his hand with a finger pointing up, but the finger sagged and he shook his head, "I sometimes wonder what your parents really think about me, what I'm getting *you* into."

"I will say what Mother said, which is not bad, and she speaks her heart . . ."

"Well, what *did* she say?"

"She said," Niizh Eshkanag replied, hesitating, "uh, you look too weak to be in woods."

"Yeah? I'm *weak* . . . and tired." The boys quieted and rolled in blankets across the fire from each other.

"We have food for two days," Niizh Eshkanag said. He stared at the fire with a tired smile. "Tomorrow, we buy groceries from Shkaakamigokwe."

"If you say . . . so," Roger said, drifting off.

Roger awoke to dawn and a blazing fire. He sat silent watching Niizh Eshkanag face the rising sun and return to the fire.

"We should set snares near the stream after eating," Niizh Eshkanag suggested. "Then pick greens and roots and bring water back. I think it is too early for ode'iminan which would sweeten our meal. In our language 'ode' means 'heart,' and there is a story we hear as children about a young couple and their love." He gazed at Roger, puzzled. "Why do you call them straw berries in English?"

"Don't know about English, but my parents would sometimes speak Polish and in that language 'truskawka' is the name for the little berries collected from low bushes that make a rustling sound. I guess lots of words have memories and stories attached to them." Roger said. Then he turned to more immediate matters and announced, "I'll cook the rice and dried meat." He stood, donned his breechcloth, and stretched. "Ooh, my muscles are breaking, and my shoulders sting, but not bad." He tied his moccasins on then took a moment to watch smoke from the fire filter up through pines, rise above trees, and waft gently eastward. "Some might say it's noisy; singing birds, yelping animals, and the wind, I mean, but to me it's peaceful," Niizh Eshkanag nodded.

The boys hung their food from tree branches to foil the four-legged thieves and headed into the valley. The morning chill was gone before they reached the creek where they scouted for future food.

"A rabbit runs here," Niizh Eshkanag said, pointing. He set a snare. "Another sleeps there." He turned, motioned to a wider section of the stream. "The water is cold, but we should at least rinse." He removed a moccasin and dipped his foot in the stream. Roger also tested the water.

"It *is* cold, but like gym teacher says, *here goes*," Niizh Eshkanag undressed and waded in, squatting to cover his shoulders. "Ooh!" He grunted, quickly leaving the steam. "It is very cold, but soon we can do that every day and enjoy it. Your turn."

"You have more goose bumps than I ever saw," Roger said as he undressed. He waded in, squatted, tried to speak, but his words erupted in staccato. He quickly waded out, and both boys dressed.

While gathering edible greens, Niizh Eshkanag pointed to some he didn't pick. "For Shkaakamigokwe or another day."

It was a short day of exploration. Back in camp, Roger gathered firewood then worked on the lean-to, while Niizh Eshkanag prepared an early meal.

Niizh Eshkanag took wooden bowls and put warmed dried meat in each with leaves for flavor and roots to chew. Then he put a tiny bit of each food on a leaf-plate and offered it to the fire. "For Shkaakamigokwe and Gichi-manidoo, who is the Great Mystery." Giving Roger one bowl, he took the other, and they sat to eat.

Roger joined Niizh Eshkanag in silence beneath the large pine, and the two watched the sun set. Later, they relaxed about the fire and listened to sounds of night drifting from the valley on cooling breezes—loons from afar, owls, and wolves.

Niizh Eshkanag wiped the bowls. "I will make tea. Will you have some?" he asked.

"But, sir, is it not *aniibiish*?" Roger decided to show off the little Ojibwemowin he knew. "I will teach you the language, which I fear you will never learn."

"There is hope," Niizh Eshkanag said with a laugh. "You have remembered your fifth word. If you study hard, you will understand enough Ojibwemowin when you are yourself an elder." He poured cold water in each bowl and added leaves.

"Cold tea tonight?" Roger questioned. "I'll have mine hot, if you please."

"I agree," Niizh Eshkanag said. He dug into the fire with a heavy green forked stick, rolled out four small round hot stones, shook the ashes off, and put two in each bowl, smiling as they simmered the water. He set the bowls aside. "We wait for the tea.

Roger stared thoughtfully into the fire. "Only a few days ago, we struggled through tests, and here I am with you. Things happen so fast; I can't imagine what comes next."

Niizh Eshkanag looked about the ridge. "Last night while you slept, I thought you might like living in forest."

"We could go longer than the week?" Roger appeared doubtful, but he stood, paced about the fire, his face aglow with anticipation, visualizing through more of the mist engulfing him since Milwaukee.

"Maybe. There is reason to stay in the forest," Niizh Eshkanag said. "Father knows but would say nothing until we ask."

"Why wouldn't he tell us or suggest something to help us?" Roger asked, puzzled.

Niizh Eshkanag looked at treetops. "We make plans; elders smile or suggest changes."

Roger nodded. "What you're saying, we use our ideas, but listen when elders suggest improvements."

"Yes sir!"

Niizh Eshkanag flicked a finger between Roger and himself. "We can live in the village after the week or visit anytime, but if you were seen, Father could not stop an agent from taking you. The village or my family would have less trouble if we live with the four-legged ones and those who fly and crawl." He motioned about. "We return as promised to the village; tell Mother and Father of this plan."

"You think it might be all right, though?" Roger persisted.

"Yep, as you would say. Mother would not like it but would agree when the one who asks is fourteen winters."

"Years."

"Okay!"

"My parents were good." Roger stared pensively at the fire. "Had Father not died I would never have thought of this life. In the end, you know, I must either go to Milwaukee or return to Uncle Elias."

Niizh Eshkanag nodded. "Enh, Mother says you'll end up with your Uncle Elias."

Roger nodded. "When I first left Big House to catch the wagon, I thought I would like to stay with you only a short while, and somehow, get to Milwaukee, but now I think more about staying in the north, going back to Uncle Elias at the end of summer, providing he'll have me."

"He will," Niizh Eshkanag promised. "In English, we read something; it went like this: 'absence makes the heart grow fonder.' Oh, and another, 'family is family,' but those are nothing new to Anishinaabe."

"Being with you, talking to your parents, I understand more about Aunt Helen than I could by living in Big House. Now, I think she just didn't seem ready for me or anybody."

Not taking his gaze off the fire, Niizh Eshkanag agreed. "I think my parents understood that."

Days of gathering, snaring, and hiking hardened the boys. Each day Roger went longer without shirt and leggings, becoming darker, hardened. The stream was now tolerable for bathing.

On the morning of day six, the boys faced east as the first rays of sunshine glistened on dew-laden grass. Both offered tobacco while Niizh Eshkanag prayed. Though it was cool, Roger no longer shivered. And living off the bounty of nature, he felt a deep awareness of sky, earth, and animals not felt near Poleville.

The sun rose above the trees, the boys began another day exploring, gathering food. Their activities similar to previous days, they swam in a deepening of the stream, rinsed their clouts, splashed and laughed, but were more thoughtful of each other, their banter less childlike, more civil.

"Shkaakamigokwe gives us a private bathtub," Niizh Eshkanag said. "In winter, we have the sweat lodge where we clean both spirit and body."

The snare held another rabbit. They put down a bit of tobacco to thank the rabbit for becoming their stew and then dressed it on the spot, saving the pelt to process later. Then the boys picked greens and roots for the evening meal.

By afternoon, their foraging took them farther west than other days, and they climbed up the west aspect of the ridge. This took them up a steep slope, almost barren of trees, with clumps of bushes and a small grove of pines.

Halfway up, around the grove, Niizh Eshkanag paused, grabbed Roger by the arm, pulling him behind bushes. "Someone is on trail!" He pointed through slightly parted bushes.

"Anishinaabe or American?" Roger whispered.

"Two Americans. At a fire . . . with horses tied near a tree."

"Could they be agents?" Roger asked. He winced and sat tight behind a tree.

"Can't say. Maybe not," Niizh Eshkanag said. "They wouldn't be looking for an Anishinaabe boy, so I will talk to them." He strode out in full view of the men and walked up the hill, watching to see if they acted suspicious, keeping rocks and other possible shelter within leaping distance.

"Hello," one man called out as Niizh Eshkanag approached.

Niizh Eshkanag stopped near a large boulder. "Hello," he called back. "Do you hunt or travel through?"

"Both," the man replied. "What is your name?"

"Little Bear," Niizh Eshkanag replied. "From Giiwedin." He pointed north.

"Come sit and talk," one man said. He motioned to rocks near where they sat.

Niizh Eshkanag slowly approached the men and sat near the fire. "Are you government agents?" *They don't seem dangerous.*

"Sort of," one man replied. "Why do you ask?"

"You are dressed like men who come to villages for government."

"I'm Fred," one man said. "This here's Steve." Fred eyed Niizh Eshkanag suspiciously. "It might be you know why we travel here and that your name is not Little Bear." He suddenly reached out and grabbed Niizh Eshkanag by the upper arm and pulled him closer. "You're not alone out here! Are you?"

Niizh Eshkanag puffed in discomfort from the strong grip on his arm, but he tried to remain calm. "We . . . I mean, I hunt for small game and have a camp not far."

"I see," Fred said. "So it is, *we.*" He jerked Niizh Eshkanag to his feet and held him facing Steve. Niizh Eshkanag grunted from the roughness.

"He could be just another Injun," Steve said. "He could also be a friend of the Poznanski brat."

"A white boy living with Indians is certain to be known by Indians of many villages," Fred said. He faced Niizh Eshkanag. "Tell me that you haven't heard of a runaway white boy."

Niizh Eshkanag grimaced from pain. "I have not heard of this. I have not been home for a long time. People in my village might know by now. Let go; it hurts."

"Not so fast, boy," Fred said. "You're lying, and we should take you into town." He took a dragging rope and tied Niizh Eshkanag's hands behind his back. "Talk! I got time." Niizh Eshkanag jerked the loose end of the rope from Fred's hands and ran awkwardly toward the hill.

Steve quickly caught him and stood him before Fred. He looked sternly at Fred. "No rough stuff when I'm with you." He untied Niizh Eshkanag's wrist. "So what if he fibs. He's just a kid and the law protects Indian kids too."

"If they catch us, that is."

Steve snorted in disgust. "I'm not sure just being with the Poznanski kid would be illegal so long as no laws were broken." He slapped Niizh Eshkanag on the back and smiled. "On your way, kid. Let someone know if you hear of the Poznanski kid."

Niizh Eshkanag frowned while rubbing his wrists and the arm where marks of the firm grasp still showed. He walked downhill but not toward Roger.

Later from a safe hiding place, Niizh Eshkanag and Roger watched the men break camp, mount their horses, and head southeast on a Poleville trail.

"The men search for a terrible one," Niizh Eshkanag said. "What was that name they said? I remember. Roger Poznanski. You are lucky I lied to protect you. Father says warriors should protect the less fortunate."

"Yeah, tell me about it!" Roger shook his head. "The one with two horns should be called Crooked Horns. Anyway, this means we could meet others."

"Right," Niizh Eshkanag agreed. He eyed Roger from head to toe. "You must change your name. If we cover your face, you could be part

Indian, so we might say you are a half blood. I give you a half blood name. How does John Bemibatood sound? It is an almost Indian name for an almost Indian."

"And the sun helps," Roger added. "What is Bemibatood?"

"A person who runs, maybe away from something bad," Niizh Eshkanag replied.

"Okay. . . . John Bemibatood," Roger repeated, thoughtfully. "It has a good sound, so long as it's not a swear word. You're sure they don't know about me?"

"They might suspect something."

"Moving right along," Roger said. He pointed east. "Is it not time to return to the village?"

"I thought you forgot," Niizh Eshkanag said. "We will return with the new day."

Chapter Nine

The east horizon brightened heralding the fire of dawn. Two boys trudged east off the ridge through a shorter forest. As the rising sun tinged treetops orange, both boys dropped tobacco, and Niizh Eshkanag prayed for a safe trip home. Continuing east, they were dressed for a warm hike, leggings and shirts in backpacks.

Without stopping, Niizh Eshkanag looked up as an eagle screeched unseen above the forest canopy, and he dropped a pinch of tobacco. "We are being watched over."

Bizaan bustled with preparations to welcome her son and his companion who would be home today if nothing terrible had happened. "Owii-azhegiiwewag giishpin gaawiin maji-izhiwebasinog."

"Owii-wiidookodaadiwag. Ikwewag onzaam-babaamendanaawaa." Migizi reminded her they would help one another and told her mothers worry too much. He turned toward the sound of running. "Esiban gimbabaaminizhikaag ina?" Migizi stretched to see behind Esiban and asked if he had been chased.

Esiban stopped abruptly twisting to look back as he said he was not and asked if Niizh Eshkanag and Roger were returning today. "Gaawiin babaaminizhikawaasiwag mii miinawaa noongom ina Niizh Eshkanag gaye Roger wii-azhegiiwewaad?"

"Jibwaa gookooko'oog wii-bimisewag bagosendamaan," Migizi confirmed that he indeed hoped they would be returning before the owls flew.

Esiban drew a deep, replenishing breath, his eyes wide beneath arched eyebrows. He pointed west and warned them of a white man leading a horse and talking to people on the other side of the village.

Migizi stood and turned to look where Esiban pointed. He watched the man appear from behind the meetinghouse and pause at a home. An elder emerged, moving little, except to point once toward Migizi.

The white man nodded vigorously, and when the elder returned inside his home, the man approached Migizi, stopping alongside the lodge. "Hello, sir," he said. "May we talk?"

"If no harm comes from it," said Migizi turning toward the door. Then he announced, "Bizaan, we have visitor," in English so the stranger would not be offended.

Bizaan poked her head out, looked up with crinkled brow at the man. "Would you like tea?" She stood and faced the man outside the lodge.

"No, thank you, I'm on business." He looked at a paper clutched in one hand. Are you the parents of Niizh Eshkanag, whom the agency requested be called Tom Horns in English?"

"Yes." Migizi said. He calmly continued working. "He is old to have his name changed." He chuckled low. "We will name our next child *Tom Horns.*"

The agent grunted with displeasure, asserting more officiously, "Could I speak to him?"

"Has he done wrong?" Bizaan questioned.

"Elias Poznanski of the government school claims young Niizh Eshkanag is friends with his missing nephew, Roger Poznanski," the man explained. "The sheriff has asked the agency to investigate the matter. First, is your son here? If not, would you know of young Poznanski's whereabouts?"

Appearing surprised, Bizaan turned to Migizi. "Did Niizh Eshkanag know a boy called . . ." She faced the agent. "What was that name?"

"Roger Poznanski."

Migizi spoke low gesturing south with one arm, "Our son speaks of Poleville Indian School. I do not remember all the names, but he speaks of an Anishinaabe boy killed by a white worker, of another Anishinaabe boy running away after being beaten by a worker. The one called Roger helped our son, Niizh Eshkanag, when his arm was broken and his chest was badly hurt by a white worker."

"I simply want to speak with your son," the man insisted, impatient.

"He might be at the other village." Migizi pointed north. "He will come home in a week, or maybe a month, I can't say. He has his own mind. But he will come home by Manoominike-giizis, your August."

"Would Roger Poznanski be with him?" The man pressed.

Bizaan appeared thoughtful. "Anyone could be with him. Niizh Eshkanag said he might go with his brother."

Migizi nodded. "They are good friends."

Irritated, the agent fidgeted briefly, then mounted his horse where he sat looking ahead, before twisting in the saddle looking down at Migizi. "There is a reward of three hundred dollars for his safe return." He cantered off.

During the discussion, Esiban ate a bit of maple sugar candy given to him by Bizaan.

Migizi turned to Esiban and, although he could not offer the same reward as the whites, he said Bizaan would sweeten the belly of the young boy with maple candy and fry bread if he would circle the village to make sure the trail was clear for his son and his brother, "Gaawiin gide-diba'amoosiinoon dibishkoo Gichi-mookomaanag, aanawi giishpin aanikeshikawad Gichi-mookomaan, niwii-nandotamawaa Bizaan giishpin daa-miizhig enigok ziinzibaakwad gaye bangii zaasakokwaani-bakwezhigan. Mii dash igo weshki-ayaajig babaami-ayaawag ge gaawiin anaamendaagozisiiwaad, daa-miigwechiwenimigoyan giishpin giiwitaashkaman agwaj-oodenang wii-debaabandaman giishpin ayaangwaamendaagwag miikanens ningaabii'anong. Mii dash iwedi waa-izhi-bimosewag ingozisiminaan gaye owiijiiwaaganiman."

Before Esiban left he warned him to be careful because the Americans seldom came alone, and another could be waiting in the forest. "Ayaangwaamizig, Gichi-mookomaanag moozhag bwaa-bi-nazhikewiziwaad, dash bezhig bebikaan daa-ezhi-akandood iidog mitigwakiing."

Esiban grinned at the prospect of looming adventure then set off promising the American would not see him. "Gaawiin

niwii-waabamigosii, dash wewiib daa-izhaayaan ji-waabamag." He
spun around and loped off.

Still within range of the faint village sounds, Esiban sat under a large
pine tree far outside the village within sight of the east–west trail, He
removed a moccasin and fiddled with the ties. *Twice round the village
and I have seen not one white man. So Niizh Eshkanag does not get
into trouble, I will wait here until near dark.* He soon tired and lay on
his back, the moccasin on his abdomen.

Moments later, a white man carrying a rifle approached the trail
from the north, paused and stared at a dozing Indian boy. Moving
stealthily, the man squatted behind a tree.

Some time passed before Esiban stirred and gazed about. *I have
been here many times and always the mother raven is quiet. I know
she sees me, but why does she scold like an angry aunt?* Esiban startled
with understanding but not so another would notice. *There is someone
near who is not from the village.*

Esiban tied his moccasin firmly on, and what a watcher might
deem innocent, he twisted to inoffensively scan a circle. Walking west,
leaving the trail after fifty paces, he swiftly circled his former resting
place. *A gun barrel behind that tree did not hide fast enough. Father
would tell me to pretend not to see it. This is a very strange game.* A
deer bolted from the west; a squirrel chattered. *Someone approaches.*
Without looking toward the hidden man, Esiban quickly stood and
ran silently north away from him. He smiled to himself at the thudding
of heavy shoes behind. Selecting each footfall carefully to miss twigs
and thickets, Esiban soon outdistanced the man and circled westward
for hundreds of paces before returning to the trail. Nothing more was
seen or heard of the white man. *I think moccasins have not yet passed
going east, but I must still hurry.*

Esiban sprinted swiftly east toward the village his footfalls heard but
paces away. Soon he stopped, squinted about while leaning against a
tree. *I am not far from the village and could meet the white man again.*
Unsure what next to do, he sat with his back against the tree.

Niizh Eshkanag and Roger rested at high sun.

Niizh Eshkanag became impatient. "We must hurry. There is no danger greater than Mother's kindness when she worries." He closed his pack and hoisted it to his shoulders.

"How's that?" Roger said while casually adjusting his own pack.

"First she crushes me. She is very strong. Then she hurts my ears, telling me that I have caused much trouble. She will feel my ribs and arms to see if I am dying for not eating. In the end, she will be nice, very nice. She thinks I am still five winters."

"Years. I wish I had your problem, but I'm happy for you."

"Winters."

"Okay."

Niizh Eshkanag stepped around the stub of a fallen tree. "You have talked of your aunt and uncle, how different they are. My father and mother argue little because they think alike." Niizh Eshkanag leaned closer to Roger. "Say nothing in the village, but Father often asks Mother what he should say to the council." His face brightened from the thought.

"Your parents are good, but I have already caused them and you too much trouble."

"Do not worry. Mother and Father like you, even before they see you. You are like a son to them."

Roger appeared horrified. "Darn! That makes me your brother. How bad is that?"

Niizh Eshkanag pointed a finger back over his shoulder at Roger. "For long time, I wanted a brother to help carry wood and pick berries."

"Hah!" Roger said with a wry grin. He sobered. "Will your parents let us go again?"

Niizh Eshkanag glanced over his shoulder at Roger, then looked ahead at distant treetops. "Maybe. First, Father will cough and point his finger at me. You, too, maybe, then toss his head and say wise things, but it's Mother who decides. For now, I am glad to return home."

"Your family and you are good to help me like this," Roger said. "But what if an agent is in the village?"

"Agents do not wait long in the village." Niizh Eshkanag shrugged, smiling as he talked. "They search, but my people stare them back into the forest. It is among the trees we see them."

"If they're even there," Roger added.

By midafternoon, nearing Waaban, but still beyond earshot of village activities, Niizh Eshkanag walked slow, scrutinizing the forest on each side and ahead of them. Doing likewise, Roger followed fifty paces behind.

Esiban sat against a tree staring absentmindedly into overhead branches. I waste time. The wanderers could sleep another night in the forest, and the white man is no longer near. He relaxed, studying loose moccasin stitches. He bent forward to retie the lacing when sudden commotion erupted from a bush behind him. A man jumped out at him and as Esiban leaped to his feet, another man jumped from behind another large tree and both grappled him into submission.

One held Esiban's arms from behind. "Now maybe we can find out what happened to the Poznanski kid," he said.

"What's your name boy," The other man said.

"Esiban," he moaned staring at the ground while squirming in the man's grasp.

"When you people gonna get Christian names?" the man asked.

"Don't know."

"You want to help us find Roger Poznanski, don't you?" the man pressed.

"Who is Roger Poznanski?" Esiban asked, forcing himself to appear surprised.

"Don't give me that. You were in school with him, and the whole village has to know Iskanak, whatever his name, and Roger!"

"I know Eshkanag," Esiban said brightly. The man twisted his arms from behind. Esiban grimaced from pain. "Giwiisagibizh! You will break my arm!"

"We're going to sit here 'til you talk, if it takes all night," the man said. He shoved Esiban roughly onto the ground between himself and the other man. One carried a rifle, the other a sidearm.

Not far west, Niizh Eshkanag and Roger walked quietly, swiftly, and did not see the white men, but Esiban heard approaching footsteps.

"Zhaaganaash!" Esiban screamed. A hand clamped over his mouth, and he was pulled roughly behind a tree. The other man raised his rifle and stood facing the trail west. Niizh Eshkanag and Roger both melted into the forest.

"Who was that?" The man with a rifle asked Esiban.

"Somebody from village, maybe," Esiban mumbled and stared at the forest.

"I'll see," the man said. He checked his rifle and started west along the trail.

"It's me and you, kid," the man holding Esiban said. "No funny stuff."

"What is funny stuff?" Esiban asked. "This is serious."

The man snorted. "Who you gonna tell? For your information, we do this according to law."

Suddenly, Niizh Eshkanag burst from behind. He grabbed Esiban pulling him toward a tree. The white man struck Niizh Eshkanag on the head while reaching for his pistol with the other hand. Just as he brought the gun to bear, a branch hit his arm knocking the gun loose. Roger jumped on the man's back, and three boys soon subdued the man.

Niizh Eshkanag rubbed his ear saying they needed to hurry before the other man returned. "Aapiji nigii-bakite'ig. Gidaa-gizhiikaamin, bebakaan dash wii-biskaabiid wayiiba." He pulled the man's shirt over his eyes so he wouldn't see Roger. "Gaawiin odaa-waabamaasiin niwiijiwaaganan."

"Let me up!" The man yelled. "You'll be sorry! I'll see your families get no supplies for a year!"

Niizh Eshkanag spat on the shirt covering the man's face, and spoke English, "No help is better than poor help we get. We will take the gun and leave it on the trail. . . . I change my mind; we will throw away the gun. We are right to rescue a captive boy." He asked Roger if he was ready and told him the man should not see his face. "Gigiizhiitaa ina? Apii dash bagidinang bazigwiid, gaawiin dash gidaa-waabamigosii gidengwe." Then Niizh Eshkanag shouted, "Azhigwa naa!" and the boys released the man and sprinted west on the trail until out of sight. Niizh Eshkanag threw the gun deep into a marsh, and the trio disappeared in the forest north of the trail.

Esiban entered the village to alert Migizi while Niizh Eshkanag and Roger circled the village until the men had gone. They entered the village at dusk, Niizh Eshkanag with his shoulders back, a firm stride and generous nods to younger boys. Roger held back, not sure how to act.

Esiban met them as they passed his home. "Migizi and Bizaan are here," he said. He called through the door of the lodge, "Two to see Migizi and Bizaan!"

"Biindigen! Bring the wanderers in!" Bizaan called.

Niizh Eshkanag turned to Roger. "Remember, no laughter when she talks. Be pleasant as you were for you Minowaki mother." Roger nodded.

Inside the lodge, Bizaan walked around, then between the boys saying nothing. She embraced her son, pushed him into Migizi and embraced Roger. Migizi warmly embraced Niizh Eshkanag and Roger together.

"Aaniin gaa-ezhi-wiisaginooganeyan?" Bizaan pointed to a scab on Niizh Eshkanag's hip and asked if he was in pain.

Nizh Eshkanag said he hadn't wanted to worry her and Migizi. "Gaawiin nigii-misawendanziin babaamenimiyeg giin miinawaa noos." Then he launched into the story of the small scar, "Aabiding dibikong, makwa ogii-bi-nandoomaandaan onaagoshi-miijiyaang. Nigii-wiindamawaa Roger wii-gopaakwiid, dash ani-gopaakwiiyaan ge niin apii makwa debibinid indayaashing gaye azhewebinid agidakamigong. Nigii-miigaadimin ginwenzh, gemaa naanan endaso diba'iganensan. Gakina gii-banaajichigaade ezhi-gabeshinaang; nisogon dash Roger nigii-giige'ig." According to his tall tale, a bear came sniffing their evening meal, and Niizh Eshkanag sent Roger up a tree. He was about to climb the tree himself when the bear caught him by the backside and tossed him to the ground. He and Roger fought a long time, maybe five white man minutes, but their camp was ruined and it took Roger three days to nurse Niizh Eshkanag back to health. Migizi almost fell off his bench laughing. Staring at the smoke hole, Roger understood most of the story and barely suppressed an urge to giggle while vigorously nodding agreement. Bizhiw and Ziigwan smiled politely. Esiban was silent but could not suppress his glee.

Bizaan spun Niizh Eshkanag around and gave his rump a stinging slap for making fun of her. She added that it was good he kept Roger safe, but they were both becoming foolish. "Number two son also need lesson." She took Roger by the shoulder, spun him around, and slapped his rear a loud slap, which stung little.

"Ooh," Roger exaggerated a moan while rubbing his rear.

Smiling during the levity, Migizi turned serious facing the boys. "Anishinaabe- wegimaad ogii-bi-izhaa naawakweg, an agent came here at noon today."

Niizh Eshkanag raised his arm to speak, "Nigii-miigaazhaanaanig Chimookomaanag jibwaa bangishimod." He recounted their battle with the Americans before sunset, gesturing between himself, Esiban, and Roger.

Migizi warned the boys that the whites had become bolder and were now willing to break their own laws, regarding the safety of the Anishinaabeg. He said another agent came days before, but they told him Niizh Eshkanag was at his uncle's home in another village or traveling between here and there. They knew two friends were gone from home at the same time, which looked very suspicious. Migizi took a deep breath and looked hard at the boys warning them but also concluding that if they had not stolen anything nor hurt anyone for seven suns, the danger to our village was no more. Though Roger is on his own with the agents, he has proven he needs no village or family to shelter and feed him, and now both boys would be free to choose where to live, though Migizi said Roger should give his family another chance.

"Anishinaabe-wegimaajig wii-bi-izhaawag," Niizh Eshkanag suggested the agents would come again and debated whether it would be better to watch for them and run or travel through the forest. "Gidaa-akawaabamaanaanig dash giimiiyang, aanawi benak dash gopiiyang." Niizh Eshkanag remembered his elders telling him a fox will not follow a trail without scent and said, "Waagosh gaawiin owii-bimizha'anziin giishpin bwaa-biijimaandang." Roger appeared bewildered at the rapid talk as Niizh Eshkanag continued with the plan reasoning that he and Roger could stay away until his fasting time, visiting the Dakota, or staying for a time in Ningaabii'an for the annual berry celebration, "Niwii-wiiji-ayaawaa Roger biinish makadekeyaan. Gidaa-izhaamin Ningaabii'an gemaa awas wii-nibwaachi'ang bwaanakiing gemaa dazhiikeyang mitigwaking. Ningaabii'anjig wii-maawanji'idiwag ji-ningaapoonowaad wayeba."

Rain pattered the bark during the night, but the sun had already chased dampness when the boys awoke. For the first time in days, Niizh Eshkanag and Roger had no firewood to collect or meals to cook.

"Wiisin! Eat!" Bizaan said, feigning grouchiness. "Many times today." She pointed to a pot bubbling over the fire. "You have eaten too little, or a four-legged has nibbled your bones while you slept."

"I am nearly as strong a runner as Niizh Eshkanag," Roger said.

"And from a distance, your back is from this village," Bizaan said, chuckling.

Migizi nodded. "He is not the pale one we saw seven suns earlier."

Strolling about the village, Niizh Eshkanag and Roger chatted with Nagamokwe and Ajijaak, visited Esiban's family, fished, and avoided sarcastic older boys.

Preparations for the coming odyssey continued inside the lodge that evening. The boys sat with Bizaan on one side of the lodge, Migizi on the other with bags of paraphernalia.

"There are leggings, repair kits, cook things, and extra clothes in the bags," Migizi explained. "Check them to see if we have overlooked anything you might need."

"Miigwech!" Roger said. "I could never live in the forest without Niizh Eshkanag and your help." *To think I once feared these people who have taught me so much.*

Chapter Ten

Roger woke to commotion outside the lodge. Standing, he yawned while dressing then shook Niizh Eshkanag's sleep robe. "Time to rise."

Disheveled, sleepy, Niizh Eshkanag lifted himself up on his elbows. "Why so early?"

"Someone is outside; I'll see." Roger bent thrusting his head out the low door. He considered backing in, but crawled out holding moccasins and a hairbrush to stand outside near the door flap. "Um, hi . . . uh, Nagamokwe, Ajijaak."

"We didn't mean to wake you," Ajijaak said.

"I was already awake."

Ajijaak smiled. "Your hair and eyes say you just woke up."

Roger ran his fingers through his hair, and looked down at his bare feet. Grinning he looked into Ajijaak's eyes. "Anything else?"

Ajijaak nodded. "You are fine. I wondered if you heard the latest."

"Not if it's today's gossip." Roger finished tying his moccasins and brushed his hair as he talked.

"The whole world searches for a runaway white boy dressed Anishinaabe."

"So? That's not news."

Niizh Eshkanag's head appeared in the doorway, and he soon stood beside Roger.

Nagamokwe gazed at Niizh Eshkanag, adding, "And the runaway is helped by one with Two Horns."

"If I am to laugh, I'll need more encouragement," Niizh Eshkanag retorted, "Are you the village criers?"

"The bullies are doing that," Nagamokwe replied. "They tell everyone and maybe even agents."

Roger understood enough and exhaled deep with a comment, "We better leave quick."

Niizh Eshkanag shook his head. "Father says we could leave tomorrow. It's only a matter of time before someone sees the agents and then the agents see you."

After eating a morning meal, two boys sauntered about the village with two girls enough apart to satisfy propriety.

"Would an agent come today?" Roger asked, glancing toward the forest.

"They must have more to do than search for a white boy in deerskin," Niizh Eshkanag said, and he did an exaggerated scan of Roger, "who is no longer white, but with pale ancestors in his face." He motioned west. "We will make the agents work very hard—we will live in the forest, move around, and visit Uncle Zhaabiiwose in Ningaabii'an, which agent and bullies must not learn about."

Nagamokwe looked past Niizh Eshkanag's shoulder. "Those two again!" Niizh Eshkanag twisted to see, then ignored Oninige and Zhingos, both who soon stood a pace away.

"The white one cannot hide behind Anishinaabe clothes," Oninige snapped in English to be sure Roger understood him. "He should leave the village; maybe someone should make him go."

Niizh Eshkanag responded testily, "Would that someone be you?"

"It matters not," Roger said, "I go in the morning."

"Where will you go?" Oninige asked.

"Here and there," Roger replied.

"You smart, maybe not smart enough," Oninige said. He made a threatening move toward Roger. Ajijaak frowned and gripped Roger's arm just as Oninige shoved him hard into her and they both fell. "I will give you a lesson!" Niizh Eshkanag stepped forward to help Roger, and the bullies turned and departed, laughing aloud.

Niizh Eshkanag helped Roger and Ajijaak get up. "No one must tell them of our plans, or an agent will be next to know. I think they will soon be in trouble with the council."

The second morning after Roger and Niizh Eshkanag returned to the village, a somber group assembled outside Bizaan's lodge. Niizh Eshkanag and Roger wore backpacks, clutched bows, and fidgeted as slivers of morning sunshine penetrated the tall forest. The boys each carried backpacks containing trade blankets, hides, and shared utensils. Each carried a bow with a quiver of arrows attached to their packs.

Bizaan had bundled three days' supply of dry food in each boy's pack along with herbs and medicines. She reminded Niizh Eshkanag of their use.

"Gidaa-ayaawaa asemaa wii-biindaakoozhagwaa gichi-ayaag gaye manidookeyan," said Bizaan as she added tobacco for elders and ceremonies to their bundles. Then she and Migizi disappeared inside the lodge.

Whether by chance or intent, two girls in neat, everyday skirts and capes approached to observe the boys' departure stopping a discreet distance apart the group.

Roger touched Niizh Eshkanag's arm while nodding toward the girls. "Is there time to talk with them?"

"We can make time," Niizh Eshkanag said, smiling. He waved to the girls, "Boozhoo miinawaa giga-waabamigom! We are off to adventure but have time to say hello and goodbye."

"Adventure? Ha!" Nagamokwe said. She and Ajijaak moved closer to the boys. "Everyone knows you are fleeing government agents." Bizaan and Migizi emerged from their lodge.

"If you plan to go with wives, you must first speak to the parents of these ones, and follow rules of suitors, not children," Migizi said, chuckling. Bizaan smiled with a nod. The girls stepped aside and waited as the boys were given tobacco pouches and final hugs.

"Ahaaw dash, John Bemibatood gaye niin dash nidaa-babaami-ayaamin, we are off on an adventure," Niizh Eshkanag said smiling. His attempt at manliness was unconvincing.

Bizaan arched an eyebrow. "Our son has given his brother Anishinaabe name, has he?"

"A secret life must be hidden behind a not secret name," Niizh Eshkanag replied. He grinned, but that faded as he gazed west. "Now we go." With that the two headed toward the westbound trail. At the edge of the village, they paused, looked back once, waved and disappeared into the forest.

The trail was now familiar to both boys, and they walked steadily until they reached the tall forest west of the village.

"We could sleep on the ridge tonight," Niizh Eshkanag said.

"The old shelter should still be good," Roger agreed. And since you fought that makwa, he won't bother us again. Gaawiin igo!" He motioned toward the ridge. "And I suppose the trees and shrubs you and makwa destroyed have already grown back."

"Enh," Niizh Eshkanag grunted. "How many winters did you say you have seen?" Speaking Anishinaabe, he teased and said it is wise to ignore the prattle of children, "Gagiitaawendaagwad wii-boonenimadwaa abinoojiiyag idamowaad." He returned to English, "If those white men suspect anything, chances are no one will search the ridge the one night we are there."

Niizh Eshkanag shifted the straps of his pack. "The packs feel heavier this time."

"I thought Indians didn't complain," Roger said. He stared at the back of Niizh Eshkanag's head, wincing as he shifted his own pack.

Familiar groves, knobs, and glens shortened the trip, and they were soon on the ridge scanning for signs of travelers. With no evidence of recent camps, they set to repairing the lean-to and building a fire. After dark, both boys sat under the lean-to near the fire studying a map sketched by Migizi.

Niizh Eshkanag pointed to the map. "Father says, we should stay here no more than one night. He thinks the mean ones might learn that we go west. But we told no one about the cliff over the Makwa Ziibi."

"Cliff??"

"Enh. I thought you would like to camp on a cliff." Niizh Eshkanag moved his finger along the map. "Tomorrow we travel through the tall forest; the next day, maybe before evening, we leave the tall forest, climb a hill. When it seems we are lost, a great opening comes. We can watch the eagles and see the Makwa Ziibi far below. Father and I hunted there three days when I was twelve. He tells of a battle between here and Ningaabii'an."

"He was in a battle?" Roger blurted.

"It was his father," Niizh Eshkanag explained. "There was a meeting in Poleville to improve relations with Indians."

"To stop the bounty?"

"There was no bounty paid in this area, but an Indian killer here could have sold a scalp elsewhere," Niizh Eshkanag explained. "Kill an Indian anyplace, sell the scalp anywhere." His face grew taut as he finished. "It was a small group of men who murdered lone Indians. Not many winters ago, Indian scalps were peddled as trophies for collectors.

Roger frowned. "Damn! Business is business." He smirked. "You said my scalp would have looked good hung outside your lodge so you could spit on it every day."

"You knew I joked," Niizh Eshkanag gently punched Roger's arm.

"I know."

Niizh Eshkanag continued. "No Indians were killed during Grandfather's battle, but a white sniper was."

"Does the story grow during the second, third, or hundredth telling?" Roger asked, smiling.

"Maybe, but it depends how excited the teller is," Niizh Eshkanag said. "Sometimes one Indian kills a few whites, but mostly the story is the same."

"Add whiskey and the tale becomes a massacre," Roger said. "My people tell stories like that, too. It's like bragging. I think both sides stretch the truth."

"If they even start with truth."

"Will we camp on a slope away from the trail, then?" Roger asked.

"If you like. It is long way down for water, but the best roots and greens are near the lake which is really a widening of the river."

"How far is that place from here? The hill over the Makwa Ziibi, I mean?"

"It is a two-day walk, but do we rush when we have weeks?"

"Guess not."

Niizh Eshkanag opened his eyes to a brightening of their forest camp. He looked into branches of the pine, then past his nose at a mouse resting on his abdomen. Howah, this little one takes heat and gives none in return. He slowly reached to touch Roger who still slept, and whispered, "Roger, a huge four-legged attacks me." Before Roger awoke, however, the mouse scampered off in a scratching of legs. Niizh Eshkanag doubled up on his side and rubbed his belly. "Hoo, that tickled, waawaabiganoojiinh, little one with the long white tail."

The sun glowed orange through the trees, fluorescing a mist in the valley as it climbed. Niizh Eshkanag and Roger stood at the rim of the bluff, facing east as giizis rose, and Niizh Eshkanag offered a song of greeting.

After the pair ate and repacked supplies, Niizh Eshkanag motioned northwest. "It could be hot today. We should travel early to escape afternoon heat, which should bring us into the tall forest."

"Where we searched for Aandeg?" Roger asked.

Niizh Eshkanag swept his arm from north to south. "The same valley, but we went west into the tall forest to escape a blizzard, we now go north in the same valley to escape the heat. Because there are hills east of the Makwa Ziibi, the wagon trail going north is west of the river, and farther north the trail returns to the east."

"It looks different than it did only months ago." Roger muttered.

Niizh Eshkanag giggled. "Much warmer."

"More Indian humor. You make me smile about what I don't know." Roger hesitated. "How come your elders make more sense?"

"I'm not old enough to know all those things," Niizh Eshkanag explained. "But Mother says, the young should search for a lighter side of trouble. Only then will they become wise elders." He frowned. "Oninige has little humor. He might have a long trail to wisdom."

"Very long."

The boys went down to the stream, which meandered in every direction, but flowed generally southwest where it emptied into the Makwa Ziibi miles farther. Filling water canisters, they immersed to cool and rinse, then began their trek northwest, not needing to re-climb the ridge.

"Today is a hard walk," said Niizh Eshkanag as he led Roger into the tall forest.

"It's hot, but not bad," Roger said.

"We can camp on the other side of the valley. We should use only half our water today," Niizh Eshkanag cautioned. "The next day we will be on the hill and camp many days."

The trek was uneventful, though tiring. Shelter that night was a simple lean-to of skins facing a low fire. The forest canopy towered overhead, shimmering in faint firelight. The call and response by creatures of the night became a natural symphony until dawn.

The tall forest brightened into perpetual twilight as the boys ate a morning meal, both silently musing about their long hot walk ahead.

Niizh Eshkanag stood and pointed. "Waaban, east, is there, I think. We see little sun today, but it will shine here and there by midday." Appearing serious he added, "Did you see the real makwa who came in the night?"

"There was a bear near camp?" Roger asked, surprised.

"Big!" Niizh Eshkanag exclaimed. He held his hand high and wide overhead for emphasis.

"Gee!" Roger murmured. "Did it go near our food?"

"It was going to eat you, but I awoke in time to tickle his ribs, and he ran away laughing. You are lucky to travel with a great warrior."

Roger yawned into Niizh Eshkanag's face. "I hope we reach your hill by night."

The trail in the tall forest divided into side trails, causing delays while Niizh Eshkanag searched for evidence of human travel. The trails were so confusing that Roger imagined walking forever on trails going nowhere in an endless forest. However, Niizh Eshkanag was able to separate tracks of wild animals from those of shod horses.

Late afternoon they traveled steadily up a gentle slope, and the twilight gave way to brightness filtering through a lower canopy.

Roger motioned ahead. "We've been climbing a long time."

"You will know when we reach the hill," Niizh Eshkanag explained. From this side, it is a hill, but from the river, it would be giishkadinaa, a cliff. We must also watch for the wiindigoo, the evil one who may hide in the woods." He glanced smiling at Roger.

"Yeah, I know," Roger said. "He or she eats young two-legged ones and likes white boys best! Har har! You gonna cook supper tonight?" Roger smiled to himself. He was beginning to sense which of Niizh Eshkanag's comments were sincere or simply talking to pass the time.

"I could," Niizh Eshkanag said.

"I'll scrounge firewood," Roger declared.

"Scrounge?

"It means search, look for, or scour the area, and before you ask, that scour is not the same as scouring pots in the kitchen, which maybe could be searching for someone to clean them."

"I like Ojibwemowin better than English," Niizh Eshkanag said.

The trail crested and ran alongside a high hill. When they stopped to rest, Niizh Eshkanag stared tiredly into the forest, "I don't remember if it is a steep climb, though it seemed easy with Father. We leave the north–south trail and go up the trail where Father and I walked up the hill." He pointed to a barely discernable animal trail. "The animals know how to travel, and we use many of their trails."

Walking for some time, the boys began traveling up a hill toward brightness. Hundreds of paces farther they made their way through a sparsely wooded area, and suddenly stood fifty barren paces from the edge of a cliff. Neither spoke as they gazed on a hazy afternoon panorama of sky and forest fading into the distance, beyond a river far below.

"An eagle would fly a long time to circle this valley," Niizh Eshkanag said.

"Do you think we are alone?" Roger asked.

"One is never alone in the forest, but maybe we are the only people," Niizh Eshkanag answered. "We should gather greens and get water at the river. Up here is a good place to camp." He pointed to a grove of short trees.

Roger pointed down at the lake. "Didn't mosquitos, pardon me, zagimeg—bother you last night? That lake down there is probably filthy with them."

"Mosquitoes, zagimeg, bite sometimes, but we rub ourselves with the juices of omakakiibag, a plant that grows near the river. Remember what we used on the ridge? The same plant probably grows down there. I will show you when we come back before night." He waved into the distance. "The wagon trail, west of Makwa Ziibi, is little more than walking trail. Whites mostly ride horses on this side."

"Then we must be careful by the river," Roger said.

"As teacher says, 'it is highly recommended,' but instead of twenty agents searching for Roger Poznanski, nobody searches for John Bemibatood."

"Hope not."

The boys made their way carefully down shrub-lined fissures along animal trails.

"I would not want to climb this at night," Roger grunted as he followed Niizh Eshkanag.

They found ample greens, and saw signs of beaver, muskrats, and fishing. There was no evidence of recent human camps, though old campfire ashes were seen.

Back on the ridge before dark, they built a fire, made a simple lean-to, and then prepared and ate their evening meal. Both boys honored the setting sun before relaxing near the fire.

Roger stared into the flames. "I'm tired,"

"Me, too," Niizh Eshkanag said. "Three days we walked."

"Uh huh."

Niizh Eshkanag glanced across the flames at Roger. "I do not think agent will follow us here." He yawned wide with a gasp.

"I don't think they will work that . . . hard." Roger was falling asleep.

The first night on the hill was comfortably cool. Cliff-top breezes kept mosquitoes at bay, and after days of walking, the boys were soon sound asleep under their robes.

Day three from their camp on the escarpment, the boys were approaching the river to fish. Two white men, naturally shielded by bushes, saw them approaching a few hundred yards up river.

"Look," one said. "Two Injun kids, looks like."

"Wonder what they're doing so far away from a village." The taller said. "The one looks different, somehow. Isn't there a white boy missing hereabouts?"

"They're Injun, anyway," the shorter said.

"Even so, we better check them out. I remember something about a nice reward for a runaway white boy. 'Cordin' to the report, he went to the Indian school with Injuns and could have taken up with them." The men lay their equipment down and began walking toward the boys.

Niizh Eshkanag watched the men start toward them. He nudged Roger motioning toward the forest at the base of the escarpment. The boys gathered their equipment and started away from the men. The men quickened their pace and held their rifles up.

"Stop!" the taller man called. He fired his rifle into the air.

"Damn Injun brats!" the shorter man said. "Should we shoot them?"

The taller man looked hard at his partner. "I hope you're not serious. We just want to talk to them, not kill them. Maybe they'll stop if we shoot off to one side, way off."

"Run in front of me," Roger said. "They suspect something. Maybe, even from a distance, they can see the white one."

"We should avoid the trail that goes uphill to our camp until we lose them," Niizh Eshkanag shouted just as a rifle shot whined off a boulder to their left, but the boys continued running.

"Another warning shot," Niizh Eshkanag said. "They are far now, and we'll lose them in those trees ahead."

Soon, from seclusion behind trees, they rested and watched the men.

"I didn't think they'd intentionally shoot us," Roger said, "but I worried they'd hit one of us by accident."

"Hard to know what a white man with a gun would do," said Niizh Eshkanag. "Indians have been killed, shot in the forest, and nothing is found out. If those men hit one of us, they would have to cover their tracks—kill both of us."

"Scary!"

"We must be more careful," Niizh Eshkanag cautioned. "They might be trappers looking for places to set traps in late fall. I think most trappers have been told to look for you."

"They look for Roger Poznanski not John Bemibatood."

"Right," Niizh Eshkanag said. "When I see the Poznanski kid, I'm going after the reward."

"I get half the reward," Roger replied with a brief snicker.

The rest of the week was uneventful, but the boys were extremely careful to scan ahead wherever they went. They became lean and weathered from their activity and exposure to sun and wind on the barren rocky hill.

One evening, Roger lazed on one side of the fire, Niizh Eshkanag sat cross-legged, and both stared into the flames.

"I miss listening to Migizi explain things," Roger said. "It might sound strange, but I miss Bizaan more than my aunt, though I miss my own mother and father most. When there is time to think, I feel strange being in the forest with an Indian friend. Not bad, because it would be very bad if you weren't with me, but guilty or something."

"I miss my parents too," Niizh Eshkanag murmured. "But . . . soon we will have fun. If we have marked the days right, there will soon be a celebration at Ningaabii'an."

"Don't you like to talk about missing your parents?" Roger asked.

"I would like to, but my mother is very sensitive and seems to know when I think of her. If my thoughts are sad, she knows."

"Wow!" Roger exclaimed. "Nothing but good thoughts from now on." He leaned closer to Niizh Eshkanag. "About that celebration . . ."

"Naanan giizhigadoon," Niizh Eshkanag said. He held his hand up and spread five digits. "Five suns to the old ones. If a white one is not afraid of being seen by an agent or called bad names because he is white, we could go."

"I'm not afraid . . . if bullets don't fly," Roger said.

"They won't," Niizh Eshkanag said. "But there are always some with small minds and big mouths. If you agree, we leave in two days. We need one day for travel, more days to rest with Aunt Boonikiiyaashikwe's cooking and Uncle Zhaabiiwose's stories."

"Those names twist my tongue," Roger smiled. "I'm beginning to think the agency's right, wanting to give you English names."

"They can give," Niizh Eshkanag said defensively, "but we still keep our Anishinaabe names. How would they like it if we give them all Anishinaabe names?"

Roger pointed to his pack hung from branches of a tree. "We're low on salt, and it would be good to get fire sticks. Using flint and steel to start the fire is hard; besides, it's old fashioned. I have no money, but maybe we could trade something."

"When we lived in Ningaabii'an, Father and I traveled to Waaban to build our home," Niizh Eshkanag said. "On the way we went to a trading post east of Ningaabii'an. If we follow a stream, we can walk there in one day. Maybe we could do that after the celebration. Father gave me one dollar and fifty cents. It is packed with my better clothes. He said it is only for when we have problems, aanimakamigad . . ."

"An emergency?" Roger said.

"What is an um-urgency?"

"When one really needs something, or is in trouble," Roger said with a shrug and an upturned palm.

"Okay," Niizh Eshkanag agreed. "We will buy fire sticks, sweets and things. That could end the emergency."

Morning was overcast, but the weather turned hot and sticky by midday. Then the sky darkened ominously, and the boys planned a quick trip to the river and back hoping to miss a threatening storm.

A muskrat was in a snare. Picking greens, filling water containers, they rinsed their clouts and prepared to head up the hill. Niizh Eshkanag pointed to rapidly darkening skies over the cliff then to a rocky overhang at the base of the hill. Thunder rumbled as rain drizzled, and the pair headed for the rock overhangs at the base of the cliff. Both were soaked before reaching shelter where they listened to thunder and watched rain pour in sheets outside. Water ran in torrents—like a waterfall—off the ledge.

Roger watched Niizh Eshkanag flinch back when a lightning bolt flashed and thunder echoed. "That one really burned!" The pair grew silent, and for some time, stood staring out until the rain ebbed.

The boys crested the hill as clouds thinned and sunshine stabbed through the overcast sky. They removed their moccasins and breechcloths, wrung the excess water out, and then put their clouts back on but remained barefoot. Building a fire, they set about drying their moccasins. The camp was intact, though damp. Formal clothes and some items had been sheltered from the rain and were dry.

"How do we find dry wood after that cloudburst?" Roger asked.

"There is always dead wood laying just off the forest floor," Niizh Eshkanag said. "Take off the wet outside bark, split the inside dry part however you want—there is fire starter."

"I . . . could've figured that out."

"Enh geget," Niizh Eshkanag murmured. "Father says, if one watches and listens, Shkaakamigokwe, Mother Earth, has everything one needs."

Night closed, cool and damp, around a warm fire on the hill. Moccasins and vests hung drying on a framework near the fire, and the boys lay under robes, staring at or talking across the fire.

"If the raven has not talked, I do not think Uncle Zhaabiiwose knows of you," Niizh Eshkanag said.

"What will they do, your uncle and aunt, I mean?" Roger asked. "When we first meet them."

"What will they do first? That will be the best part. Their eyes will go funny, then they lift your flap behind to see if you really have Indian ancestors. They will not believe we are alone and will look far to see who comes with us." Niizh Eshkanag paused to savor the image. He lifted his head to see Roger across the fire. "Aunt Boonikiiyaashikwe will say little to start, but she will study you. When she sees you have an Anishinaabe heart, she will fix you up good for the celebration . . . I hope cousin Giigoo is home."

"I have relatives out east who would feel bad if they knew I live in the forest with an Indian." Roger smiled then grew pensive. "They would make me see a head doctor, but that is because they know so little about Indians."

"Like when you first came to Poleville?" Niizh Eshkanag needled. "Head doctor? They look inside the head?"

"Well, some doctors treat people's minds—try to decide who's crazy or not," Roger began to explain, but Niizh Eshkanag was already asleep.

Chapter Eleven

Niizh Eshkanag rubbed his eyes as dawn probed through his eyelids. Rolling to see Roger sleeping across the fire ring, his gaze settled on a filament of smoke curling up from a char. He called softly, "Is the pale Anishinaabe awake?"

Roger moved without opening his eyes. "The sign reads, 'do not disturb.'"

"A woman mooz almost stepped on you, and the man mooz made a terrible noise," Niizh Eshkanag said with a sleepy grin.

Roger sat. "They're called cows and bulls; even I know moose wouldn't be on the ridge. They'd be down by the water and all."

Niizh Eshkanag talked softly while he dressed and donned moccasins, "We hope Gichi-gezhaadiged, the Great Guardian, watches us on our way to Ningaabii'an."

"Okay, but first things first." Roger stood and stepped away from their camp area.

After the boys honored the rising sun, Niizh Eshkanag stirred ashes and blew coals into flame.

Roger murmured as he started toward the rim of the escarpment. "One more look where we swam and fished."

"And ran from bullets," Niizh Eshkanag added.

"Yeah." *Niizh Eshkanag could, but I might never see this place again,* Roger mused as he scanned the panorama, absorbing it along with memories of adventure with Niizh. *Bill was right, there's adventure here; hopefully not more than I need.*

"Beaver meat is cooked, lazy one," Niizh Eshkanag said after Roger returned to the fire.

"You're happy 'cause you visit relatives," Roger said as he sat down. "Maybe you're leading me into a trap. What did your Father say, three hundred dollars reward? Hey, thanks!" Roger stretched to catch a piece of flying meat. "Anyway, I'll make sure Uncle Elias won't have to pay it."

Niizh Eshkanag snickered once. "He can pay it to your new brother."

"To Niizh *Ashcan-yuck*?" Roger retorted. "I don't think so." He held up one of his leggings. "Would we wear leggings and shirts in the village?"

"If it is cold, but it will not be. I will wear what is comfortable, but we should wear leggings going through brush on the shortcut between this trail and the road outside Ningaabii'an. We can wash in the stream, put on fresh clothes. Villagers like young visitors who are neat and polite."

"Girls like clean boys, too," Roger said. "We learned that in Milwaukee. Pardon me—Minowaki." He turned serious. "Anyway, I'd get different looks than one who has Anishinaabe ancestry. But I'll be polite and hope they don't throw stones."

"Not all will look for your ancestors," Niizh Eshkanag said. "The elders will, which is not bad."

Roger motioned north. "Is it a long trip to the village?"

"Most of the day, but we should be there before dark. The village will know of a search for Roger Poznanski, but I do not think they know of John Bemibatood."

"I hope not." Roger grew pensive as he adjusted Niizh Eshkanag's pack, and turned so Niizh Eshkanag could adjust his pack. Both boys then studied the sketched map, with nods and a great deal of pointing.

The duo traveled northwest along the trail below the hill, then veered straight north into a trackless forest to shorten the distance. The trek went easier than expected. No one was seen on the way, but scurrying animals helped pass the time. After a long stop for water and rest at midday, they were, by late afternoon, on the horse trail heading west toward the village. Carrying heavy packs and tired from their adventure and excitement, the boys were ready to rest and refresh as they arrived late afternoon at the stream.

The stream was shallow, and after a brief, rejuvenating rinse, the boys waded across, carrying all their gear. Drying off, they donned aprons, dress moccasins, and put on beaded necklaces. Trail gear and other clothes were stored in backpacks.

Niizh Eshkanag pointed. "The village is a short walk through trees."

After skirting the village perimeter from a knoll, scanning for unusual activities, the boys relaxed behind low dogwood bushes.

"No white ones in sight," Niizh Eshkanag whispered. He faced Roger, grinning. "Uh. Except one." Before Roger could respond, he grew serious, "Wait here while I find my cousin's home. My uncle will suggest what to do."

"Okay," Roger said, and he settled back on a clear spot among bushes.

Niizh Eshkanag stood, adjusted his pack, and strode proudly into the village. He stopped near a boy who stared wide-eyed. Then he introduced himself and asked about his aunt and uncle. "Aho, niijikiwenh. Gimikwenimiyan ina? Niizh Eshkanag indizhinikaaz, inawemagwaa Zhaabiiwose miinawaa Boonikiiyaashikwe."

"Gigii-nitaawig," the boy commented on how much older Niizh Eshkanag looked, gestured to a group of lodges near a large pine, and asked if Giigoo was his cousin. "Noongom besho a'aw zhingwaak endaawag. Gigoo ina gitaawis aawi?"

"Enh, aawi." Niizh Eshkanag confirmed his relations and asked when the celebration would happen. "Aaniin apii jiikakamigag?"

"Niizh giizhigadoon," the boy replied.

"Gimiigwechiwi'in." Niizh Eshkanag thanked him and headed for the large pine tree.

The proud youth who strode through the village suddenly disappeared, and an excited boy rapped gently at the entrance to one of the lodges. A woman poked her head out, squinting in surprise.

"Boozhoo," Niizh Eshkanag said, and he forced a nervous smile.

"Boozhoo," the woman returned, speaking soft with a questioning air. Then she asked who was at her door, "Awenen aawiyan?"

"Boonikiiyaashikwe!" Niizh Eshkanag blurted and then explained his identity, "Niizh Eshkanag indaaw, endaayaan Ningaabii'an noongom."

Boonikiiyaashikwe's voice changed little, but her eyes glistened with understanding as she invited him in and commented on his age, "Howah! Biindigen, gichi-nitaawigiyan ani biboong. . . ."

"Ashi-niiwin nimbiboonigiz," Niizh Eshkanag pointed out he was fourteen winters now.

"Mii sa!" Boonikiiyaashikwe exclaimed. She looked about and beyond Niizh Eshkanag for a traveling companion. "Awenen wiiji-ayaawad?"

"Niwiijikenh waabishkiwi eta, naasaab biboonigizid," said Niizh Eshkanag to assure her the only other visitor was a white friend his own age.

Boonikiiyaashikwe strained to look farther, then backed into the lodge motioning for Niizh Eshkanag to follow. Inside, she pointed to a bench near the fire pit with embers deep within and asked if his friend was hiding because he is white. "Giwiijikenh onji-gaazo ina waabishkiwid?"

Niizh Eshkanag told his aunt that Roger was dressed Anishinaabe-style outside the village and waiting for an invitation, "Anishinaabekwaniye agwajiing oodenang mii baabii'od ji-wiikamaagod."

"Gida-giiwashkwanimaa nebwaakaad naagadawendang inendaminid. Biizh waabishkiwid wii-maadaa-ashangeyang," Boonikiiyaashikwe smiled and told Niizh Eshkanag he could confuse a wise man, but he should bring the white one so they could begin to feast.

After Niizh Eshkanag left him, Roger lay nearly dozing, oblivious of approaching footfalls. Two boys, carrying a deer, passed the bush hiding Roger just as he stirred in doze, rustling leaves and twigs.

The boys stopped at the sound behind a bush.

"Nashke!" The younger boy pointed over to the bush. They peered at Roger and wondered if he was white. "Aabita-waabishkiwi ina?"

"Gaawiin wiika ingii-waabamaasii," the older boy said he had never seen this one before.

The younger whispered they might need to speak English to him, "Indinendaan aabdeg zhaaganaashiimotawangid."

Roger opened his eyes, saw two boys staring down at him, and quickly stood.

The taller, a boy of seventeen, wore trade pants, moccasins, a necklace and earrings. The smaller boy, Roger's age, was shorter. He wore a necklace, moccasins, and a simple deerskin skirt.

Sheepish, Roger smiled looking around. "Boozhoo. I am John Bemibatood, from Waaban near the Poleville Indian School."

The older boy spoke fair English with an accent, "You dress Anishinaabe, but are white. I am Nenaginad." He motioned to the smaller boy. "This Apane."

"My father is white," Roger said quietly.

"What are you doing here?" Nenaginad asked.

"I am with a friend who is in your village. I will join him now."

"If you are half Indian, you should wear half Indian clothes," Nenaginad said. He laughed, an unfriendly laugh. Roger frowned, shifted his stance and looked aside to avoid what he perceived as a hateful stare. Nenaginad took Roger by the wrist and jerked him toward the village. "Maybe, you are spy for the agents."

"Hey, not so rough!" Roger yelled. He reached down with his free hand and awkwardly grabbed his backpack, which slapped the bushes, then his legs. Desperate, he lunged to free himself, but Nenaginad was too strong. "It hurts!"

"You can tell Ogimaa Niigaan why you here," Nenaginad demanded as he twisted Roger's arms behind his back. Roger would not let go of his pack and it banged the back of his legs harder.

"He told us he was here with Niizh Eshkanag," Apane protested. "Why do you hold him?"

Niizh Eshkanag approached from behind a lodge and asked the boys what they were doing when he saw Nenaginad mauling Roger. "Bemibatood! Aaniin ezhichigeyeg?"

Grunting displeasure, Nenaginad shoved Roger so hard toward Niizh Eshkanag he fell, scraping a knee and elbow. Nenaginad left, motioning Apane to accompany him. Niizh Eshkanag and Roger headed to Boonikiiyaashikwe's home. Roger rubbed his arm and shoulder.

"That older boy grabbed me, not for the reward, but he thought I was in cahoots with agents."

"You are lucky I came . . ."

"Yeah, I know—great heroic warriors. . . ." Roger laughed at the zaniness of their jokes.

"You said cahoots? What's that?"

Roger shrugged. "People working together. I think it mostly means less than nice." "Some might say you and I are in cahoots, but we could deny that. Anyway, about your relatives, what did they say about us, about me?"

"Zhaabiiwose was not home, but Boonikiiyaashikwe waits to see the white Anishinaabe." Niizh Eshkanag paused. "I remember something about the one who was mean to you. Was he called Nenaginad?"

"Uh huh," Roger confirmed. "The smaller boy my age was called Apane who says he will see us later."

"Nenaginad, was never friendly, but he never hurt younger ones before. Giigoo will know if he is trouble."

Outside her home, Boonikiiyaashikwe watched Roger and Niizh Eshkanag approach. When they stood before her, she used English for Roger and told them, "I saw two Anishinaabeg from a distance, and I wondered how these two came together, but tell me only what you wish."

"I know John Bemibatood many moons, uh, months," Niizh Eshkanag said.

"Then he is no stranger," Boonikiiyaashikwe said, guiding the boys into the lodge.

A man soon entered, and Niizh Eshkanag stood raising his hand in greeting. "Aho, Ninzhisheh! It is good to see you again my uncle."

"There is only one your age who calls me Zhisheh. You have grown some, Niizh Eshkanag. Who is the one who looks like one of us from a distance, but who is not one of us?"

"Roger Poznanski is from the school. He learns of our people and loves the forest. Where is Giigoo?"

"He met a friend, and they stopped to tell stories." Zhaabiiwose motioned about. "He will come when he is out of words."

Boonikiiyaashikwe pointed to stew and fry bread warming near the fire. "We wait no longer for Giigoo."

Boonikiiyaashikwe and Zhaabiiwose settled around the fire to eat with their guests, and a boy appeared from around a neighboring lodge. He stopped when he saw Niizh Eshkanag with another boy.

"Boozhoo!" Niizh Eshkanag pointed to Roger, "Niwiijikenh Roger Poznanski gaa-izhinikaazo, but now we call him John Bemibatood."

"He is Anishinaabe ina?" Giigoo looked closer. "Howah! I see. Bangii eta ina, is he part Anishinaabe?"

"Waabishkiwi gwiiwizens eta, all white boy," Niizh Eshkanag said.

Roger smiled at the ground. *Here we go, again.*

"It started in Minowaki," Niizh Eshkanag began. As he listened, Roger couldn't stop shaking his head or smiling.

Boonikiiyaashikwe listened to the growing saga. "Your family does not know you are with Niizh?" She stood back, studying Roger from head to foot, dwelling on his face and hair. "A white man came many days before; he gave council a paper with picture. The picture is of a pale white boy, short hair. White man said this boy is friend with my nephew, Niizh Eshkanag. Maybe you are the one, but I see two brothers who come to visit their aunt and uncle." She motioned them into the wigwam.

Inside the lodge, facing Roger, Boonikiiyaashikwe acted joyful. "I need a new dress. How much is the reward?"

Niizh Eshkanag elbowed Roger's side as he replied, "Enough to buy a new dress every day from one moon to the next."

Boonikiiyaashikwe chuckled. "I make a joke. There is stew warming, enough for hungry travelers." She sobered. "Niizh speaks of an uncle and aunt who do not treat you good. A child should find happiness living with relatives; relatives should be happy to have a child."

"It's mostly my aunt, and she acts like I'm burden. I think it is sadness for my dead cousin, her son, more than hate for me," Roger explained.

"The end is the same," Boonikiiyaashikwe reflected. "If her heart is on a journey of sadness, you are better on your own journey."

Niizh Eshkanag glanced to Roger, then Giigoo. "We have been many days in the forest. The first seven days so my village could not be blamed for stealing Roger."

Zhaabiiwose thoughtfully gazed at Roger then Niizh Eshkanag before breaking into a brief smile. "I do not think your skin was 'bright like the sun' as Niizh says. He motioned about and sipped the last of his stew. Live in the forest good if parents agree, but running away . . . I don't know. Niizh has experience in the forest, but you, maybe not enough. And it is not good when a boy walks a crooked trail to manhood. I agree with Bizaan and Migizi; it is better Roger be away from family for a while, but maybe not too long. Give your aunt and uncle more time to learn what is important."

Zhaabiiwose set his bowl down, took a deep breath, and squinted at Roger. "It will also help a nephew learn what is important." He motioned about. An agent came fifteen days before, looking for a white boy. There was a name to remember, but I gave it no thought, for I did not know this white boy traveled with my nephew. When they learn I am Niizh Eshkanag's uncle, they came again, six days ago and say the boys could be together. We must be careful, for they could return. There might not be many who would seek that reward, but it takes only one."

"I will not stay if it means hardship to your family," Roger said.

Zhaabiiwose raised a hand, "About the reward, which could tempt anyone, good or bad; it is for your safe return, not a bounty." He motioned between Niizh Eshkanag and Roger. "Will you go to the forest, then return for celebration?"

"We would like to stay for celebration then go to the trading post," Niizh Eshkanag said. "After that we go back to the forest."

"Celebration is two suns," Zhaabiiwose said. "Help us pray for a good berry harvest."

Niizh Eshkanag and Roger helped Giigoo with home and village chores, which included preparing the dance circle for dancing and gathering wood for fires. That evening after eating, they sat yawning at the family fire.

"Daga inda-wiijiiwaag ina adaawewigamigong?" Giigoo asked if he could go with the boys to the trading post, looking first to his father then his mother.

"Niwii-inendaamin," Zhaabiiwose told Giigoo they would think about it and then said in English for all to hear, "You boys are young to be without an adult, but maybe old enough to join those who do well in the forest. It is up to them and your mother."

Boonikiiyaashikwe nodded. "We will talk after celebration. It is soon dark, and our guests are tired from a long walk with heavy packs." She faced the boys. "I have robes and blankets inside when you are ready." She pointed to the wigwam.

"I will sleep by the outside fire," Niizh Eshkanag said.

"If it rains," Boonikiiyaashikwe cautioned, "there is room inside."

Zhaabiiwose yawned and stretched. "I must be up early to work on celebration plans with elders. I will sleep now."

Niizh Eshkanag smiled at Roger, "I will help you sleep, then we both help with celebration."

"Good night!" Roger said, shaking his head in feigned dismay. Both boys spread their blankets near Giigoo and lay down.

The morning sun touched the treetops, and the boys still slept beside a freshly stoked fire. The aroma of hot fry bread and jerky teased Niizh Eshkanag to peer from under his blanket then to quickly sit. Roger sat propped on one elbow, his hair half over his face, rubbing sand from the corner of his eye.

"Aaniindi ayaad noos?" Giigoo asked where his father was.

"Gchi-ayaayan owiidokawaan goos," said Boonikiiyaashikwe as she prepared the morning meal and shared that he had gone to help the elders and would return soon to eat. "Owii-azhegiiwe wayiiba ji-wiisinid."

Zhaabiiwose returned, and after eating, the family began preparations for the Berry Celebration. Niizh Eshkanag and Roger worked with

Zhaabiiwose in the morning, and after midday, picked greens with
the girls and women.

One girl moved close to Niizh Eshkanag as they worked and said
she remembered when he lived in Ningaabii'an. "Ingii-mikwendaan
apii endaawaad gidinawemaaganag omaa. Ogii-bami'aan ina
aabitaa-anishinaabewinid? Did they adopt a half blood?" She nodded
toward Roger who worked apart from other boys.

"John Bemibatood izhinikaazo miinawaa Poleville onjibaad," Niizh
Eshkanag explained who Roger had become after his parents died.
"Ingitizimag ogii-nibowaad mii dash wiiji-babaamaadiziyaang."

The girl whispered to Niizh Eshkanag that his friend looked like trouble,
but he was cute. "Aanimakamigizi iidog gaye wawiiyazhinaagozid."

"Mino-doodaanan dash daa-wiidookawaad Anishinaaben misawaa
aabitaa-anishinaabewid eta," Niizh Eshkanag, slightly embarrassed,
shifted the conversation from looks to say that Roger was a good
person and would do anything to help the Anishinaabe people.

During the evening meal, Boonikiiyaashikwe looked at Giigoo. "If you
go with Niizh Eshkanag and Roger, you should wear good clothes in
the trading post, but not on the trail."

Giigoo brightened. "Gimiigwechiwi'in! Thank you!" He turned to
Niizh Eshkanag and Roger. "It is yes for me to join you?" he asked.

"All right," Niizh Eshkanag agreed. Roger nodded.

Boonikiiyaashikwe faced Niizh Eshkanag and Roger. "Giigoo is
young. You will be the leaders, and he must listen to both of you. I
think you will watch him so he will not get hurt."

The next day, Roger, Niizh Eshkanag, and Giigoo hunted small game,
fished, picked berries with the women and girls, and gathered wood.
Late afternoon, they worked on the dance arena, sweeping, picking
twigs and other matter. It was dirty work, and when they finished,
streaked with grimy sweat, they headed for the stream.

First to awaken on the day of the berry celebration, Roger stirred the
fire, and soon Niizh Eshkanag and Giigoo stood with crossed arms
near the flames to chase an early morning chilll.

"The sun is soon up and people from everywhere trample us," Giigoo moaned. He pointed to a tent at the outskirts of the village. "Those drank whiskey all night."

"I saw white people last night. There could be an agent here," Niizh Eshkanag cautioned. "Father says the agency makes villages get permission to dance and would like to stop all celebrations." He faced Boonikiiyaashikwe, smiling brightly. "We are up early to help my favorite aunt, a duty I endure for no other."

"I must speak to Bizaan of a coyote with a clever tongue. Wait, get my trade mirror, you see him yourself." Boonikiiyaashikwe chuckled adding, "After sunrise ceremony, we eat. Then the coyote and his brother will bring wood for the celebration."

"When we carry wood don't pass close to white strangers, brother John Bemibatood," Niizh Eshkanag cautioned, then with an artful grin, "I would be angry if another got the reward."

"Dancers and traders might look for Roger Poznanski who shines in the dark, but all they will see is John Bemibatood," Roger said. "I'll try not to sound or look too white-boyish."

Three boys strolled about the village and explored the nearby forest, which teemed with tents and lean-to shelters. To not disturb a meeting of elders, they bypassed the meetinghouse, and finished putting greens over benches around the dance circle. On their way to the arena, they met three older boys.

"Nenaginad," Giigoo greeted with a half-hearted wave.

Weaving with inebriation, Nenaginad squared off to Roger and told him to go back to the white village. "Giin, giwaabishkiw mii dash izhaan waabishkiwi-oodena!"

Roger shifted uneasily glancing to Niizh Eshkanag who shrugged and pulled Roger's arm. "We go around these ones," Niizh Eshkanag said. "They are giiwashkwebi with whiskey."

Roger followed his friend, both stepping around the older boys. "We want no trouble."

"Go live to white village with your other half," Nenaginad snarled in English this time. He grabbed Roger's arm, glaring at him.

Giigoo pulled on Roger's free arm. "Let's go, Bemibatood!" He said.

"Let him go!" Niizh Eshkanag shouted. He forced his way between Nenaginad and Roger, but was kicked in the back by Nenaginad's friend. Nenaginad released Roger and struck Niizh Eshkanag in the abdomen. Roger jumped on Nenaginad, but another bully pulled him off and threw him against a tree.

On hands and knees, Niizh Eshkanag struggled to stand. He sagged flat on the ground moaning, but somehow gathered breath to scream, "Giigoo! Naazh goos Zhaabiiwose!" But Giigoo had already headed home to fetch his father.

Niizh Eshkanag lay gasping. Roger crawled to sit against a tree holding his stomach. Nenaginad stared at the boys then drew back to kick Niizh Eshkanag again, even as his friend grabbed Roger's shoulders to further maul him.

"Ishkwaataan baabige!" Zhaabiiwose yelled for Nenaginad to stop immediately. He was with another elder. Zhaabiiwose tended Niizh Eshkanag, the other elder helped Roger while talking to Nenaginad,

The elder scolded him saying it was terrible that he was not only drunk but also a bully who hit younger boys, "Geget maji-izhiwebad ge-giiwashkwebiiyan, gaye bakite'adwaa oshki-gwiiwizensag wenji-zhaagode'eyan." He motioned to Zhaabiiwose who cradled Niizh Eshkanag in his arms and warned Nenaginad that if either of the boys suffered a lasting injury, the council could banish him and his friends from the village. "Giishpin ongow gwiiwizensag wiisagishinowaad, zegaswe'idijig dash gidaa-giichigonigowaag oodenang." He then sternly announced there was no time for a council meeting, and warned they were not to leave their homes while he fulfilled his peacekeeping duties. They were to wait until later when the council would determine their fate. "Gaawiin noongom dash daa-zagaswe'idisiiwag, gaye wii-gizhaadigeyaan, daa-maajaayeg oodenang gemaa dazhiikeyeg ezhi-daayeg. Zegaswe'idijig owii-naakonaanaawaa ishkwaa maawanjiweyaang."

Zhaabiiwose carried Niizh Eshkanag, and with the elder helping, Giigoo supported Roger walking to Zhaabiiwose's home.

"Weshki-ayaajig banaajichigaazowag apii minikwaadamowaad ishkodewaaboo, awashime banaaji'iwendamowaad," Boonikiiyaashikwe fumed about whiskey ruining weak young minds as she helped settle Niizh Eshkanag and Roger inside on robes.

Zhaabiiwose prepared an herb drink for Niizh Eshkanag and said Nenaginad had been trouble since the age of fifteen and now had clearly forgotten the words of the First Grandfather, no longer walking the trail of the ancestors. "Ogii-wanendaan gaa-gikinoo'amaagod Gichi-mishomis gaye dash bwaa-bezhigwedang ge gidaanikoobijiganibaninaanig gaa-ezhi-inaadiziwaapan."

Niizh Eshkanag stood up saying he felt as if he fought a bear, "Makwa ingii-miigaazh'aa moozhitooyaan." Then he asked what happened to Nenaginad and his friends. "Aaniin gaa-inaakonigaazowaad Nenaginad gaye . . . gaye owiijiiwaaganiman?"

"Giwii-booniikaagowaag," Boonikiiyaashikwe said they would not trouble him again. She gave Niizh Eshkanag a cup of herb tea but after one sip he frowned with a wry grin and asked if it was poison. "Gimiizh ina bichibojigan?"

Giigoo told Niizh Eshkanag to drink it all so he would never have to taste it, "Gidan dash gaawiin wiikaa daa-biijipidanziiwaan."

Boonikiiyaashikwe pretended to frown while swiping Giigoo's head then asked the boys where Nenaginad had gotten the whiskey, "Aaniindi gaa-wendinamowaad i'iw ishkodewaaboo?"

"Gichi-mookomaan wedaawed ogii-biidoon," Zhaabiiwose explained a white trader brought it.

Moments passed, Niizh Eshkanag's eyes sharpened, and he looked at Roger who sat nearby holding a wet rag on his face while in a forward lean trying to listen to their conversation. Niizh Eshkanag suddenly lay back, one hand dramatically covering his eyes. "I am failing, Aunt," he moaned with an overdone wince.

Boonikiiyaashikwe twisted, slapped Niizh Eshkanag on the chest with a laugh. "When the coyote wags his tongue in foolishness, he is far from his end unless he angers his aunt." Zhaabiiwose nodded with a smile.

The boys soon recovered enough from the assaults to prepare for the dance circle.

"Niizh Eshkanag and, uh, Bemibatood will look good at the dance," Zhaabiiwose remarked to Boonikiiyaashikwe as he watched the boys preen feathers inside their lodge. "It is good we found a few dance feathers for them."

"Will they laugh at a white boy?" Roger asked. "And what is this ceremony for?"

"It's for a good berry harvest," Zhaabiiwose said. "We are early so that two weeks later, we can travel to another village and help them celebrate their harvest."

"Mm, more excitement, I see," Roger murmured.

Zhaabiiwose explained to Roger that other young half bloods follow their Indian side. Wise ones see a dancer's spirit, quicker than his race."

Boonikiiyaashikwe looked straight at Niizh Eshkanag. "Roger is like a warrior facing the enemy," she said. "He faces more hardship when he brings white blood among Anishinaabe dancers."

Dancers lined up outside the entrance to the arena, warriors first, women next, and finally youths.

"Must Boonikiiyaashikwe and I protect you from girls?" Zhaabiiwose asked. He cast an admiring glance at the boys.

"I wish Nagamokwe were here," Niizh Eshkanag said, his face aglow with excitement.

"Ajijaak, too," Roger said.

The celebration went well, during which the boys enjoyed meeting people, and nothing more was seen of drunk older boys. There seemed to be enough whiskey circulating, but most was imbibed within the confines of civility. Other than standing out as part white, no negative suspicion appeared to follow Roger.

Late at night, Zhaabiiwose sat with the boys around the outside fire while Boonikiiyaashikwe prepared travel packs in the lodge.

After warning the boys to be careful with all strangers—Indian or white—Zhaabiiwose gestured toward the boys' sleeping spaces. "Sleep so you can awaken with the sun."

Chapter Twelve

Niizh Eshkanag stepped behind Roger, inspected his pack, and unsuccessfully shielded his anxiety—*I must protect a white runaway boy who must help how he can, and both of us must look out for Giigoo.*

"I'm ready," Roger declared. He shrugged, jostling his pack for fit.

"Most Anishinaabe would not capture a friend for reward," Zhaabiiwose said. "But money and whiskey are powerful temptations. Be careful near the trading post." He thought a moment. "Anishinaabe family is usually all right to visit. Those with children, have little time to plan mischief."

Boonikiiyaashikwe approached nodding at the boys. "Children, even of white ones, could be with mischief." She smiled as the boys squelched the urge to giggle. She held out two large beaver pelts. "These are from winter traps, are cured, and worth much money. Niizh Eshkanag should do the trade; the trader is honest, knows our furs, and will give an honest price. Everyone will share the money."

"The journey is two short days for a family," Zhaabiiwose said, "but one day for yearlings, with another day to rest. We look for you in three maybe four days."

Each boy carried dress clothes to appear neat and businesslike, but circumstances limited that to beaded moccasins, colorful headbands black aprons, and necklaces. They each carried their own knives and youth bows and arrows, and divided the remaining camp gear between them. For travel they wore heavy trail moccasins, an everyday breechcloth, doeskin shirts and leggings, which they would use if nights turned cool or when traveling under difficult circumstances.

The day turned warm and humid as the boys hiked east against the west-flowing stream. By midday with little breeze, and damp with perspiration, they stopped to rest and snack. Niizh Eshkanag noticed Giigoo's shoulders tinged red from the chaffing of the backpack strap. "We travelled far today," he said. "We can take some of your load. We are used to carrying things, and you are smaller than us."

"Miigwech, but I can carry it," Giigoo said.

"We think of ourselves." Niizh Eshkanag handed food to Roger, while talking to Giigoo, "If you stay healthy, we will not have to carry one who is much heavier than his pack."

Roger smiled. "Good point."

The boys followed the stream until it veered north where the trail wound through a tall forest with little ground foliage. Before dark, they arrived at a rough wagon road, which coursed from the north, past a trading post two hundred paces from an east-flowing stream. The road crossed the stream over a wood bridge and continued southeast to eventually cross the Zagime Ziibi, and miles farther to Waaban.

The trio camped along the stream among pines and bushes near an Anishinaabe family. While Giigoo prepared a fire and lean-to, Niizh Eshkanag and Roger approached the neighboring camp where a man, woman, and a child were seen.

Niizh Eshkanag waved his hand high overhead. "Boozhoo!" he greeted as they neared the fire. Roger's wave was subdued at shoulder height.

"Boozhoo!" the man returned the greeting then asked the boys where their parents were. "Aaniindi ayaawaad gigitizimag?"

Niizh Eshkanag explained they were students from Poleville Indian School travelling alone and introduced himself. "Ge niswi niinawind ninazhikewizimin. Niizh Eshkanag indizhinikaaz miinawaa Waaban onjibaayaan." He nodded aside toward Roger. "John Bemibatood izhinikaazo Waaban onjibaad miinawaa." He motioned behind. "Nitaawis Giigoo aawi onjibaad Ningaabii'an."

The man smiled and introduced himself and his wife and daughter, "Netaawichiged indizhinikaaz mii niwiiw izhinikaazod Bagakaabikwe miinawaa nindaanisinaan Nenookaasi aawid." Netaawichiged looked at their packs and asked if they were afraid to be alone knowing there are sometimes evil people around trading posts. "Gaawiin ina gizegizisiim wii-nazhikewiziyeg? Aangodinong wiindigoog ayaawag besho adaawewigamigong."

Niizh Eshkanag briefly described how they struggled with one government agent near Waaban. Netaawichiged smiled and said they would probably be fine at the trading post but should be careful. "Indinendaan daa-ayaangwaamiziyeg iwedi adaawewigamigong."

Niizh Eshkanag explained they had one dollar and fifty cents and planned to trade two tanned winter pelts to buy a few things: matches, salt, and candy. "Indayaawaanaanig bezhigwaabik gaye naanimidana zhoomaanikeg, gaye wii-meshkwadoozhangidwaa niizh bibooni-awesiiwayaanag. Ninandawendaamin ishkode-zaka'iganan, zhiiwitaagan, ziinzibaakwadoon, gaye anooj gegoon."

With a chuckle Netaawichiged said they had already traded and were resting two more nights before traveling home. "Zhigwa nigii-adaawemin gaye niizhogon wii-anwebiyang biinish giiweyang, niizhogon waabanong." He asked if they were planning to stay another night and generously said they were welcome at the fire even with John, who was clearly white. "Giwii-bi-ayaam ina bakaan dibik miinawaa? John Bemibatood waabishkiwe, aanawi dash geyaabi nandonjigaazoyeg ezhi-baamendamang ishkode."

Niizh Eshkanag said they would be staying the night in the woods again and had been there for many days. "Ningii-gabeshimin niibiwa dasogon mitigwakiing."

"Giiniwaa nayenzh gidinaagozim." The older man laughed and said they definitely had that look.

Niizh Eshkanag motioned toward Giigoo working near a blazing fire. "Aambe maajaadaa." Exchanging waves with the family, Roger and Niizh Eshkanag returned to their camp.

Roger studied the shelter with a comment, "Giigoo made a good shelter!" Then added, "ogii-nitaa'ozhitoon," to show he was working to learn Ojibwemowin.

"Onizhishin! It is good!" Niizh Eshkanag agreed as they sat under the lean-to.

"Wiisinin! Eat! I have prepared food for a chief," Giigoo declared with pride. "Did the family know of Roger?"

"No more than that he could be part *Injun*," Niizh Eshkanag replied with a snicker.

Roger snorted. "You said it, I didn't!"

"I joke."

Roger smiled, "I know, more *Injun* humor."

Niizh Eshkanag pointed to the stream. "Clothes should be neat and clean and our hair brushed before we trade tomorrow."

Wrapped in robes ready to sleep, the boys talked with occasional yawns. Giigoo slept quickly, but Roger and Niizh Eshkanag, stared longer into the fire past robes wrapped to their noses.

Niizh Eshkanag awoke to a fresh fire then jerked to sitting, staring at a young girl who stood near the fire.

"Boozhoo," the girl said as she set down a small load of wood saying that her mother was worried they might let their fire go out. "Ninga ogii-inendaan waa-aatawebiyeg."

"Gimiigwechiwigo!" Niizh Eshkanag thanked her then asked how many winters she had seen. "Na'aa . . . Nenookaasi. Aaniin endaaso biboonigiziyan?"

"Midaaswi nimbiboonigiz miinawaa gegaa waniikenindaman izhinikaazoyaan." She informed him she had seen ten winters and teased him for nearly forgetting her name. She then stood there barefoot wearing a simple strap dress, and a necklace of red glass beads. A small eagle plume adorned her neatly brushed and braided hair.

Niizh Eshkanag yawned while stretching, and pointed out that she must have gotten up early. "Gigii-onishkaanaaban wayiiba."

"Enya," she confirmed she had.

"Gidandawendaan waabandaman wawiiyazh gegoo?" Niizh Eshkanag asked in a whisper if she would like to see something funny. . . . He picked up a large green worm, lifted Roger's blanket off his abdomen and set the worm on his navel. Roger stirred as though to awaken, but settled again to gentle breathing. He twitched in his sleep as the worm crawled toward his ribs. Nenookaasi covered her mouth with both hands to stifle giggles and her eyes twinkled when the worm crawled toward Roger's neck. Giigoo was now awake, sitting up.

Roger suddenly sat, brushed the worm off, and smiled at Nenookaasi. "Hello." He turned to Niizh Eshkanag. "What's so funny? Did I miss something? Hey, you put that worm on me!"

"Gidandawendaan ina ziinzibaakwadoons?" Giigoo asked Nenookaasi if she would like a piece of his maple candy.

"Enya daga!" she smiled.

Giigoo dug into his pack, produced brown lumps, handed one to Nenookaasi, and thanked her for bringing firewood. "Gimiigwechiwigo misan gaa-miizhiyaang."

"Ningashki'o waabandaman gigabeshiwinim megwaa izhaayeg adaawewigamig," said Nenookaasi, offering to watch their camp site while they went to the trading post.

Niizh Eshkanag nodded.

The boys ate, bathed in the stream, donned their best clothes, and returned to their camp to finish dressing. They fixed each other's hair, put on necklaces, and though each boy wore a necklace, Niizh Eshkanag and Giigoo had a spirit pouch attached to theirs. Taking money and furs, they went to their neighbor's camp.

"Awenen aawiwaad ongow miikawaadizininiwag?" Bagakaabi asked who the handsome young strangers were.

Niizh Eshkanag grinned and thanked her for sending Nenookaasi. "Gimiigwechiwi'in gaa-anoozhad Nenookaasi ji-wiidookawiyangid." Then he asked if her daughter could watch their camp while they are busy trading. "Owii-waabandaan ina gidaanis ningabeshiwanim megwaa adaaweyaang?"

"Mino-biboonI-awesiiwayaanag aawiwag," Bagakaabi observed his nice winter pelts and confirmed that Nenookaasi could watch their camp for the day while her father was fishing upstream. "Giga-waabamininim onaagoshig," she waved the boys off, said she would see them later, and watched them make their way toward the trading post.

At the hitching rail, Niizh Eshkanag stopped, scanned carefully about. Two riding horses and a wagon team; it should be safe enough. *I have never traded alone with a white man, but Boonikiiyaashikwe and Zhaabiiwose say this trader is honest.* Fidgeting, he stepped toward the door. *One must go in or go away.* He walked to the door with Giigoo and Roger behind. Roger held back as though unwilling to enter. "Do not worry," Niizh Eshkanag added, twisting to see behind, trying to appear confident. "You think whole world wants Roger Poznanski. When I went with Father to a trading place, we see only trappers and travelers. This place—like teacher says—is remote 'stablishment. The search is for full-blood pale boy who is very not strong."

Roger shook his head in disbelief. *Joker.*

Niizh Eshkanag opened the door and entered heading for the counter followed by Roger and Giigoo.

Inside, the soft sliding fall of moccasins on a wood floor suddenly became the only sound. Niizh Eshkanag became uneasy, pausing until Roger and Giigoo were abreast of him, and all approached the counter. They scanned the display of wares and about the room. The proprietor had just served a man and boy at a table to Niizh Eshkanag's left and now returned to the counter. *Netaawichiged also said the trader is an honorable man.* A spoon clinked a cup directly behind Niizh Eshkanag, and a man coughed aloud. Niizh Eshkanag looked back at two bearded men nearly hidden behind the open door. One did not blink or turn away when his eyes met those of Niizh Eshkanag. *Two men behind the door look to be trappers who might not be friendly, but they should be no trouble.* He faced the trader, but was compelled to glance at the table to his left. *That man with his son does not look at us with hate, but he is a thoughtful one.*

Niizh Eshkanag smiled at the trader. "Boozhoo. We have two tanned winter beaver pelts from Zhaabiiwose and Boonikiiyaashikwe of Ningaabii'an," he said.

"I know them, and need only to measure the hides," the trader said. "I'm Chuck. Boonikiiyaashikwe sends only the best pelts." He began writing the terms of the transaction, paused and looked closely at Roger, talking pleasantly, "You are not Anishinaabe, unless you are only part Indian."

Roger threw a pleading glance to Niizh Eshkanag.

"John Bemibatood is my brother with a white father," Niizh Eshkanag said. He smiled as though for Boonikiiyaashikwe, and stretched to watch the trader write. "Are you busy with furs?"

"Not this time of year. Travelers stop and the mail comes twice a week. Pretty quiet. I give more if you take it in trade."

Looking behind at the trappers who still stared at him, Niizh Eshkanag shifted his gaze over their heads to posters on the door. Resisting an urge to stare the trappers down, Niizh Eshkanag turned back to the trader. "Bemibatood and I will trade," he said. *So! One poster behind those men is an old picture of a white boy in school clothes, short hair. I wonder what the writing says? We must be very careful.*

Roger nudged Niizh Eshkanag out of his muse. "Boozhoo. nindadaawemin," he said, trying to use the little Ojibwemowin he knew to convince the trader he was from Waaban.

"Pick what you want," Chuck said, "and we'll see if it comes to this." He shoved a paper between Niizh Eshkanag and Roger.

"I would like a folding knife," Niizh Eshkanag said to Chuck. Then he turned to ask Roger what he wanted, "Aaniin andawendaman Bemibatood?"

"Gaawiin gegoo," Roger said nothing at first but then reconsidered and said maybe a bit of candy. "Na'aa, ganabaj ziinzibaakwadoons."

"Adaawetamawaadaa gidagiigin gigaminaanig wii-oshki-majigoodenhkewaad," Giigoo said they should trade for some calico so their mothers could make new dresses.

"Must be a half breed!" a young voice from the table whispered, but it was heard easily about the room. "Taking after his Injun side!"

Niizh Eshkanag spun and glared at the boy, then the father. *Father would never let me speak like that before strangers, Indian or white!* The man put his hand on his son's shoulder and admonished him with a look.

Roger stood facing the father and son. "Rather a half blood than a halfwit spewing nonsense!"

Niizh Eshkanag glanced about the room and caught the trapper's surprised look. He saw the poster, resembling Roger at the beginning of the school year. *It is Roger. The writing is small, but the picture says enough.*

Without using Ojibwemowin, Roger was suddenly an educated schoolboy. Quickly concluding the trade, the boys started toward the door. The trappers were expressionless as the boys passed them.

One trapper, Dan, stood and gazed out the window watching the boys depart. He was sullen, aggressive with heavy boots and a hat that slouched about his head. He pointed at the poster. "See what I see?"

"Yeah, let's see where they go," the other, Brady, said. He was mild-mannered, content to follow another's lead.

Chuck walked over and looked closer at the poster. "It's possible," he said, "but why take with Indians? Appears to been living with 'em a bit. 'Cording to this, the Poznanski kid's been gone less than a month."

"Anybody could look like that in a month," Dan said, "if'n they lived outside."

"There's half bloods here bouts; could be a look-alike," the trader cautioned.

"Take away the weather, put clothes on him, cut his hair. That'd be him fer sure!" Dan declared.

"Remember, it hain't a bounty," Chuck said. He squinted, scratched the side of his jaw. "The reward is fer a boy to be returned *safely* to his family. He can't be captured like a criminal. "'Pears to be doin' right smart fer himself. I'll write the school that a boy, like what the poster showed, came through. I'll tell 'em he looked real good."

"We'll jest talk him into going home," Dan said, winking toward Brady.

"Yep! We'll make his folks real proud to git him back," Brady said.

"You goin' after the reward?" Chuck asked.

"You might say we jest wants to bring a poor boy and his family together," Dan replied, an ominous purse twisting his mouth.

"You can't hurt 'im, or those with 'im, either, whatever you do," Chuck cautioned. "Like when you killed that Indian boy charged with stealing a horse."

"The law wanted an Injun, paid us fifty dollars to catch one," Dan argued. "The law didn't bother none to check it out neither, except to make sure he was dead."

"Even so, don't bite off more than you can chew," Chuck said. "Those youngsters seem right smart."

The boys disappeared over a knoll toward the river. Brady and Dan hurried out the door following the boys until certain where they camped, then returned to their river camp.

"The bearded ones know who you are," Niizh Eshkanag said as they neared their camp. "It was when you spoke. Did you see the picture behind the door?"

"No, but I think you're right. I better go alone."

Niizh Eshkanag gazed into the treetops, at the ground and then into Roger's face. His cheeks dimpled from a taut face, and his eyes glowed. "You would have a hard time alone in forest. I could not leave you and my family would not want me to leave you. You helped me and Aandeg last winter." His eyes softened. "We will leave early in the morning, carefully, together!"

Roger gently punched Niizh Eshkanag on the arm. "Thanks, Brother Too-Many-Horns."

Meanwhile, Dan and Brady plotted how to capture Roger. "We go afore dawn, follow the brats, wait for our chance and nab the one," Dan said. "If the Injun kids make trouble, we slug 'em." He sat against a tree. "They'll be scared and hightail fer home."

"Don't seem right to hurt kids, even Injun kids," Brady said. "Maybe jest slap 'em hard." He spat a chaw into the fire.

"Now we can get new guns an' clothes," Dan said. "I'm gittin one of them new-fangled high-powered rifles, and a pistol too."

Brady sat erect. "How we gittin' him home anyhow?"

"If he don't go peaceful-like, we lead him like a horse," Dan replied. "Guess it'll be harder than tracking Injuns for the law. They can be killed without a fuss."

"Did we ever bring any back alive?" Brady asked, frowning.

"Now that you mention it, maybe not."

It was near midday when the boys returned to their camp. Peering anxiously about, they built a fire and cooked a meal. Then they went to visit Nitaa's family.

Nenookaasi met them as they approached. Giigoo dug into his pouch then offered a closed hand to Nenookaasi. "Ziinzibaakwadoons ina?"

"Enya geget ziinzibaakwadoons!" Nenookaasi gleefully confirmed she would like a piece of candy and held her hand out expectantly.

"Aaniin ezhi-adaaweyeg?" Bagakaabi asked how the trading had gone as the boys approached the fire.

"Niizh wanii'igewininiwag ningii-waawaabamigonaanig." Niizh Eshkanag reported that two trappers had stared at them.

"Ningikenimaanaanig Dan miinawaa Brady. Aangodinong maji-ininiiwiwag mii eta igo wii-babaameniminegwaa giishpin gegoo ayaameg andawendamowaad." Bagakaabi said she and Netaawichiged knew the two trappers who could be evil but said they would only bother the boys if they had something the trappers wanted.

"Gonemaa gegoo nindayaamin andawendamowaad." Niizh Eshkanag motioned toward Roger and said they might have what the trappers wanted.

"Aaniin dash?" Bagakaabi asked if they were looking for Roger, "Onandawaabamaan Bemibatoonid?"

"Owii-diba'amaagoziwag giishpin odaapinaawaad Bemibatood." Niizh Eshkanag then explained the traders would be paid if they captured Roger and shared the long story of their summer adventures.

Bagakaabi listened intently as the tale unfolded. When Niizh Eshkanag finished, she nodded understanding. "Netaawichiged booch indendaan gaa-ezhiwebag." She wanted her husband to think about what had happened because Bemibatood, who was also Roger Poznanski, was old enough to decide some things but not others. "Bemibatood aawi Roger Poznanski miinawaa gashki-onaakonang gegoon miinwaa bebikaan gegoon gaawiin onaakonanzig." She handed jerky to each and motioned them to sit.

Netaawichiged returned and listened as Niizh Eshkanag recounted their adventures again, then offered thoughts between bites of dried meat. He nodded at a rifle leaning against a rock and considered the situation saying that to fight the trappers before they do anything is like trying to put out a fire that is not burning. Then he suggested the boys move their camp closer and perhaps the trappers would leave them alone. "Gida-gabeshim besho gabeshiyaang mii gonemaa wii-boonikoonegwaa."

The three youths spent the remainder of the day visiting, swimming briefly in a large pool, and walking along the stream with Nenookaasi.

Midafternoon, while swimming, just out of sight of their camp, Niizh Eshkanag pushed Roger toward shore. "Don't look now, but a man is across the stream watching us from behind a tree," he said, shielding urgency with a smile. "Aambe! We should go back to camp. Azhigwa! Now!"

Back at camp after air-drying, and with help from Netaawichiged the boys moved their camp near Netaawichiged's family.

The night wore on, and though they planned to stay awake, fatigue took its toll, and the boys slept.

In the morning, Bagakaabi stood smiling over Niizh Eshkanag who leaned on one elbow gazing with bleary eyes at the fire. "Goshkozin. Gigiishkaabaagwe ina?" she urged him to wake up and offered him a cup.

Niizh Eshkanag asked what was in the cup through a yawn. "Awegonen awang? Niwii-zhiibaa'aabanjige ina giishpin minikwaadamaan?" He stood and walked to the fire.

"Makademashkikiwaaboo izhinikaade." She handed a steaming cup of coffee to Niizh Eshkanag.

Niizh Eshkanag took the cup and cautiously sipped as he remembered having the same drink in the employee's dining room at Poleville Indian School.

The day brightened, and the boys shared their supplies and ate a community meal with their neighbors. After goodbyes, which included cautions from Nitaa, they headed west, cautiously scanning ahead and aside at trees and rocks—anything that could conceal trappers.

By midday, with no evidence of being followed, the trio stopped to rest and eat. Then Niizh Eshkanag led them at a slower pace.

"It will be late when we arrive," Roger said. "Will Boonikiiyaashikwe be worried?"

"Maybe," Giigoo said, "but she will not stay awake waiting. Father and I have been days late, and she was not surprised."

"But with your father along, she had less worry," Niizh Eshkanag countered.

Roger nodded. "I can hardly walk. We could camp one night before reaching Ningaabii'an. It would be better to enter the village rested than crawl in on hands and knees."

Niizh Eshkanag nodded in agreement. "Debwemigad."

The boys camped an hour before sunset on a knob over the west flowing stream. With no sign of anybody, they prepared a fire and spread skins to rest.

"There were no signs today of the evil ones, but we must be careful," Niizh Eshkanag said, peering in every direction.

Roger sat beside his pack, then lay resting against it looking up at Niizh Eshkanag who stopped near him. "Niizh, we are a long way from the trading post, but hours from the village, I think. The trappers might not come this far to find me." He paused. "But some would do anything for three hundred dollars. Wouldn't they?"

Niizh Eshkanag smiled with his hand on his chin. "I would do anything for three hundred dollars, except what my parents thought was wrong. I wonder if capturing a runaway is wrong."

"Could be," Roger replied through a yawn.

The boys ate, and, to be on the trail at dawn, they prepared to sleep early.

Niizh Eshkanag stretched and looked around. A whippoorwill sang near the stream. He tipped his flask to drink. Shaking it, he muttered, "No water."

"Roger is most tired," Giigoo said, "I will go with you to get water." As he talked, he bent, tying the lower thong of his knife sheath to his thigh.

"Miigwech," Roger said.

"It is short way to the stream," Giigoo said.

"If you need us, yell. We hear a long way," Niizh Eshkanag said. Roger watched Niizh Eshkanag and Giigoo disappear down the slope. He checked his bow and then sat to break wood into small pieces for a low fire.

Edgy, Roger strolled to the down slope listening for sounds heralding the return of his friends. Returning to the fire, he fingered his bow, then laid it down. He paced to a large pine and was about to return to the fire when a figure leaped out with encircling arms. A penetrating sense of helplessness forced Roger to pause long enough for Brady's large hands to grab one of his arms. With a surge of energy borne of desperation, Roger tore his arm loose and bounded past the fire heading for the hill.

"Niizh Eshkanag! Giigoo!" Roger screamed just as a figure loomed in his side vision. The figure swung something striking him above the left ear. He did not know he sprawled unconscious at Dan's feet.

Chapter Thirteen

Roger sprawled, grotesquely twisted, a clenched fist slowly relaxing, blood oozing from a head wound.

"Mighta hit 'im too hard," Dan muttered. "Git water, cool his head."

"Yer in big trouble if he dies," Brady said.

"Nobody knows we's here," Dan barked. "You saw him fall, hit his head. Besides he ain't gonna die."

Brady walked to horses tethered a hundred paces east and returned with water. Rolling Roger onto his back, he laid a wet bandanna over the seeping bruise. "Ain't coming around too fast. Longer he's out, the worse he'll be if'n he wakes up."

Dan motioned away. "Help me carry him to our horses afore the Injun brats come."

As he was carried, Roger opened his eyes to a bleary, unreal world. He felt his arms and legs held by strong hands, and he moaned, "Niizh Eshkanag? . . . Giigoo?"

"Quiet," Dan hissed.

Roger wanted to feel his aching head, but his arms were held. The men laid him near the horses, and prepared to ride.

Roger saw only outlines in dim moonlight filtering through the tall forest. "You hit me. Why am I tied?"

"'Cause you wouldn't come peaceable," Dan retorted, "and so you don't get notions about walking off."

"Yeah . . . the reward," Roger mumbled. "If they find out . . ." his talk slurred, "that you beat the tar out of me, tied me up . . . you'll get no reward."

Dan sneered. "We'll get the money afore you even talk to 'em!"

"We best be goin'," Brady said. "Those Injun brats might've heard, and we don't want 'em seeing where we gone."

Dan held a rope leashing Roger by the waist and lifted him to his feet. Bushes lined the trail where the men camped. Light-headed, Roger lost his balance tumbling awkwardly onto the bush where he lay, his breathing marked by escaping moans.

"What's the matter, kid?" Brady asked, nudging Roger's ribs with his boot.

"Mm, must've fainted," Roger muttered. His senses cleared somewhat, though his head ached and he became more rational. *With horses they will have to use the main trail south and this trail to reach it. Niizh Eshkanag will know.*

Brady retied Roger's wrists in front, and lifted him onto the horse. Mounting the horse, he followed Dan on the trail south.

In spite of dire circumstances, Roger pondered scenarios of escape. *Will Niizh Eshkanag go to the school to tell Uncle Elias who will then get the sheriff or Mr. Murphy to surprise them? Anyway, they've got me, and that's that.*

Niizh Eshkanag and Giigoo were halfway up the knob when they heard Roger scream.

"Wanii'igewininiwag! Trappers!" Niizh Eshkanag spat as he realized they must have Roger. "Odayaawaawaan Rogeran!" The two hastily climbed the hill, and as expected, found the camp empty.

"Wiindigoog!" Niizh Eshkanag hissed. He looked carefully about the camp. They saw Roger's knife and pack and decided to hide them in a hollow tree near the stream to pick up later. They knew the traders were on horseback and had to follow the trail below their camp on the escarpment. "Niibaadaa omaa miidash maajaayang gichi-gigizheb." He gazed west and asked Giigoo if he thought his mother and father would worry when they did not show up in Ningaabii'an.

"Ningitizimag owii-nisidotaanaawaa," Giigoo said he was sure they would understand because one night of worry was worth it if they could help Roger.

As dawn broke, the boys checked their supplies.

Aunt Boonikiiyaashikwe had given them enough dried venison to last many days, and they knew they could dig roots along the way so they knew they would have enough to eat and headed south tracking the kidnappers.

"Wadikwanan biigoshkaawan gonemaa awiya gii-namadabi gemaa bangishing," Giigoo paused and pointed out an area with broken branches where it looked as if someone sat down or possibly fell.

"Bebezhigooganzhii-bimikawaanan," Niizh Eshkanag said pointing to horse prints in the ground. Near the remains of a fire, they found Roger's bow, arrows, skins, and his share of food. Knowing they could move quickly and the trappers had tired horses, they pressed on.

"Nashke! Obabagiwayaan miinawaa aasan atenoon," Giigoo saw Roger's leggings and shirt near the fire where he must have slept.

"Onashkinadoon," Niizh Eshkanag suggested they pack Roger's clothes with hope they would find him. "Nimbagosendaan wii-mikawang."

Later, traveling at a fast walk, Niizh Eshkanag and Giigoo soon came upon signs of a camp and more hoof tracks heading south.

"Howah!" Giigoo exclaimed. He realized they had missed the kidnappers who left early and might be far ahead by now. "Onji-gii-maajaawaad wayiiba gigii-wani'aanaanig. Gaawiin gide-debibizhaasiinaanig gemaa."

Niizh Eshkanag gazed thoughtfully at the trail realizing that one horse must be carrying two people. "Niizh bemaadizijig daa-babaamoomigowag." He told Giigoo they would almost certainly pass Roger and his captors within two days because although they had a head start, the horses would need to stop for water and rest. "Giwii-gabikawaanaanig jibwaa izhiseg niizhogon."

The horses thrust over mounds on a twisting trail, and Roger's headache was aggravated by a bouncing irregular gait and the fact that he was tightly bound. There was brief respite when the trappers stopped to water horses at holes made by the unearthed roots of giant toppled trees.

"This is the only water on the trail," Roger said. "Horses will be thirsty and need more grass than can be found in the forest; you and the horses need water." With his wrists tied together, Roger tried to hold his head by both hands trying to ease his headache. "I have a bad headache."

"Horses will eat at night, get water from the dew," Dan growled.

"What dew is there in a tall forest?" Roger asked. *It will not be enough. The horses will soon balk.* Roger was hoisted to ride with Brady and the kidnapers continued on.

Near high sun, the trappers passed a deep forest glen with scattered bushes and sparse grass. The sun flickered through the high canopy but not enough to leave shadows on the ground. During an episode of dizziness, Roger sagged against Brady who reined his horse as he caught Roger.

"Kinda figured ya hit 'im too hard," Brady said.

Dan reined his horse and looked back. "Damn brat!"

"Better rest or we're going to have a dead kid on our hands." Brady untied Roger from the saddle, dismounted, and lowered him to the ground.

Roger soon became more alert looking up at Brady, pain in his face. "Do you hafta tie my wrists? Makes my headache worse."

Grumbling, Dan cast a piercing look at Roger. "He's p'tendin'. Oughta bang him on the other side fer slowin' us."

"Best ta keep 'im alive 'stead of gitting there faster," Brady said. "Besides, we got no hurry. The Injun brats won't follow, and his relatives ain't 'spectin' us."

Niizh Eshkanag and Giigoo were only an hour behind the trappers at the onset of pursuit, and they soon arrived at the glen where the trappers had rested and fresh horse droppings etched the trail.

"Howah!" Giigoo showed Niizh Eshkanag signs on the ground where three people had been sleeping and the smaller space looked as if someone in pain, or in restraints, did not move much. "Roger ogii-bi-anweshimo; ininiwag abiwaad imaa. Gaawiin ogii-mamaajiisii iidog dash daa-wiisagishing." Niizh Eshkanag said. He took a look and agreed they were getting closer. He told Giigoo it could be dangerous, but there was still a good chance they could save Roger. "Daa-zegindaagwad aanawi giishpin bezhigwendaman, daa-zhaagoozikamawangwaa ishpaadinaang gaye gemaa zhaabwizhang Roger."

"Gaawiin nizegizisii," Giigoo insisted that he wasn't afraid but wondered how two boys with bows could outsmart two sly men with horses and guns. "Gaawiin nizegizisii, aaniish dash waa-ezhi-doodamang ge gwiiwizensiwiyang gagwe-bakinawangwaa niizh gegiitaawendangig ayaawaawaad bebezhigoogaanzhiin gaye baashkiziganan?"

"Gegoo indenendaan . . ." Niizh Eshkanag explained his plan motioning with glowing eyes south along the trail. Giigoo nodded with understanding of the plan unfolding between them, but his smile of approval was edged with concern.

"Gidaa-gizhiibizomin biinish gabikawangwaa," Niizh Eshkanag said they needed to speed up until they passed the group ahead. Giigoo followed Niizh Eshkanag who began a brisk trot. While jogging, they talked—whisperings on puffs of air accompanied by soft rhythmic footfalls on forest humus.

Niizh Eshkanag warned they should not kill anyone unless their own lives were threatened because the Americans always ruled against the Anishinaabe people. "Gaawiin gidaa-nishi'aasiinaanig biinish giinawind naniizaaniziyang. Gichi-mookomaanag apane gimaji-dibaakonigonaanig Anishinaabeg."

"Awiya ayaa," Giigoo suddenly said someone was nearby, as he and Niizh Eshkanag slid behind large trees.

"Wanii'igewininiwag," Niizh Eshkanag said it must be the trappers. The boys watched as the trappers peered about while horses nibbled sparse vegetation. Roger lay with his forearm shielding his face. The boys' black hair and brown bodies, when unmoving, made them all but invisible among the browns and blacks of tree trunks in the dim forest.

"Moozhag anwaatin mitigwaking," Niizh Eshkanag noticed the wind picking up and whispered to Giigoo that he knew the horses might pick up their scent, but he wanted to try something from a story his father once told him. "Bebezhigoogaanzhig nitaa-minaanjigewag, geyaabi dash bakaan ezhichigewaangwen, gegoo noos gii-dibaajimid. . . ."

Dan lifted Roger up behind Brady then mounted and reined his horse south. Looking cautiously around at first, Dan became more concerned with their slow progress than the chance they might be followed.

Roger was silent, though soft moans escaped when the horse passed over obstacles lurching him about.

The trappers stopped for the night near a large pothole, still with water after a recent rain. While cooking the evening meal, they released Roger's hands, but tied each ankle with triple knots and fastened his waist rope to a tree.

Brady set a tin of food near Roger. "Eat, git some meat on ya. Looks like we bin luggin' a skeleton around."

Dan dug into his pack and pulled out a dirty underwear shirt with shoulder straps. "Put this on 'im. We can see him better at night, and it'd give him something to wear. Reminds me of a stinking Injun."

Brady handed the jersey to Roger. "Ya know how to wear reg'lar clothes?"

"Funny," Roger mumbled, softly to not further anger his captors. He donned the shoulder strap shirt, which covered little of his chest, appearing more like a skirt with straps.

Roger yawned after eating, sleepy instead of exhausted. He leaned against the tree where he was leashed. *Will Niizh Eshkanag and Giigoo, if they try to follow us, know where we are? If I go to Uncle Elias like this, he'll pay the reward, and I'll never live it down. I've got to escape!*

"Time to sleep, kid," Dan said while laying wood on the fire.

The night before, hundreds of yards north, Niizh Eshkanag and Giigoo slept early and arose long before dawn. They built a low fire, ate their morning meal, and using fallen cedar twigs, smudged their bodies and equipment for good luck.

Niizh Eshkanag said the horses would smile and look the other way when they passed, "bebezhigoogaanzhiig wii-zhoomiingweniwag gaye animikogaawaad." Ready to travel, the boys quietly crept against an almost nonexistent breeze until near the trapper's camp. Peering from behind a large tree, Niizh Eshkanag observed the horses on the far side of the camp and sleeping forms near the fire. He stole close, broke green branches without snapping them and placed them in an obvious pile close to the sleepers. Nearby, Giigoo crouched with strung bow and fitted arrow. Now ahead of the trappers, the boys took their packs and began a long day of hiking.

Almost rested, Roger awakened as dawn filtered into the forest. The horses had snorted in the night briefly waking him, but they soon quieted. And Roger had sensed something during sleep—an image, like a dream.

The forest brightened and the trappers prepared to travel.

"I have to pee," Roger declared. "Or do I go here?"

Brady checked Roger's bonds while Dan heated food.

"Ain't enough we got to bring the runt back home, we got to nursemaid him too," Brady muttered.

"Let me go and I'll show you who needs a nursemaid," Roger said. "Tell it like it is; I'm a captive, tied up, beaten. . . ."

"Aw, shut up," Dan interrupted. He pointed to bushes. "Don't go too far; make sure he don't piss me shirt."

Roger wrinkled his nose. *What a joke, his shirt would gag a skunk.*

Brady released Roger's ankles, but held the tether to his waist. "C'mon, do yer duty."

"Yeah, I'm coming." Roger went ahead of Brady who held the rope from behind. After relieving himself, Roger turned to face Brady, but stopped when something seemed out of place. *Those twigs in a pile look fresh.* Restraining elation, he pretended to stumble toward the bush, which jerked the rope from Brady's hand.

"Gotcha, kid," Brady said lunging forward, grabbing the rope. "You ain't gittin' away that easy."

"Who's trying?" Roger said. "Just stumbled."

The trappers packed camp gear after the morning meal and headed south, allowing Roger looser bonds so he could ride easier.

Roger was all but certain what Niizh Eshkanag had in mind. *The men will try to reach Poleville by tonight, and Niizh Eshkanag, hopefully, wants them to camp on the ridge tonight—we have to camp one more night! On the ridge!* Given sufficient water and food, he felt better but pretended to be sickly.

Dan became irritated as the horses moved slower, responding less to prodding. "Keep this up and it'll take a week to git there," he said.

Beginning a slow incline through a grove of shorter trees, the trail was now familiar to Roger. *We're going too fast and they won't camp on the ridge. I have to slow us down.* Roger swayed and bent over hard against Brady, then began to slide off. "Don't feel good," he moaned.

"Bitch! Now what? Keep going!" Dan shouted.

Roger moaned, straightened in the saddle, suddenly lurching sideways again.

"Damn! We got to rest again," Brady grumbled as he caught Roger and pulled him back.

"Awright! Carry that ass, so's he don't die on us," Dan snarled.

Brady dismounted and hoisted Roger like a sack on his shoulders with Roger's head hanging behind.

Gad! Brady sure has got hard shoulders. Roger was gently enough laid on the ground, but when Brady paused to stare at him, he moaned as though in excruciating pain.

"We'll rest 'til he comes out of it," Dan declared. He broke a chaw of tobacco as he stared at Roger. "If we're going to collect the money, I s'pose we gots to keep him alive."

Roger's legs were free, but he was tied to a tree. In spite of the headache, he was ready to spring and run, but he worried the trappers would see him untie the rope. *Anyway, Niizh will somehow send a signal to me when he's ready to move.*

The sun moved lower in the west. Roger sat up, looked up at treetops then at Brady. "I feel better. Can I have water?"

"Humph," Brady grunted. He brought water and waited as Roger slurped, spilling more than he drank.

Dan frowned, "now I s'pose ya got to piss?"

"How'd you guess?" Roger said. It was too bland. He flinched sideways as Dan raised his fist in a threatening gesture.

Later, Roger masked excitement as they wound through a forest with scattered openings. We're coming to the ridge! He wavered in the saddle and appeared frail.

"Looks like a hill in the trail," Brady observed.

"Yeah, it's downhill from there to Poleville," Dan said. "Maybe we'll have smooth sailing to the school—git our money!" But the horses responded slower to prodding, snorting from lack of energy.

"Horses goin' mighty slow," Brady said. "Got to water 'em soon or we be walkin'."

As though on cue, Roger moaned audibly while suppressing a sense of elation. He twisted in the saddle pointing ahead. "There's water near that hill. It's best to camp and water the horses; there's no water from there to the school."

"We keep goin'," Dan muttered.

"I feel weak, and my head hurts," Roger moaned. "If you rest on the ridge, you can still get there tomorrow. I'll feel rested, and this terrible headache might be gone." He lowered his head, grimacing.

"The brat's right," Brady said. "We can still get our money tomorrow. Why not have 'im lookin' better when his uncle sees 'im."

Dan scrutinized Roger. "Awright," he snarled. "He's more trouble than a whole tribe of wild Injuns. I could shoot the whole shebang. My granpappy told how he shot 'em out west fer scalp money. But Injuns are still here, huntin' and trappin', makin' it hard fer an honest trapper to make a livin'. Top it all, they's got their own lands, and we ain't s'posed to bother 'em. Bah!"

The kidnapers topped the ridge. Roger looked about with hope but appeared wan and listless to the trappers who tied him to a tree and set to making camp.

Roger was tied against the tree, though his hands were free. Looking about, he focused on the edge of the ridge where the ground fell away toward the valley. *What will Niizh Eshkanag do? Be careful, of course.*

Dan is sly and a bow cannot best a gun. And I'm no help, tied and all.
Roger stared at his moccasins, and a heavy boot appeared shoving his
legs together.

Brady lowered a plate to Roger. "Just to be sure." He bent and tied
Roger's legs together at the ankles.

"Can I have water?"

"We's about out of water," Brady replied.

"Does that mean I don't get a drink?" Roger said. "Your horses
haven't had water either."

"Where'd you say water was?" Brady asked.

Appearing weak, Roger pointed. "There's a creek down there. Take
maybe hour for a man with two horses to go down and back.

Preparing a fire, Dan looked at Brady and nodded toward the slope.
"Okay, water the horses and fill the canteens. I'll make camp."

Niizh Eshkanag and Giigoo had been far ahead of the trappers. Instead
of following the trail when they arrived in the late afternoon at the
incline to the ridge, they skirted it heading instead to the creek.

"Owii-nibaawag giishkaabikaang," Niizh Eshkanag knew the
trappers would sleep on the escarpment. He also knew one of them
would need to water the horses, leaving the other to watch Roger. Niizh
Eshkanag stared into the distance, firming up their strategy. Thinking
about his friend, he turned to Giigoo and pointed out that as Roger
started to look less white his spirit had grown brighter, "Gaawiin geyabi
gichi-waabishkiwisii Roger mii dash noongom waase-ojichaagod."

"Gigii-nitaagikinaamawaa," Giigoo nodded saying Niizh Eshkanag
had taught him well.

"Gaawiin," Niizh Eshkanag disagreed, adding that his mother
would say Roger was simply good at learning from the world around
him. "Niga odaa-idaan ge Rogeran gikinoowaabandaminid." Niizh
Eshkanag paused to explain how two boys could capture the adult
trappers. "Booch igo dash gidaa-doodaamin giishpin oditinangid awiya
ge awashime apii giinawind mindidod . . ."

Brady took one gun and, leading two horses, started toward the edge of the ridge. He turned while yet within talking distance. "Is it straight down?"

Roger appeared annoyed and weak, but he motioned as he talked, "The trail goes back and forth; it is good for horses. Follow it to the stream. It's good water, can't miss it."

Brady started down. He held the halter ropes in one hand, his gun in the other. It was an easy trip down, and he was soon at the stream. While the horses drank, Brady stooped to fill the canteens. When the horses raised their heads and whinnied, Brady looked nervously around until the horses returned to drinking, and he continued filling canteens. The last canteen full, Brady set it on the bank, stood, and turned around. He stiffened erect, his face frozen in surprise, eyes wide. Two, tautly drawn bows holding arrows with iron points were aimed straight at his chest. The boys had quietly crept up on him as he filled the flasks and were less than ten feet away and ten feet from each other.

"Do not call out," Niizh Eshkanag hissed, "or my finger slips. Do not reach for your gun!"

Giigoo picked up the gun and inspected it. "Father has one like it. It is a single shot cartridge load."

"Zhigweyaabam giishpin onashkinadeg," Niizh Eshkanag said to Giigoo. He looked at Brady. "Lay on ground, face down," he ordered, trying to sound older.

"Who are you?" Brady asked. He squinted, eyes widening as Niizh Eshkanag pulled the arrow farther back.

"You know us!" Niizh Eshkanag replied. "On your belly!"

"You won't get away with this!" Brady complained as he lay down.

"You took our friend and gave us much worry," Niizh Eshkanag said. "My hand tires holding this arrow. My cousin knows of your gun and how to use it. If you do not make trouble, his finger will not pull the trigger."

Niizh Eshkanag put his bow down, took a rope from the saddle, removed Brady's shoes and threw them in the stream. Trussing the kidnaper's arms behind his back, straining them upward in a tight leash to the saddle so that he could not get on to ride away and would be dragged if the horse decided to run. He used Ojibwemowin to tell Giigoo he had learned this trick from a white trader. "Noos nigii-waabanda'ig, dash gii-gikinoo'amaagod Gichi-mookomaan-wedaawenid. Gaawiin ode-akwaandawesii geyaabi, miinawaa giishpin bebezhigoogaanzhiin bimibatoonid, wii-nibod." Then he turned to Brady, speaking English, and said, "I will go up the hill. Giigoo will watch you from that bush." Niizh Eshkanag pointed. "If you try to escape or call out, my cousin will shoot and kill you or scare the horses, maybe both. The end is the same."

Niizh Eshkanag started off but stopped and faced Brady, muttering angrily, "If something bad happens to me or my white brother, my father and my uncle will make you wish for a speedy death." Giigoo aimed the gun at Brady as Niizh Eshkanag spoke and backed out of sight behind a bush.

"Maajaan, giizhiitaayaan," Giigoo told Niizh Eshkanag to go from the bush.

Brady watched Niizh Eshkanag climb the hill and disappear among brush and trees along the slope. He did not think that Giigoo was anywhere but nearby watching him.

Niizh Eshkanag waited up the hill where Giigoo soon joined him and whispered that Brady still feared he was being watched. "Ozegizi gaye inendaan geyaabi ganawaabameg." Giigoo told Niizh Eshkanag to take the gun and the extra cartridges because it was too hard to aim good from a distance, "Odaapinan baashkizigan gaye anwiiwizhensan gii-odaapinamang, gaawiin gwech waasa zhigweyaabisiiyaan."

Niizh Eshkanag admitted he also did not want to use the gun because they had more control of their arrows. He suggested bringing the gun to Roger. "Gaawiin niin gaye, aanawi gikendamaang ezhi-bimojigeyaang. Roger niwii-biidawaa baashkizigan gaye wii-bimojigeyang." They knew the trapper with Roger would be suspicious if his friend is gone too long, so they needed to move soon. "Gidaa-bi-izhaa onji-waabanong ge wii-bi-izhaayaan onji-ningaabii'anong. Gaawiin gidaa-gaganoonidisiimin noongom, aanawi dash daa-waabanda'idiyang gagwe-wiindamaageyang." Niizh Eshkanag decided he would come from the west and Giigoo should come from the east. Then he moved up the hill and, carrying the loaded gun, while Giigoo went east.

To get to the trappers' camp, Niizh Eshkanag stole through a grove of scrubby pines with low branches and crouched behind a tree away from the fire where Dan held cooking utensils. Roger sat bound against a tree closer to where Niizh Eshkanag waited. The tree hid Roger from Niizh Eshkanag, but Roger's bound legs could be seen alongside the roots. Looking up often from his cooking, Dan became increasingly edgy.

An arrow's flight to the east, Giigoo crouched low and worked his way closer to the fire. Whenever Dan looked elsewhere, Niizh Eshkanag signaled to Giigoo, once pointing to a rifle leaning against a tree behind Dan. After short spurts stealing up to Roger's tree, Niizh Eshkanag lay flat behind the tree where Roger sat. He whispered, "It is Niizh Eshkanag; do not move. A rifle is behind on your left. I think you can reach and hold it with tied wrists."

"I can," Roger whispered.

"Count to ten and lay flat," Niizh Eshkanag said. "I hope no one journeys to the afterlife today."

One, two, three, Roger counted to himself.

Hidden by the tree, Niizh Eshkanag stood erect and set the gun near Roger, fitted an arrow and prepared his quiver.

Eight, nine, ten, Roger quickly lay beside the tree squirming to grasp the rifle.

With time only to swipe once with his knife, Niizh Eshkanag cut Roger's tether, but not his wrist bonds, and he was able to only cover half the distance to Dan's gun before Dan leaped to his feet racing toward his gun with drawn knife.

Niizh Eshkanag had erred. Dan would reach the gun first! Niizh Eshkanag slid to a stop, knelt, and drew his bow back. "Stop," he cried.

When Dan did not slow, an arrow appeared in his thigh, but he fell toward the gun, grabbed it and crawled behind some rocks.

Niizh Eshkanag scurried back to Roger, manhandled him to shelter behind the tree just as a bullet whined through bark over his head.

"I could not work the rifle," Roger said.

"It's hard," Niizh Eshkanag said, cutting Roger's bonds. "Take it now, and we capture this one. He is wounded and could weaken."

"We are now three and have a gun," Niizh Eshkanag yelled toward Dan. "Throw your gun and your knife, and we end this trouble." In reply, a bullet kicked dirt near their tree and whined past.

Niizh Eshkanag pointed toward the rocks that were shielding Dan. He told Giigoo he would work his way south behind the evil one and cautioned Giigoo because Dan now had the gun and was wounded. "Niwii-izhaa zhaawanong, ishkweyaang Wiindigoo. Ayaangwaamizin, ayaan baashkizigan gaye wiisagishing."

No sooner had Niizh Eshkanag worked his way behind Dan than he saw Giigoo creeping nearer. He motioned at Giigoo just as Dan twisted, saw him, raised his rifle and fired. Niizh Eshkanag released his arrow and lunged toward the shelter of rocks, but his leg burned near the knee and his bow flew out of reach. He doubled up and tried to crawl away as another gun shot echoed. He stiffened in anticipation of being shot then relaxed as his friends approached.

"Giwiisagishin Niizh," Giigoo saw that Niizh Eshkanag was hurt and told him they needed to stop the bleeding. "Gidaa-nooginaamin ezhi-zaagiskwagiziyan."

Niizh Eshkanag said he did not feel well and his leg was growing numb, "Gaawiin gwech nimino-inamanji'osii giikimanigaadeyaan gaye ... maji-inamanji'oyaan."

Roger winced at Niizh Eshkanag's complaint, but he remained outwardly calm. "A bullet has gone through your leg above the knee inside," he said. He straightened Niizh Eshkanag out. "It does not spurt, so maybe no arteries were cut, but we must stop the bleeding."

"What about the wiindigoo?" Niizh Eshkanag asked. "My leg hurts more."

"The wiindigoo is dead," Giigoo said.

"Your arrow might have killed him," Roger said, "but when you fell, he was after you. I took no chance and shot him."

"I hoped it would not come to killing," Niizh Eshkanag murmured, "for whites listen to whites first."

"It matters not that your arrow might have killed him for I shot him and the law will only know that." Roger went to Dan and stared down at him, frowning while cutting his shirt off. Returning to Niizh Eshkanag, he cut strips and bound the leg and gave him water.

"We must move fast," Giigoo said. "The one below the hill has heard the shooting and could get free." He laid a gun near Niizh Eshkanag. "The hole seems clean. I think we must leave you and get this one's friend."

Roger and Giigoo took one gun and headed into the valley listening for sounds of horses. When they found Brady, he showed signs of freeing himself, but returned peacefully with the boys.

The fire burned bright, and Dan had been buried in a shallow grave until he could be retrieved. Brady was trussed and tethered where Roger had been tied.

Roger took Niizh Eshkanag's medicine pouch and laid the contents on the ground. "You'll have to tell me what everything does," he mumbled.

"I will tell you," Giigoo said, taking a bag of powder. "First we wash with this and warm water. Then we pour these two things in the hole and cover everything."

"What are those two things?" Roger asked.

"One is old medicine, the other," Giigoo smiled, "was given to Mother by a white doctor."

"Your village is closest, Niizh Eshkanag," Roger said, looking east. "We need to get you to a doctor. Lucky we have horses."

"To go in morning will be good," Niizh Eshkanag said.

Niizh Eshkanag's wound was painful in the morning, but he was not feverish. Roger and Giigoo prepared one horse to carry a wounded rider and crafted a long splint to immobilize Niizh Eshkanag's leg during travel.

Roger faced Brady. "You ride one horse. Niizh Eshkanag will ride the horse behind you. I will lead your horse. Giigoo will lead Niizh Eshkanag's horse, and they will watch from behind with guns." He helped Niizh Eshkanag up, fastened the stiffly wrapped leg to the saddle horn, and handed him a rifle.

This strange entourage moved slowly along the ridge on the trail heading east then down into the tall forest.

Chapter Fourteen

Niizh Eshkanag did not complain when he was jostled erratically as the horse walked on a narrow trail used more for human hikers. Rest stops required both Roger and Giigoo to get him off the horse and on again.

As they traveled, Niizh Eshkanag watched the trail ahead and aside, and he mused about their circumstances. *Everything seems different than when we left Waaban. . . . How much different—and better—our adventure would have been without greedy trappers. Roger should not be blamed for shooting the trapper. . . . It will work out. Somehow.*

The group met no one, and according to the moon, arrived at the village near midnight. After a brief exchange between Niizh Eshkanag and the peacekeepers, Brady was taken to the meetinghouse, and Niizh Eshkanag was carried to his parent's home followed by Roger and Giigoo.

"Bizaan, Migizi," one of the peacekeepers called out that Niizh Eshkanag had returned. "Niizh ogii-bi-dagoshin."

In spite of fatigue and soreness, Niizh Eshkanag cracked a wan smile when frenzied bustling issued from within.

Bizaan thrust her head out the doorway asking with shock if her son could speak for himself. "Gaawiin ina ode-gaagiigidosii?" She stared mute at her son cradled in the peacekeeper's arms, then motioned them in. The peacekeeper handed Niizh Eshkanag through the doorway to Migizi, who laid him gently on his sleep robe.

Migizi looked at the wrapped leg, and except for the injury, covered Niizh Eshkanag, with a robe. He faced the peacekeeper, thanked him, and said they would wait to hear the story with Gekendaasod. "Gimiigwechiwi'in. Niwii-baabiitoomin dibaajimowin."

The peacekeeper said Gekendaasod was on the way, and others were waiting outside, "Aanind baabii'owag agwaj-ayi'iing."

"Waabi-Anishinaabe ina ogii-dagoshin?" Bizaan asked if the white Anishinaabe had also arrived. She stroked Niizh Eshkanag's face as she talked.

"Bezhigo gwiiwizens ge niswi gii-dagoshinog daa-aawid," the peacekeeper replied that one of three boys who brought a captive might be the one she mentioned. He added that the story could take some time to tell because the boys were very tired. "Ginwenzh dash indaa-inaajim. Aapiji ayekoziwag."

"Bemibatood ayaa omaa." Bizaan was certain one of the boys must be Roger but said she did not know the other boy. "Gaawiin nigikenimaasii wa'aw oshkiniigid." She took a lantern and cleared the door. She stared into the darkness at the two boys and asked what kind of evil turns young boys into old men and who was the stranger with her son. "Aaniin ezhiwebag ge zezika wenji-nitaawigiwaad weshkiniiwigijig mii miinawaa awenen ayaayan?"

"Boozhoo, ninosheh. Giigoo indizhinikaas, ingitizimag ezhinikaazowaad Zhaabiiwose gaye Boonikiiyaashikwe." He greeted her and explained he was her nephew, the son of Zhaabiiwose gaye Boonikiiyaashikwe."

"Nigii-daa-gikendaan iidog dash Niizh gaye owiijiiwaaganiman daa-mikawaawaad wiitaawisiman." Bizaan gently herded them to the lodge muttering that is was no surprise that Niizh Eshkanag and his brother found a cousin. She told them to get inside and then said she would make a stew to help them sleep. "Biindigeg. Niwii-naboobike ji-naadamaagooyan nibaayan."

Relieved that they might not to be blamed for the shootout on the ridge, Niizh Eshkanag smiled wanly, *I'm home.* Feeling secure amid family and elders. Roger, too, felt and displayed relief but was still edgy—feeling responsible for his friend's wounding.

"Aaniindi ayaad wiindigoo?" Bizaan faced the peacekeeper and asked where the evil one was being held, thinking she might like to help him into the afterlife, though he likely had nowhere to go.

"Zagawe'idigamig ayaa," the peacekeeper told her one white man was at the meetinghouse and another white man was said to be dead on the ridge. The plan was for the council to consider the events in the light of a new day.

Niizh Eshkanag weakly sipped stew and chewed warmed dried venison as Gekendaasod prepared a cleansing solution. Roger and Giigoo watched as they ate.

"Giwii-boonisaadaan ina infection?" Roger spoke Ojibwemowin, except for one word.

"In-ec-shun?" Gekendaasod questioned. "Ho, enh," he said yes and explained it was from the Poleville doctor, and works only when used by skilled healers. "Poleville mashkikiwinini nigii-miizhig, dash eta noojimo'iwemagag apii nenaandawe'iwejig aabajitoowaad." He twisted, casting a sly smile between Bizaan and Migizi, and explained their son was fortunate because the shot missed bone and artery, almost missed him entirely. The damage was less because he was so thin, but was still very painful, and because some muscle was damaged, he should not walk for some time without a crutch.

Roger and Giigoo slept the instant they lay back and did not see all of Niizh Eshkanag's treatment, and Niizh Eshkanag slept before Gekendaasod finished treating him. Bizaan washed Niizh Eshkanag; Ziigwan washed Giigoo while the boys slept, then both mothers helped clean Roger who barely moved, though he briefly, opened his eyes.

"Roger ozhaashaagondibe, gaye gegaa miskwiiwid oninjimaang miinawaa obikwaakoganaaning." Zigwan commented on Roger's bruised head, and his nearly bleeding wrists and ankles. "Gii-daa-aapidapizogoban," she surmised he must have been tightly lashed to have such marks.

Later, Gekendaasod sipped tea with Bizaan and Migizi and summarized the situation. "Ingiw gwiiwizensag aakode'ewag gaye gagiitawendamog. Dibishkoo gaa-izhiwebad, gwiiwizensag miigaazhaawaad ininiwan, bimoojigewaad ge baashkizigenld." The elder was pleased as he noted how brave and clever the boys were, adding that it was like the old days, boys fighting grown men, bows and arrows against guns."

"Enh," Migizi agreed and commented that Roger had helped his friends who in turn helped him, which is how Creator shows the young ones the many circles of life. "Roger ogii-naadamawaan owiijiiwaaganan ge naadamaagod dash Gizhemanidoo ezhi-waabanda'aad oshkiniigiwan ge onjineyaang."

The boys awoke for morning food, slipped back into deep sleep, and remained at rest until evening when they were summoned to the meetinghouse. Roger and Giigoo walked. Niizh Eshkanag was carried to the meetinghouse where the boys sat in the center of the room, facing the council members who were seated in the east, with most of the villagers lining the remaining walls.

Elders whispered among themselves. The boys looked around, and as though of one mind, settled their gaze on Brady, who sat bound to their right, facing council elders.

"The trapper is still here," Roger said, staring at his moccasins.

"I think they will banish the white Anishinaabe," Niizh Eshkanag said, nudging Roger. His humor failed, and he grimaced from pain.

"I mean, really." Roger said. "Will they send me back? Okay then, banish me because the trouble is over me."

A crier entered. "Gigiizhiitaamin. We are ready," he announced in both languages, which quelled whispers permeating family groups.

The chief stood, sprinkled tobacco into a copper bowl, and nodded to Gekendaasod who rendered a durable prayer while offering a pipe to the four winds. The chief beckoned to the boys and explained that before the council decided what to do with the white prisoner, all three boys must each tell what they did and saw. He asked Niizh Eshkanag to begin because he was injured. "Maadaajimon. Begin your story."

"Gimiigwechiwi'in." Niizh Eshkanag looked at his father and mother then elders. "Gaawiin onjida. I am sorry to be unable to stand." He motioned west. "Giigoo is long overdue in Ningaabii'an. Can a message be sent to Zhaabiiwose and Boonikiiyaashikwe that he is all right?"

The chief smiled as he explained. "Two runners left before sunrise. After today, his family should no longer worry."

"Gimiigwechiwigo. Thank you. We were on our way to Ningaabii'an on our return from trading post. John Bemibatood—Roger—was captured, injured and nearly died. It was that man and his friend." He pointed at Brady. "We chased the trappers, so had no time to tell Aunt Boonikiiyaashikwe and Uncle Zhaabiiwose that we would be late, which is now very late. Creator made us lucky and we captured one, but the one called Dan shot me once, was going to kill me, but Roger saved me by shooting him."

After Roger and Giigoo finished recounting their experiences, the chief spoke. "The council knows of these men, Dan and Brady. They have been paid by the white government to hunt Anishinaabe people who were said to be criminals. They killed them without proving their guilt and without asking Anishinaabe councils whether it was right or wrong. We find no fault with the young warriors for killing Dan." The chief paused gazing straight at the bound trapper then continued. "In the matter of Brady, two runners have gone to Poleville and will explain to the white lawman what happened. Lawmen can get the body of the dead one and take Brady." He gazed straight at Roger. "The runner is to tell only what three young Anishinaabe boys did, though Brady will surely claim to have seen the missing white boy. We have a number of white-man days to think on that. The wind should then become a breeze, and everything will have more meaning. Mii i'iw." Roger breathed a deep sigh, and the lines of his face relaxed.

The sheriff and an Indian agent rode into the village four days after the boys' return. They would stay two days in a guest lodge, make reports, record complaints of villagers against white people, and investigate complaints by white people against Waaban villagers.

The Indian agent met first with the tribal council. Migizi and Bizaan had talked to the council, and that business was quickly settled. The Indian agent departed forthwith to be at a northeast village the following day.

The council then met with the sheriff who produced a warrant to take custody of Brady. It was an informal meeting marked by casual dialogue. Boys sat around the outside wall with villagers, Roger partially concealed amid deep shadows.

During a break for refreshments, the sheriff spoke to Migizi. "I have been asked to search for a white boy named Roger Poznanski who is thought to be a friend of your son, Tom Horns."

Showing no anger, Migizi looked straight at the man. "My son answers to the name Niizh Eshkanag. If you give him another name, do not feel bad if he does not hear it. This friend of Niizh Eshkanag; what is his name again?"

The sheriff eyed Roger as he replied, "Roger Poznanski, age fourteen." Roger gazed innocently back at the sheriff.

"Roger Poznanski," Migizi murmured. "A boy with that name goes to Poleville Indian School with Niizh Eshkanag." He motioned past Niizh Eshkanag at Roger's feet. "The one had great sadness when he came to us in late spring. Speak to John Bemibatood directly if you like."

"May I speak to him alone?" the sheriff asked.

"A young man of fourteen must answer that question," Migizi replied. He motioned to Roger.

Though anxious, Roger stood, motioned toward the door flap. "I will talk with you alone." The pair exited the lodge and walked away from the meetinghouse.

"You are of white blood," the sheriff began. "Why do you live with Indians?"

"Whites say too much about blood, which in truth, runs the same in the veins of all races. Then you talk about color, which makes no sense because you can see I am now much closer to the color of my Anishinaabe brother."

"I don't know what to say," the sheriff breathed. "By law you belong to your white relatives." He peered into Roger's eyes, watched them corner in avoidance. "If you come with me right now, I'll see no harm comes to you."

Roger's eyes flashed, but he remained calm. "Do you think I'm in danger here? If you take me by force, where would you take me? My greatest danger is from greedy white men."

The sheriff smiled. "Our investigation says Roger Poznanski belongs with his uncle at the school and has relatives in Milwaukee."

"I have family here, and I am well off, except when trappers kidnap and beat me," Roger said. He smiled down. "My Anishinaabe family says a boy of fourteen is nearly a man and can choose where he lives."

The sheriff squinted, scratched his jaw then gripped Roger's shoulder. "You are certainly healthy and appear to have a handle on your own affairs. Shooting Dan to save a friend was courageous and also proves you can make quick decisions." He looked up, then at the lodge. "Nevertheless, the Indian agency would dearly like to know about you. They strongly disapprove of white minors living with Indians—corrupts them they think." He paused. "If the Indian agency knew a white boy was here, they might force me to take you into custody. For your own protection, you see."

Masking belligerence with a pleasant face, Roger nodded west. "Up to now, my only danger has been from white men, not Indians, though I know there are bad ones in all races. I am familiar with the forest, can travel far and will, if necessary. But will you report me to the agency?"

"Let's go inside and talk this over with your, uh . . . parents and the chief." The sheriff pleasantly motioned at the lodge. Inside, he grouped with elders including Migizi and Bizaan.

"It appears," the sheriff said, "the matter of a missing boy cannot be resolved at this time. I must at least report the presence of a half blood boy who is very much Anishinaabe and should not be forcibly removed." He grinned while concluding, "Off the record, I think this relative of yours, might at some time, wish to return to his white family and should be encouraged to do so." He faced the chief. "I will register the rifles and release them and the horses for disposition by the village. In the matter of the shooting death of Dan, I'll file a report of self-defense, and if necessary, ask the court if any papers need to be signed, or if anyone has to appear in Poleville or Hutford to finalize things."

The chief used both Ojibwemowin and English to address the sheriff and the Anishinaabe who were gathered. "Nimbagosendaamin wii-gwayako-doodawad Brady. We hope you do what is right for the one called Brady. Meji-doodangig gigii-debibinaag noongom, gii-maji-doodamowaad, gegoon dash Gichi-mookomaanag gaawiin bezhigwendanzigwaa maji-doodaagemagag. The evil ones were caught this time, but not before they had done many bad things, which some white ones do not call bad. Gimiigwechiwi'igoo gii-bwaa-gaganoodaman ezhiwebizid John Bemibatood. We thank you for not interfering in the matter of John Bemibatood. Midaaswi-ashi-niiwin beboonigizid ge ininiwid gii-dibaakonang, dash miinawaa gwiiwizensiwid giishpin biskinikezhind. A man of fourteen, who has proven he can make wise decisions, could again become a child of fourteen if others force their decisions on him. Anishinaabe odinawemaaganiman gikinoowizhaa, bwaa-biskinikezhind. His Anishinaabe family guides him, does not force him."

The meeting ended, and villagers dispersed.

"Wonder how Giigoo is," Roger murmured. "The ones who went with him, who are they?"

"Runners and one peacekeeper who carried a message to Ningaabii'an," Niizh Eshkanag replied. "Like us, Giigoo needed to be home. He has his first story of adventure to tell his parents, and one that can be told around many winter fires."

"Ingikendaan, I know," Roger said smiling, "where it will grow more exciting with each telling,"

Before sunset, on a cool day, late August, while heading to his foster home, Roger watched Niizh Eshkanag approach and enter the home of Gekendaasod to begin his vision search. He will be very hungry. Roger then entered the home of Bizaan and Migizi.

Inside the lodge, Bizaan talked softly with concern in her eyes about Niizh Eshkanag's fast and the cooling weather, "Wii-dakaayaa apii Niizh makadeke."

"Debwemigad," Migizi agreed and noted that it would have happened earlier were it not for the kidnaping. "Ogii-daa-doodaan zhaye giishpin bwaa-odaapinind."

"Sorry, Gaawiin onjida," Roger said trying to understand more of the Ojibwemowin he heard around him.

"One should not be sorry for what is caused by evil ones," Bizaan said to Roger, kindly switching to his mother tongue. "The kidnapping was dangerous for three boys but helped the village *very* much."

"And you all will be honored," Migizi said. "Giigoo will receive an eagle feather by two special runners who will escort him in a ceremony in his own village."

While Niizh Eshkanag fasted, Roger hunted and fished. One day he watched Bizaan prepare to gather berries with women, young boys, and girls. Migizi repaired a basket beside her.

"Shall I gather wood while you pick berries?" Roger asked Bizaan.

"You are old to pick berries, mawinzo," Bizaan replied, "but I thought you still might like to go."

Roger straightened his back, responding pleasantly. "Since I am a man of fourteen, should I not pick berries with girls and women?"

"Though you are on the road to manhood, you are not yet a man," Migizi said. "There is wood enough, and you might find berry-picking pleasant," he paused, staring up. "Ajijaak also picks."

"Ah," Roger beamed. "It occurs to me that a man must humble himself when duty calls." Bizaan suddenly searched for leather scraps.

"Exactly," Migizi said. His mouth twisted to one side, but he appeared pleasant then tested Roger's Ojibwemowin by telling him to wear his vest and leggings in case he was asked to gather berries deep in the bushes, which Migizi did as an older boy. "Biizikan gigibide'ebizon gaye gidazhiganan. Gidaa-nandomigoo wii-mawinzoyan noopiming, gaa-ezhichigeyaan iw apii zaziikiziyaan." Roger nodded, happy to understand the advice.

His fast and vision search ended, Niizh Eshkanag met with and related his dreams and observations to Gekendaasod, the meanings of which would be only between a boy and his family.

In the lodge that evening, Roger asked Migizi and Bizaan about honor ceremonies.

Bizaan explained, "You and Niizh Eshkanag should give Gekendaasod a gift. We will work on that before the feast and ceremony; we have five days yet.

It was before bedtime in Big House. Elias had finished work in the study, Helen and Karen were reading in the parlor.

Elias entered the parlor from his study, and Helen looked up from reading. "About that letter you received from the Indian agent, was it important?"

"It was an advisory of incidents involving reservation Indians near here. Didn't appear to involve any of our students."

Karen stopped reading and sat erect. "Any specifics?"

"Two trappers kidnaped an Indian boy, and two other Indian boys rescued him, resulting in one dead trapper and an injured Indian boy. Apparently the death of the trapper is being deemed justifiable, and the surviving trapper is in custody."

Karen closed her book and stood. "Did they release names of the Indian boys?"

"Not yet. If it involves any of our students, we'll be notified when the investigation is over."

Helen clasped her hands on her lap. "I hope Roger is not injured by such foolishness."

"Roger can take care of himself," Karen said. "I hope he comes back from wherever he is."

Helen stared at the floor. "I didn't realize that Roger could take the place of Donald . . . until he left us." She faced Elias. "Any word about the reward?"

"None."

Karen looked first at Elias then her mother. "If he should return . . . would you smile at him . . . maybe hug him?"

Helen nodded. "I'm sorry I was not a loving aunt. I would like to make it up to him."

Karen felt the change in her mother and breathed, "Where is he?"

"Now dear," Elias said. "If he's in Milwaukee, we should hear before school starts. Relatives will tell us."

Karen spoke softly, "If Roger is with Indians or working in Hutford, he would not give up on education." His friend Niizh Eshkanag is just like him—both have visions beyond their circumstances.

Elias nodded. "I understand why Roger didn't feel at home here. I do hope he returns. Things will change."

"For the better, it seems," Karen added.

At the feast, before the ceremony, Niizh Eshkanag and Roger were dressed in their best clothes. Their oiled hair, just long enough for short braids, framed faces beaming with pride. For the first time in their lives, Niizh Eshkanag and Roger were hosted and served by other boys after elders were served, and they ate with the warriors.

As they ate, Roger spoke while chewing venison, "I hope Gekendaasod likes the moccasins Bizaan made for him."

"For you, for him," Niizh Eshkanag said around a mouthful of wild rice sweetened with sugar.

Roger shook his head. "Hey, this is no time for jokes. Anyway, putting childish thoughts aside, Bizaan put five dollars in the moccasins she made for me for Gekendaasod."

"Same for me," Niizh Eshkanag confirmed.

Roger became thoughtful. "I had planned to make my way to Milwaukee before the summer ended, but traveling and being with you and your family . . . made me think, and listening to what your parents said, I realize that's not the way to go."

"Mother thinks you will go back to Big House," Niizh Eshkanag said. "She knows us, you and me, better than we know ourselves."

"She is very wise," Roger said. "When I go back to the school, if they'll have me, I'll ask Uncle to give twenty-five dollars to your family."

"If I capture you, my family will get three hundred dollars," Niizh Eshkanag said, grabbing Roger gently by an arm.

"You forget, though you can catch me running. I can escape from you . . . I think."

"Maybe. We are almost equal." Niizh Eshkanag smiled. "Mother says, your aunt has had a long time to think, and you must be missed at Big House."

First the grand entrance, then a number of warm-up dances, and it was time to honor those giving service to the village. The chief called out the names of those to be honored, giving each a gift and eagle feathers according to their honor, and having them escorted in an honor dance.

Later, two eagle feathers each draping from their braids, Niizh Eshkanag and Roger sat together. Nagamokwe and Ajijaak sat together a short distant away from the boys, all intoxicated with pride, feeling a sense of the surreal.

Chapter Fifteen

The celebration wound down except for small groups, couples in beautiful slow dancing, and the rhythmic sound of muted drums. Villagers began to disperse into family gatherings around fires or inside homes. Bizaan and Migizi sat inside their lodge on one side, two boys, still in dance dress, feathers safely put away, sat on the other side, everyone sipping cedar tea.

"Wayiiba aabdeg gida-izhaam gikinoo'amaadiwigamigong." Bizaan mentioned that it was nearly time for school. "Ingo-giizis . . . about three weeks."

"Bizhiw gaye niin nigii-nandomigonaanig miinawaa wii-odaapinangidwaa gikinoo'amaaganag." Migizi said he and Bizhiw had been asked to take students to school again.

"Ah sa," Bizaan sighed and said, after a busy day, they should just relax and get some sleep. "Gigii-ondamitaamin noongom, aambe bizaanendandaa jibwaa ani-nibaayang, gagiizhawisedaa."

Earlier before sunset, two older Anishinaabe youths made their way outside the village and stopped at a campfire. Two white men sat near the fire talking low, smoking pipes.

"Hello." The greeting was soft and came from beyond firelight.

"Show yourself," one white man, named Paul, barked. He stood brandishing a pistol.

Oninige and Zhingos entered the camp area and stood by the fire. Oninige spoke, "We hear you search for Roger Poznanski. I am Oninige; this is Zhingos."

Paul talked as he opened his case. "We are on other business now, but . . ." He paused while scanning records. "Yes, the agency searches for a thirteen-year-old boy with that name. Looks like he would be fourteen now. Sit and tell us what you know of this." The youths appeared nervous and glanced about as they sat.

"Uh, is there a reward for him?" Oninige asked.

"If he is brought safely home, yes."

"How much?" Zhingos asked.

The other man, named Jake, scanned the file. "Mm, three hundred dollars. Even if we help, you get the full amount. We simply do our job; take nothing but our salary."

"How long are you here?" Oninige asked.

"How much time do you need?" Paul asked. He tossed wood on the fire.

Oninige replied, "We might bring him tonight. That one who is not Anishinaabe."

Paul smiled, retrieved a small whiskey bottle from his pack, and offered it to Oninige. "There's more besides the money if you bring him to me." He motioned in the direction of the dance circle. "We watched part of the celebration. There was a boy who looked to be part white. Can you tell us about him?"

Oninige hesitated. *If he captures the white boy, we get no reward.* "I will not say what you saw, but we will bring the one you want."

"And the eagle feathers he wore?" Paul pressed. He looked into the youths' faces. "I'm not sure you are the right ones for this. I warn you, if the boy is harmed, you get no money. No rough stuff!"

"We will not hurt him," Oninige promised, smiling broadly. The youths took the bottle and returned to the village. The men continued to talk and smoke, sitting around the fire.

"Money talks," Paul murmured.

"As always," Jake replied.

Later that night, the celebration still going with slow muted drumming, Roger and Niizh Eshkanag stowed their dress clothes and donned everyday breechclouts and moccasins, ready to relax.

"Abaate. Giwii-wiidosem ina jibwaa nibaayang? It is a warm night. Should we walk before sleep?" Niizh Eshkanag asked. "My leg is stronger, but Gekendaasod says I need more exercise to make it limber."

"Mino-inendagwad. Good idea," Roger agreed. "We can see who's outside the village."

The boys sauntered amid scattered tents outside the village, careful to stay away from campfires.

"The moon shines, yet it is hard to see, and it grows cool." Niizh Eshkanag said. "Giiwedaa. Let's go back." He walked as swiftly as he was able with Roger following. Still outside the village, the boys passed two older youths, one holding a lantern, which he held up to Roger's face. Blinded by the light, neither Niizh Eshkanag nor Roger recognized the youths, both thinking it to be an innocent gesture. Niizh Eshkanag continued on, Roger stopped to tie a moccasin.

"I'm right behind you," Roger said, just loud enough for Niizh Eshkanag to hear.

"Giga-waabamin endaayang," Niizh Eshkanag called out to say he'd see Roger at home.

Roger straightened and was about to jog after Niizh Eshkanag, but flinched, lunging away from one set of encircling arms into the arms of someone strong enough to subdue him. His attackers had set a lantern on the ground nearby.

Roger struggled for his knife, but his arms were pinned. He stared up into Oninige's face, looking past him at Zhingos, who wore moccasins, pants, and no shirt. Oninige wore a heavy leather vest, baggy pants, and white man's boots.

"What do you want? Are you after a reward?" Roger hissed.

"It is not for you to know," Oninige snapped. He forced Roger on his abdomen, roughly pulled his arms onto his back, and tied them above the elbows and at the wrists. Both youths then lifted Roger to his feet shoving him to walk away from the village toward the river trail.

"Agents wait," Zhingos snapped.

Puffing in discomfort, Roger stood unmoving. "I'll not walk to help you get the reward." Zhingos shoved him, and Roger sat down hard with a grunt. Oninige kicked him in the back and hit his ribs with a fist.

"Uh! . . . Uh!" Roger grunted from the blows. "You'll get no money if I'm hurt." The older boys stared a long time at Roger. "Help! Wiidookawishin!" Roger yelled. Oninige clapped his hand over Roger's mouth, and the plea was lost amid serenade drumming and singing.

"Shut your mouth!" Oninige hissed. He turned to Zhingos. "I watch him and make fire over there." He pointed near a tree. "Bring agent there. Ajijaak need Anishinaabe man, not white snake!"

"Ajijaak and I are only friends," Roger said between gasps for air. *Will this trouble ever end?* He watched Zhingos move swiftly toward a distant tent.

Oninige lashed Roger's legs together, and with some difficulty, hoisted him to his shoulder and carried him away from the main camping area and built a low fire. Zhingos and Paul soon arrived.

Paul looked down at Roger. "Did you have to tie him up?"

"He would not move so I will carry him," Oninige explained.

"So you're the runaway," Paul said. "Are you ready to return home? If we untie you, will you run?"

"Maybe," Roger said. "Why do you want to take me back?"

"The agency frowns on white minors living with Indians. Also your relatives want you back. They're your guardians, you know. By law, I have no choice but bring you back."

"I'll go with you if the reward isn't given to these two," Roger declared.

"I have no control over that," the agent said. "My only responsibility is to get you safely home."

"I'm certainly not safe now," Roger said, as he struggled against the discomfort of being bound. "So untie me."

"Okay," Paul said. He motioned to Oninige. "Untie him. After I deliver him safely home, I will report that you found him for us. However, if he does not arrive with me, there will be no reward. If you want to go with us to make sure he gets home, that's all right with me."

"We will go with you," Oninige stated.

The agent gazed thoughtfully at Roger. "I suppose we should put handcuffs on him overnight. Just in case. He's certainly reluctant to go." Roger was untied and handcuffs put on his wrists.

"We will come back in the morning," Oninige said. He and Zhingos departed.

When Roger failed to come home, Niizh Eshkanag faced his father and told him something must have happened because Roger was not home. "Gegoo gaa-ezhiwebag. Gaawiin ayaasii Bemibatood."

Migizi said it was too late for Roger to be alone. He told Bizaan that he and Niizh Eshkanag would ask Bizhiw for help. "Niwii-gagwejimaanaan Bizhiw ji-wiidookawiyangid." Father and son made their way to Bizhiw's lodge, rapped on the bark, and waited, gazing around.

"Biindigen," Bizhiw invited them in, but after they explained their concerns he said he had seen nothing. "Gaawiin gegoo ingii-waabandanziin."

"Zanagad gegoo ji-waabandan dibikong." Ziigwan said it was difficult to see at night.

"Gichi-mookomanag gabeshiwag mitigwaking gonemaa awiwaad Anishinaabe-wegimaajig," Esiban said white men were camping in the forest, and they could be agents.

"Aaniin minik ininiwag gii-waabamadwaa, Esiban?" Migizi asked how many men Esiban had seen.

"Niizh eta ogii-gaganoozhaan," Esiban said he saw two men speaking to the others.

Niizh Eshkan's eyes sharpened. "Oninige and Zhingos?"

"Enh," Esiban confirmed the bullies had been speaking to the men.

"Roger geget iwedi ayaad," Niizh Eshkanag declared Roger must be there.

"Wiindigoowiwag!" They are evil, Ziigwan snapped, worried they would hold Roger against his will.

Migizi was silent for some time, then he told Bizhiw they should not be seen helping to take Roger from American agents. "Gaawiin giwii-waabanjigaazosiimin Roger zhaabwizhangid."

"Debwemigad." Bizhiw agreed that was true.

Niizh Eshkanag suggested he could find Roger, make sure he is all right because white men would not worry if a boy walked by.

Migizi considered the offer but cautioned Niizh Eshkanag to not be gone long, "Gego ondendiken ginwenzh."

"Ingikenimaa awiya gagiitawendang wii-naadamawid," Niizh Eshkanag said he knew someone clever who could help.

"Niin!" Esiban offered.

"Gigagiitawendam idash oshkaya'aayan." Niizh Eshkanag kindly told Esiban he was clever but too young, glancing at Esiban's mother who smiled, nodding assent. "Nagamokwe indinenimaa."

Ziigwan guessed correctly that Niizh Eshkanag was thinking of Nagomokwe and warned him to be careful. "Ayaangwaamizin."

"Da-onizhishin. Gizhemanidoo giganawenimigoonaan giishpin naadamawandgwaa nindinewemaaganaanaanig." Migizi said this plan could be fine because the Creator protects those who help their relatives.

Niizh Eshkanag went to the home of Bedose, and knocked on the bark, fidgeting as sounds of stirring came from within. Bedose poked her head out, and seeing Niizh Eshkanag, motioned him in.

"Boozhoo, biindigen. Gibabaamendaan ina?" Bedose asked if something was worrying him. Niizh Eshkanag glanced at Nagamokwe.

Niizh Eshkanag asked politely if he might borrow their pretty daughter who is very clever, like her parents, to help him find a missing boy. "Daga giwii-awii'aazomininim ina gidaanis? Miikawaadizi miinawaa dibishkoo giinawaa gagiitawendang."

"Apii awiya wiisagazii-maa'iinganinitaagozid, gegoo bebakaan idang." Bedose said, when someone speaks like a coyote, there is deeper meaning to what he says, and she motioned to Nagamokwe, who had moved to stand beside her.

"Waabi-gwiiwizens ina andawedaan naadamaawind?" Nagamokwe asked if it was the white boy who needed help.

"Enh."

"Miinawaa?" Nagamokwe was surprised he needed help again and asked if he was helpless or simply had many enemies. "Bwaanawichige ina gemaa baatayiinowag zhiingenmaad?"

"Wiindigoog zhooniyaawan omisawenmaawaan zhiingenimaawaad Rogeran. Wiindigoog zhooniyaawan ozaagi'aawaan dibishkoo makwag aamoo-zhiiwaagamizigan zaagitoowaad." Niizh Eshkanag explained the evil ones who want money are his enemies because they love money the way bears love honey. He said Roger could not be far but may have been captured by white men again. Then he asked Nagamokwe to help him. "Daga, naadamawishin."

Nagamokwe threw a robe over her shoulder and moved beside Niizh Eshkanag. She said she would go with Niizh and suggested they ask Ajijaak to join them to see that Roger is all right.

Three youths, including Ajijaak. stole into the forest where Esiban said he had seen the camp of white men.

Ajijaak suddenly pointed to a dying fire near a tent with a lantern glowing inside. "Niizh ininiwag niwaabamaag miinawaa gikendamaan da-ezhichigeyaan." She whispered to the others that she saw two grown men in the shadows, but she had a plan.

The two girls moved behind the tent and began to talk loud, giggling and laughing. Soon a man's head showed through the door flap. Niizh Eshkanag watched from behind bushes. *So, they are white ones.* The girls became louder as the first man stood tall outside. Another man emerged and looked behind the tent at the girls.

"Quiet, please," one man said. The girls moved away and continued laughing, speaking loud Ojibwemowin.

Niizh Eshkanag waited until the men moved far enough away then he ran to the tent, shoved his head in and saw Roger lying handcuffed with free legs. "Aambe, izhaadaa! Come on, let's go! Now! Fast!" Niizh Eshkanag hissed. He helped Roger up, shoved him through the tent flap, and soon both boys were hundreds of paces away.

"We cannot go to our home," Niizh Eshkanag cautioned, "nor do I think you can stay in the village with me. My parents and I cannot be seen helping you." Niizh Eshkanag and Roger soon connected with Ajijaak and Nagamokwe.

"Now what?" Roger asked, holding up his manacled wrists for emphasis.

"I did not know white boys wore bracelets," Ajijaak said. Her smile was just discernible in moonlight as she glanced innocently at treetops.

"Ha, ha," Roger retorted.

"The village peacekeepers have these things," Niizh Eshkanag said. "But we better not, *push our luck*, as you say, by asking them for key."

"They might be forced to give me to the agents," Roger said.

"To stay out of trouble themselves," Niizh Eshkanag said thoughtfully. "The agent will first come to my home. So it should look normal, which means I must be home with Father and Mother." He paused, gazed around then looked straight at Roger. "It is time for you to end this trouble. Do you agree, brother Roger, wiijiwaagan Bemibatood?"

Roger stared at the ground for some time, then glanced south. "Yes," he said, softly in resignation. "If they will not take me back in Poleville, I will go to Milwaukee."

"They will take you back," Niizh Eshkanag declared. "Father says they would not offer such a big reward if they did not want you."

"Can he go like that?" Ajijaak asked, frowning.

Roger fidgeted, staring at his shackled wrists. "I can try, but it will be hard for me," he looked at Ajijaak and trying to find his sense of humor, added "wearing bracelets."

"Anything could happen if you were alone wearing those things, but I must be in my own house if agents come," Niizh Eshkanag said. "Someone else must take you home."

"Then I will take him, niin sa," Ajijaak declared.

"She and I can split the reward!" Niizh Eshkanag said, expressing delight.

Ajijaak looked at Roger. "It is tempting." She tried squelching a grin. "But my mother and father love Roger, too, and would never forgive me—you either—Joker. Bebaapinizid."

Niizh Eshkanag turned serious then. "Ajijaak, you should get food and blankets. You and Roger will need to sleep on the trail. I will tell Father and Mother that you both have gone to the school. The agents have horses so you should take Roger to school using the trail this side of ridge. It takes only a few hours longer, and the agents should not find you there, if they even think you might be going to the school."

"I will be back soon with food, water, and a bow," Ajijaak said. Niizh Eshkanag watched her disappear then faced Roger and Nagamokwe.

Ajijaak returned with provisions and a backpack, which she set on the ground and began sorting things, stuffing them into the pack leaving space on top for food. She threw a blanket over Roger's shoulders and pulled the ends so he could hold them under the handcuffs.

Roger and Ajijaak took the west trail toward the ridge, making fair progress in spite of an awkward gait imposed on Roger by the handcuffs. They walked two hours west until they arrived at a southbound trail, yet some distance from the ridge.

"We should sleep here," Roger said. "This trail goes to the ridge." He pointed west. "This trail goes to Poleville and the school." He pointed south.

Ajijaak hung their provisions in a tree away from them, then they each rolled up in a blanket and soon slept.

Chapter Sixteen

Lying on his side, Roger opened his eyes, and moved his blanket off his face and grimaced as he moved sore, manacled wrists. Sensing movement behind, he rolled to see sunlit treetops and Ajijaak quietly preparing food, sorting equipment.

"G'morning, minogizheb," Roger said. He threw the blanket off his shoulders, and held it around his waist. He tried stretching, but could only extend both arms together still holding the blanket. The effort painfully aggravated wrists as he walked, and moved during sleep.

"How long you been up?" Roger asked, interrupting himself with a yawn.

Ajijaak smiled. "Just like a man, sleeping while the woman works. I was up early to watch for agents, fix food while you talk silly in your sleep."

Roger frowned, mumbling, "Just like a woman searching for gossip." He stood, speaking louder, "My wrists are red, and they hurt from the handcuffs."

Ajijaak walked over to Roger with a tin of food, "Poor boy. Gigoopazinaagoz. Eat. Wiisinin." She sat near Roger and held the tin of food so he could use both arms to move the spoon. "We must eat and go or the agents will find you. It might be better if I feed you."

"Just hold the plate."

After eating, the couple headed south on the trail toward the school. Snacking at midday, they traveled hard with only a few rests to ease the chaffing on Roger's wrists, allow him to recover from fatigue worsened by the awkward gait.

Near dark they arrived at Poleville Indian School and made their way to Big House. Roger tapped lightly on the door and waited, fidgeting, glancing around. The door opened and Karen peered into the dimness,

"Father!" Karen called over her shoulder. "Two Indian children are here."

"Students aren't due for days yet," Elias replied. He left his study and moved to join Karen.

Karen peered closer at the two and, suddenly, "No!" She breathed in, her tone incredulous. "Ajijaak? She looked at the girl. Hesitant, she scanned the boy in breechclout. "Who?" She fingered his long hair held by a thong touching his hard shoulders, appearing darker in the dimness.

Roger was mute, overcome with emotion. Finally he stammered, "Karen! I'm Roger. He motioned. "Uh, Ajijaak." He held his wrists up.

"You *are* Roger! Come! Come in! Both of you!" Karen herded them into the kitchen. She faced her parents, both standing silent in the parlor doorway staring at Roger and Ajijaak. "The adventurer has returned."

Helen looked sharply toward Elias. "Get those things off his wrists! The very idea!" A suppressed smile worked the corner of her mouth. "No need asking where he's been."

Recovering from surprise, Elias headed for the door. "You have caused us much worry," he began . . . "Never mind, you're here, and that's all that matters. We have those here. I'll have Mike get them off and ask him to send the nurse."

"Goodness!" Karen exclaimed. "Almost forgot to welcome you properly." She pulled boy and girl together into a warm embrace, though Roger was unable to reciprocate. She stood back to look them over. "I think you both need a bath. Those clothes might do in the forest, but they certainly won't do in school." She felt Roger's hard shoulders. "You're stronger than you were last spring. I see why Ajijaak likes you." She smiled at Roger then faced her mother. "May they both bathe here?"

"Certainly," Helen replied. "I'll heat water." She headed to the bathroom.

"Now that Mother can't hear," Karen whispered into Roger's ear, "she has changed a lot, a whole lot! And I know she wants you to stay. She always did but couldn't admit it."

Roger nodded. "She's more pleasant than I can remember—how she talks and looks."

Mike entered the house with Elias. He looked at Roger, grinning as he produced a key. Roger held up his wrists. Mike unlocked the handcuffs and stood back as Roger sighed with relief rubbing chaffed wrists.

"I asked Nurse Pierce to check the youngsters," Elias said, "after they've bathed. She'll be along shortly."

"The bath is ready for one," Helen called. "I have clean clothes for both."

Roger nodded to Ajijaak. "You go first." Roger offered Ajijaak. Elias nodded assent. Ajijaak bathed and soon appeared wearing one of Karen's dresses, which hung quite loose on her.

Roger came from the bathroom wearing pants and holding his shirt. Emma had arrived and now applied salve on his badly irritated wrists, and scrapes where the bullies had kicked his back and ribs.

"You've had quite a summer of it, I'd say," Emma said, her face reflecting deeper concern. "Bet you never expected this much excitement when we rode together on our way here last year. You were afraid of Indians then."

"Seems like years instead of months, but . . . yeah, it was not the Indians giving me trouble except two that helped the agents. It was the reward, but I can't blame my Uncle or Aunt; they just did what they thought was best for me."

"You say the reward gave you the most trouble?" Elias questioned.

"First the trappers," Roger began, hesitating.

"Yes? Trappers you say?" Elias pressed. Roger frowned, fidgeting with his hands.

Karen interrupted, "Don't you see, Father, Roger has to be one of the Indian boys the sheriff talked about in a shootout with trappers." She faced Roger. "Did you do the shooting?"

"Yeah." Roger breathed. "To save Niizh."

"Well, I'll be," Elias breathed. "The trappers were after the reward then."

Roger nodded. "And so were the Indian bullies who worked for the agent or with them anyway. The agent was the one who put the handcuffs on me after the Indian bullies captured and beat me."

"By the looks of his injuries, it was a violent beating," Emma added.

Elias nodded. "Perhaps I'd better have a talk with the tribal council. No doubt those two are a bad influence on many young Indians. I'll have a word with the agents, too. The very idea, handcuffs on innocent children! By the way, do you know the agent's name?"

"Paul," Roger replied. "I don't know his last name."

"Paul seemed to be civil in dealing with Indians," Elias said. "But I don't know him that well. Maybe I'd best talk to village elders myself, within the pretext of school business."

"You have every right!" Karen declared. "Village bullies attacking our kin. Just a little more violence, and he wouldn't be here today."

"You're right!" Elias admitted.

"Who was beaten beside you and who was shot?" Karen pressed.

"Niizh was shot and beaten helping me," Roger explained. "He's fine now but limped for weeks."

"It was during the shootout, I suppose," Karen guessed.

"Uh huh." Roger nodded.

"Tomorrow Mike and I will take Ajijaak to the village, and I'll talk to the chief," Elias said.

"Father," Karen interrupted.

"Yes, dear."

"Why doesn't our whole family go, Mother, too," Karen said, her eyes shining. "We can meet the families that helped Roger."

"My family should meet yours," Ajijaak said. "But some elders will not feel comfortable with white people." She fingered the dress she wore. "Your clothes are good, but I would wear my own clothes to village." Helen nodded.

"Well, Cousin Brother," Karen said, giving Roger a knowing look.

"You're right, Cousin Sister," Roger said. "I would like to wear the clothes Niizh's family gave me." He faced Elias and Helen. "Only if Uncle Father and Aunt Mother agree."

"I don't approve of naked boys running about the house," Helen remarked, but she smiled, adding, "I suppose there are as many adages to legitimize behavior as there are to condemn them." Karen smiled with a wink at Roger and faced her parents.

"All right," Elias said, "Considering they helped Roger through a difficult experience, and, it occurs to me, were the reverse true—an Indian needing help from a white family might not be so lucky." He thought a moment as he stared out a window then shared a concern: "It appears that we have slowly changed our focus with our native students from what the boarding school system seems to expect. We've limited the use of corporal punishment, but are required to cut student's hair and prevent their use of native languages and religion."

Karen nodded while adding, "Roger helped find Aandeg and assisted other students with their school work. If the truth were known, the Indians were more eager to help Roger because they knew he was willing to help them."

"You're absolutely right!" Elias exclaimed. "It's a start we can build on."

In the morning, Mike brought the carriage to Big House and, holding the horses, watched as the Poznanski family boarded. He handed the reins to Elias and pointed to Roger. "Is he one of the new students from Waaban?"

Elias cast a side-glance at Ajijaak and Roger. "They are, indeed, students from the Waaban. The one may choose to live with us this winter, but his heart is definitely at Waaban." With that he slapped the reins, and the carriage headed north.

The family made good time arriving well before dark at the village.

Roger asked Ajijaak as she headed toward her home if he would see her later. "Giga-waabamin ina?"

"Enya," the call came back.

Roger led his family to the home of Bizaan and Migizi and rapped on the bark beside the doorway. Bizaan thrust her head out.

"Ingikendaan bi-ayaayeg," Bizaan said, speaking Anishinaabe. She looked up at the elder Poznanskis. "Your faces say you are friends."

"Bemibatood onoshenyan miinawaa ozhisheh miinawaa omisenyan Karen." Niizh Eshkanag announced the arrival of Roger's aunt, uncle, and cousin, then said he would make a fire outside. "Niwii-boodawe agwajiing."

Darkness descended, everyone sat around the outside fire. Bizhiw, Ziigwan, and Esiban joined them, and later, Ajijaak and Nagamokwe arrived. The Anishinaabe parents used as much English as they could to be polite.

"Our parents do not feel comfortable with the white headmaster and did not wish to come," Ajijaak said, speaking for both girls.

When Roger explained the kidnaping and how he was handcuffed and beaten by Oninige and Zhingos, Bizaan glanced sharply at Migizi.

"It is time you spoke to the chief about those two," Bizaan snapped.

"I plan to discuss that matter with the chief, as well," Elias said.

"I will get him," Bizhiw said. "This concerns everyone in the village." He stood and headed for the chief's home.

The chief arrived, and Roger again described the latest events.

"I have considered contacting the sheriff concerning the way in which the agent and the two Indian boys kidnaped Roger for the reward," Elias explained. "However, the right and wrong of it is hazy at best, and it would be difficult to prove it was kidnaping, only that Roger was beaten and bound."

"Gaawiin ingikendanziin gaa-ezhiwebag eta go manaadenimangid Roger Poznanski ezhinikaazod Bemibaatood." The chief's said he knew few of the details, but the village respected Roger who they also knew as Bemibatood. His attitude then went from pleasant to stern as he said he knew more about Oninge and Zhingos who no longer remember the words of the First Grandfather. The chief asked that the village be allowed to deal with the two young men who were still young enough to change. Niizh Eshkanag translated for Elias when the chief finished his statement.

"I leave it to you, and will clear it with the Indian agency," Elias said.

The chief replied to Elias."Owii-wiidookawaan zhiigaan ji-maawandowaatigwewaad dash ji-gwaaba'igewaad mii dash giiwosewaad gaye zagawe'idigamig biinitoowaad. Aabdeg nanda-gikendaanaawaa ezhi-mino-bimaadiziyaang. Giishpin gaawin owii-ezhichigesiiwag miidash zaagijiwebiniganiwiwaad." Niizh Eshkanag served as translator again and reported that the offenders would be asked to help the widows, gather firewood, clean the meetinghouse, and learn a good way of life; if they did not do these things, they would face banishment.

"I will write a paper to confirm what we have said today and leave it in your hands," Elias said. Be sure to notify the agency or us if it comes to banishment.

"While here, I can take the list of students attending school this year," Elias said.

"It is only a week yet until school," Roger said. "May I stay here and come with the students?"

Glancing to Helen, Elias seemed surprised. After a very long moment, Elias put his hand under Roger's chin and lifted it so their eyes met. "I guess a week longer is short after a summer away from home. We do love you and want you home." He retrieved his hand. "Like the Anishinaabe say, a boy of fourteen is also a man of fourteen, and according to all reports, you are becoming a man. However, there will be chores while you're in school, and before you ask, you will be able to spend a month or so next summer with your friends at this village." He paused. "Or should I say, you may wander the triangle next summer."

"Without a reward on my head," Roger added, "I will have to pick berries with the girls for excitement." Elias coughed. Helen shifted amid a round of laughter.

The Poznanski family departed in the morning with much of the village waving them off. Niizh Eshkanag and Roger wore Anishinaabe dress clothes with two eagle feathers each draped aside their head as they waved them off.

It was Saturday; students arrived at the school from villages by wagon and carriage, and Mike Murphy's grandson arrived from St. Paul.

"Too bad, Jack, about your father," Mike said. "I hope you like it here. You'll live with me but go to school with the Indians." He pointed to a line of students. "For now, get in line there and register for school, then follow them to get your uniform."

Jack appeared sullen as he muttered, "They're savages, and those two are naked. The one looks like a half breed. Why do I have to go to school with Injuns?"

Mike flashed a knowing smile. "You'll get along just fine."

Jack stood in line behind Esiban and Nagamokwe's younger sister, and he felt insulted as Esiban looked at him while speaking Anishinaabe. He glared at Esiban, snapping, "Are you talking about me?"

"I ask if you will go to school with us," Esiban said.

"Oh," Jack said. "Who's the half breed?"

"Roger Bemibatood Poznanski is all white, and he is Niizh Eshkanag's brother."

"Who's Niizh Eshkanag?" Jack asked.

"The one ahead of him,"

"How can they be brothers?" Jack asked, puzzled.

"Long story, it would take all winter to tell."

MII I'IW

Glossary

Margaret O'Donnell Noodin and Michael Zimmerman Jr.

This glossary is a list of the Ojibwe words used in the book. It is made up of many words that can be found in The Ojibwe People's Dictionary but also contains words from other sources as needed. The spelling conventions and dialect used throughout the book is western Ojibwemowin, which matches the region where the story takes place. As verbs appear on this list, they are shown in the third person form, which is often considered the "root" verb. You will see them used with pronoun prefixes and suffixes in the book, which means a bit of knowledge about Ojibwemowin and other Anishinaabe languages would be helpful for language learners using this glossary. You can find a basic introduction to the grammar at www.ojibwe.net and through the language and culture departments of many of the 143 nations in Anishinaabewakiing where Ojibwemowin, Nishnaabemwin, Neshnaabémwen are spoken by Ojibwe, Odawa, and Potawatomi people. Audio files for this glossary also can be found at www.ojibwe.net. You can find a map of the nations here: https://ojibwe.net/inawe-mazinaigan-map-project/.

A

aabawaa—it is warm

aabiding—once

aabita—half

aakode'e—to be brave

aakwaadizi—to be strict

aambe—come on, a gesture of invitation

aamoo-zhiiwaagamizigan—honey

aanawi—but

aandeg(oog)—crow(s)

aangodinong—sometimes

aaniin—hello, what

aaniin apii—when

aaniin dash—why

aaniindi—where

aaniin minik—how many

aanikeshikaw—follow someone's trail

aanimakamigad—difficulty, trouble, an emergency

aanind—some

aapidapizo—to be tied up securely

aapideg—must

aapiji—really, very much so

aas(an)—legging(s)

aatawebi—let a fire go out

a'aw—that (animate)

aawenan—to know by sight

aawi—to be

abaate—warm weather

abi—sit quiet in a place

abinoojiiyens(ag)—baby(s)

adaawe—to trade

adaawewigamig—trading post

adaawetamaw—to buy something for others

agidakamig—the ground

agwajiing—outside

ajijaak—sandhill crane

ajina—a short while

akandoo—to wait in ambush

akawaabam—be on the alert for someone

akawe—first

akwaandawe—to climb up

anaamendaagozi—to be blamed

anaamimaakaniwi—to be accused

anami'aa—to pray

anami'etamaw—to pray for someone

anami'etaw—to pray to someone

andawendan—to want something

aniibiish—tea

animikogaa—turn away or look away

Anishinaabe—the larger language and culture group which includes the
   Ojibwe, Odawa, and Potawatomi

Anishinaabekwaniye—to dress Anishinaabe-style

Anishinaabemowin—the language of the Anishinaabe people

Anishinaabe-wegimaad—Indian agent

Anishinaabewi—to be Anishinaabe

anokii—to work

anooj—more

anwaatin—to be calm or still

anwebi—rest

anweshimo—to rest, try to sleep

anwiiwizhens(an)—gun cartridge(s)

apii—when

apikaadizo—to braid one's own hair

asemaa—tobacco

ashange—to feast people

ashi-niiwin—fourteen

asigibii'igan—number

awas—go away

awashime—more

awegonen—what

awenen—who

awii'aazom—borrow from someone

awiya—someone

ayaa—to be

ayaan—to have something

ayaangwaamizi—to be careful

ayaaw—to have someone

ayekozi—to be tired

azhegiiwe—to return home

azhegiiwem—return someone home

azhen—return someone

azhewebin—throw something back, push something back

azhigwa—now

B

baabaabii'o—very, very much to wait

babaamoomigo—to ride on horseback

baabige—immediately

baabii'o—to wait

baabiitoon—to wait for something

baashkizigan—gun

babaamenim—to bother someone

babaami-ayaa—to wander around, go on an adventure

babaamiwizh—to guide someone

baamaa—later

baatayiinowag—many, of an animate group

babaamaadizi—to travel around

babaamendan—worry about something

babaaminizhikaw—to chase someone

babaapinizi—to joke around

babagiwayaan(an)—shirt(s)

bagidanaamo—to breathe

bagidin—to release someone

bagidinan—to allow something

bagidini—to allow someone to do something

bagosendan—to hope

bagwanawizi—to be ignorant

bakite—to hit someone

bakite'igaazo—to be hit by someone

bamendaan—to care about something

bami'—to adopt someone

banaajichigaade—something is damaged, ruined

banaaji'iwendamo—ruined thinking, a weak or damaged mind

bangii—a little

bangishimo—sunset

bangishin—to fall down

bashanzhe'—to punish someone physically

bazigwii—make someone rise up

bebakaan—completely different, other one

bebezhigooganzhii(g)—horse

Bebooniked—Winter Maker

besho—near

benak—a little more, a little better

bezhig—one

bezhigwaabik—one dollar

bezhigwendan—agree on one thing, think the same thing

biboon—winter

bibooni-awesiiwayaan(ag)—winter pelt

biboonigizi—to be a certain age, have a certain number of winters

bichibojigan—poison

biidaw—bring something for someone

biidoon—to bring something

biigoshkaa—it is broken

biijipidan –taste something

biindaakoozh—make a tobacco offering

biindige—enter

biinish—until

biinitoon—clean something

biinjaya'ii—inside

biiwide—a stranger

biizh—to return

biizikan—to wear something

biizikigan(an)—clothes

biizikonaye—to get dressed

bimibatoo—to run

bimikawaan(an)—tracks

bimise—to fly somewhere

bimizha'—to follow someone

bimojige—to shoot with an arrow

bimose—to walk

biskaabii—to return

biskinikezh—to force someone to do something

bizaan—to be quiet, still, or at peace

bizaanendan—to have calm thoughts

bizhiw—lynx

bizindaw—to listen to someone

booch—necessary

boonenim—to ignore someone

booni—to stop something

boonigidetaw—to forgive someone

boonikaw—to leave someone alone

boonisaadan—to stop something

boozhoo—greeting

boozi—to get into a vehicle

bwaa—failure or inability to do something

bwaanakiing—Dakota country

bwaanawichige—to be helpless

D

daga—please

dagoshin—to arrive

dakaayaa—to be cool weather

dakon—to hold someone

dash—then

dayaash—butt

dazhiike—dwell or settle somewhere

debaabandan—to see something far away

debibin—grab something, seize something

debibizh—to catch someone

debwe—to be correct or truthful

debwe'endan—to believe something

debwemigad—it is true

debwetaw—to believe or agree with someone

debweyenim—believe in someone

denaniw—tongue

dengwe—face

dewe'igan(ag)—drum(s)

dibaajimo—to tell a story

dibaajimowin(an)—news, story, narrative

dibaakonan—decide about something

dibaakonigewin(an)—law(s)

diba'amaagozi—to be paid or rewarded

diba'amaw—to pay someone, to reward

diba'iganens(an)—minute(s)

dibendaagozi—belong someplace

dibenindizo—belong to oneself

dibik—night

dibishkoo—like, as

doodan—to do something

E

endaa—to live somewhere, make a home

endaso—every

enh—yes, used by all

enigok—to do something with effort

enokii(jig)—worker(s) from anokii, to work

enya—yes, used by women

eshkan(ag)—horn(s)

esiban(ag)—raccoon

eta—only

eta go—except

ezhichige—to do something, be occupied

ezhiwebad—it happens, an event, occurrence

G

gaagiigido—talk

gaagwe—to attempt something

gaaskanazo—to whisper

gaawiin—no

gaawiin awiya—no one

gaawiin gegoo—nothing

gaawiin wiikaa—never

gabeshi—to set up camp

gabikaw—surpass, pass by, overtake someone

gagaanwaanikwe—to have long hair

gaganoonidi—speak with each other

gaganoozh—talk to someone

gagiibaadizi—to be foolish

gagiitaawendaagwad—it is wise

gagiitawendam—to be clever

gagiizhawise—to relax

gagwejim—to ask someone

gagwekwaniye—test wear, try on an item of clothing

gakina—all

ganabaj—maybe

ganawaabam—to watch someone

ganawenim—to protect someone

ganoozh—speak to someone

gashkadino-giizis—November, the Freezing Moon

gashkichige—to deserve something, be able to do something

gashki'o—to be able to do something

gegaa—almost

gegapii—finally

geget—for sure, certainly

gego—don't

gegoo(n)—something

gekinoo'amaaged—teacher

gemaa—or

gete-—old

geyaabi—still, continue

giboodiyegwaazon(ag)—pants

gichi—a prefix meaning big, large, or very

gichi-ayaa(yag)—elder(s)

Gichi-gezhaadiged—Great Guardian

gichi-gigizheb—early in the morning

Gichi-manidoo—Great Spirit

Gichi-manidoo-giizis—January, Great Spirit Moon

Gichi-mishomis—First Grandfather

Gichi-mookomaan(ag)—American, literally "the long-knives" which is the term used for Americans because many soldiers carried bayonets with knives at the tip.

gichitwaawendaagozi—to be holy

Gichi-zaaga'igan—Big Lake

gidagaakoons(ag)—fawn(s)

gidagiigin—calico print cloth

gidan—drink all of something

giichigon—to remove someone

giige—nurse someone, heal someonee

giigoo(yag)—fish

giikimanigaade—to have a numb leg

giimii—to sneak away, run away

giin—you

giishkaabaagwe—to be thirsty

giishkaabikaa—a ridge or escarpment

giishkadinaa—a place where the ground is cut off, a cliff

giishpin—if

giishpinazh—buy someone or something animate

giiwashkwanim—to confuse someone

giiwashkwebii—to be drunk

giiwe—to go home

giiwedin—north, and the name of one of the villages

Giiwedinanang—the North Star

Giiwitaashkaa—go in a circle around something

giiwose—hunt

giizhigad(oon)—day(s)

giizhiitaa—to be ready

gikendaaso—to be smart

gikendan—to know something

gikenim—to know someone

gikinaamaw—to teach someone

gikinoo'amaadiwigamig—school

gikinoo'amawaagan(ag)—student(s)

gikinoowaabandan—to learn by observing the world

ginebig(oog)—snake(s)

ginoozhe—a northern pike

ginwenzh—continuing, a long while

gisinaa—cold weather

gitaawis—your male

gizhaadige—to serve as a guard

Gizhemanidoo—the Creator

Gizhewaadizi—to be generous

gizhiibizo—to travel quickly

gizhiikaa—to hurry

gonemaa—maybe

gookooko'oo(g)—owl(s)

goopazinaagozi—to be pitiful

gopaakwii—to climb a tree

gopii—to go inland, go into the brush

goshkozi—to wake up

gwaaba'ige—to draw water

gwayako-doodaw—to do right by someone

gwayakwaadizi—to be honest

gwech—enough

gwiiwizens(ag)—boy(s)

H

howah—oh my! oh no!

I

idamaw—to say something to someone

idan—to say something

igo—an emphasis marker

iidog—maybe, possibly

i'iw—that

ikwe—woman

ina—question marker

inaadizi—have a way of life, practice a culture

inaajimo—tell someone

inaakonigaazo—to be judged

inamanji'o—to feel a certain way

inawem—to be related to someone

inawemaagan—relative

inendan—to think about something

inenim—to think of someone

ingitizimag—my parents

ingoding—someday, sometime

ingodwaaswi—six

ingozis—my son

inini—man

ininiwi—to be a man

initaagozi—to sound like something or someone

ishkodekaan—fireplace or fire pit

ishkodewaaboo—fire water, whisky, hard liquor

ishkwaa—after

ishkwaaj—since

ishkwaataa—stop an activity

ishkweyaang—to be located behind

ishpaadinaang—high hill or ridge

Iskigamizige-giizis—April

iwedi—there

izhaa—to go

izhi-niimi'iding—the dance circle, the powwow grounds

izhinikaade—it is called, it is named

izhinikaazh—to call someone something

izhinikaazo—to be named

izhise—a certain way or direction

izhitwaawin(an)—tradition(s), custom(s)

izhiwebad—it happens

J

jaka—to sting someone

jibwaa—before

jiibaakwe—to cook

jiikakamigad—a celebration is happening

M

maadaa—before

maadaajimo—begin telling a story

maa'iingan(ag)—wolf(s)

maajaa—to leave

maamakaajichigaade—it is wonderful

maanenim—challenge or mock someone

maanzhi-doodaw—harm someone

maawandowaatigwe—gather wood

maawanji'idi—gather together

maazhichige—to do something wrong, to be wrong

maji-dibaakon—to judge badly or judge harshly

maji-doodaw—to treat someone badly

majigoodenh(yan)—cloth dress

maji-ininiiwi—to be an evil man

maji-izhiwebad—a bad happening

maji-manidoowaadizi—behave as a bad spirit

makadeke—to have a fast, coming of age ceremony

makademashkikiwaaboo—black medicine water, coffee

makizin(an)—moccasin(s)

makwa(g)—bear(s)

mamaajii—move around

manaadenim—to respect someone

mane—a prefix meaning something is needed

mangodaasiwi—to be selfish

Manidoo-giizisoons—December, Spirit Moon

manidooke—to have a ceremony

Manoominike-giizis—August, Wild Rice Moon

mashkawizi—to be strong

mawidishiwe—to go visiting

mawinzo—to pick berries

megwaa—during

megwayaak—the woods, forest

meshkwadoozh—to trade someone or animate things

metisin—to miss, long for someone

mewinzha—long ago

michaa—it is large

migizi—bald eagle

mii—so

miigaadi—to fight

miigaazh—to fight someone

miigiwe—to give a gift

miigwech—thanks

miigwechiwenim—to give thanks for someone

miigwechiwi—to thank someone

miikanens—small road or path

miikawaadizi—to be handsome or beautiful

miinawaa—and, also, again

miizh—to give something to someone

mikaw—to find someone

mikwendan—to remember something

minaanjige—to smell something

mindido—to be large

minikwaadan—to drink something

mino-ayaa—to be fine

mino-bimaadizi—to live a good life, be on a good path

mino-doodan—be good to something, responsible for something

mino-inendagwad—it is a good idea

minogwaan—rest well

Minowaki—Milwaukee, good land

minwaadizi—to be a good person

minwendaagozi—to be happy

minwendan—to like something

minwenim—to like someone

misan—firewood

misawaa—even though

misawendan—to want something

miskwiiwi—to bleed

mitigwaki—the dense forest

mooz(oog)—moose

moozhag—usually

moozhitoon—feel something

N

naa—emphasis

naagadawendan—contemplate something

naanan—five

naanimidana—fifty

naanogonagad—five days' time

naasaab—same

naawakwe—at noon

naazh—to fetch someone

nagadenim—to be familiar with someone, and the name of the chief of Waaban

nagamo—to sing

nagamootaw—sing to someone

nahaaw—okay, correct, amen

namadabi—to sit

Namebini-giizis—February, Moon of the Sucker Fish

nandagikendan—study, seek to understand something

nandawaabam—to search for someone

nandonjigaazo—to be invited, welcomed

nandoomaandan—to sniff something

nandotamaw—to request something for someone

nashke—hey!, look!

nayaazh—too long

nayendaagozi—to be comfortable

nazhikewizi—be alone

neyaab—go back

nibaa—to sleep

nibo—to die

nibwaachi—to visit someone

nibwaakaa—to be wise

niibin—summer

niigaanii—to lead or be in front

niijikiwenh—friend

niin—me

niinamizi—to be weak

niinawind—just us

niitaawis—my male cousin

niizh—two

niizhogon—two days' time

niizhwaaswi—seven

nindaanisinaan—our daughter

ninga—my mother

ningaabii'an—west

ningaapoono—gather and eat berries

ninzhisheh—my cross-uncle

nishkaadizi—to be angry

nishi—to kill someone

nishki'aa—to make someone angry

nisidotan—to understand something

nisogon—three days

niswi—three

nitaa—a prefix to say something was done well

nitaawigi—to grow up, become older

niwiiw—my wife

noogin—stop something by hand

noogishkaa—to stop moving

noondan—to hear something

noondaw—to hear someone

noongom—today, now

noos—my father

O

obikwaakoganaan—his/her ankle

odaapin—take someone, capture someone, take something animate

ode'imin(an)—strawberry(s)

oditin—grab and attack someone

odoozhiman—his nephew

ogimaa—leader or chief

ogitiziiman—his/her parent

ojibwe'inendan—to think in Ojibwemowin

ojibwemo—to speak Ojibwemowin

Ojibwemowin—one of several languages spoken by Anishinaabe people

Ojichaago—to have a soul

ozhichigaade—to be built

omaa—here

omakakiibag(oon)—plantain(s)

omisenyan—his female parallel cousin

omishoomeyan—uncle, father's brother

Onaabani-giizis—March, the Crust-on-the-Snow Moon

onaagoshi-miijin—to eat something for dinner

onaagoshin—evening

onaakonan—to decide about something

onasham—to command someone

onashkinade—it is loaded (a gun or weapon)

onashkinadoon—pack something

ondamitaa—to be busy

ondendi—stay away

ondinan—to get something from someplace

ongow—these animate ones

oninige—to put things in order

oninjimaan—his/her wrist

onjibaa—to come from a place

onishkaa—get up from laying down

onizhishin—it is good

onjine—something happens to someone as a response to something they did

onoshenyan—his aunt on his father's side

onowe—these (inanimate)

onzaam—too much

oodena—town, village

oshkaya'aawi—to be young

oshki—new, young

oshkinawe—a young man

ozhaashaagondibe—to have a bruised head

ozhibii'igaadeg—it is written

ozhitoon—to build something

S

Shkaakamigokwe—Mother Earth, woman who renews the land

W

waabam—to see someone

waabamojichaagwaan(an)—mirror(s)

waaban—east, tomorrow

waabandan—to see something

waabandaw—to show something to someone

waabanjigaazo—to be seen

waabishkiwi—to be white

waagosh(ag)—fox(es)

waasa—far away

waasezi—to be bright

Waatebagaa-giizis—September, Moon of Leaves Changing Color

wa'aw—this one (animate)

waawaabam—stare at someone

waawaabiganoojiinh(sag)—mouse(s)

waawaashkeshiwegin(oon)—deerhide(s)

wadikwan(an)—branches

wanendan—forget or ignore something

wani'—to notice the absence of someone

wanii'igewinini(wag)—trapper

waniikenindan—to forget something

wawiiyazh—funny

wayiiba—soon, early

wendaginzo—to be cheap

wenji—because, for a reason, from a place

weshki-ayaa(jig)—a youth

wewiib—hurry

wiidigem—to be married to someone

wiidookaw—to help or assist someone

wiidookawishin—asking others, "help me"

wiidosem—to walk with someone

wiigiwaam(an)—lodge(s)

wiiji-ayaaw—to be with someone

wiijiiw—go with someone

wiijiwaagan(ag)—a friend(s), ones who are together through life

wiindamaw—to tell someone something

wiindigoo—evil, greedy, cannibal

wiisagazii-maa'iingan(ag)—coyote

wiisagendam—to hurt someone mentally

wiisagibizh—to hurt someone physically

wiisagine—to be in pain

wiisaginoogane—to have a pain in the hip

wiisagishin—to be hurt

wiisini—to eat

Z

zaaga'igan(an)—lake(s)

zaagijiwebiniganiwi—to be banned or expelled

zaagiskwagizi—to bleed

zagawe'idigamig—meeting house, council house

zagime(g)—mosquito(s)

zanagad—difficult

zegaswe'idijig—council members, the ones who smoke together

zegi—to scare someone

zegindaagwad—it is scary

zegizi—to be afraid

zhaabiiwose—to walk through the water

zhaabwii—to survive

zhaabwizh—to rescue someone

Zhaaganaash—English

Zhaaganaashimong—in the English language

zhaaganaashiimotaw—speak English to someone

zhaagode'e—to be a coward

zhaagoozikaw—outrun someone

zhiibaa'aabanjige—to be focused, see a way through something

zhiigaa(g)—widow

zhiibaa'igan—passage between

zhiingenim—to hate someone

zhigwa—already, a while

zhigweyaabam—aim at someone

zhigweyaabi—take aim

zhingos(ag)—weasel(s)

zhingwaak(oog)—red pine(s)

zhoomaanike(g)—cents

zhoomiingweni—to smile

zhooniyaa—money

ziibi(wan)—river(s)

ziigwan—spring

ziinzibaakwadoons—candy

Character List

Aandeg (Crow) / Allen Crow—boy from Waaban

Ajijaak (Sandhill Crane) / Sally Crane—girl from Waaban, friend of Roger, born 1879

Bagakaabikwe—mother the boys meet in the woods

Bemised (One Who Flies)—a young man in Waaban

Bizaan (Peace)—sister of Boonikiiyaashikwe, wife of Migizi, mother of Niizh Eshkanag

Bizhiw (Lynx)—husband of Ziigwan, father of Esiban

Boonikiiyaashikwe (One Who Is Like The Land That Stops The Wind From Blowing)—sister of Bizaan, wife of Zhaabiiwose, mother of Giigoo

Esiban (Raccoon) / Billy Coon—son of Bizhiw and Ziigwan, born 1880

Gekendaasod (One Who Has Knowledge)—the spiritual leader of Waaban

Giigoo (Fish)—son of Boonikiiyaashikwe and Zhaabiiwose, born 1879

Ginoozhe (Pike)—boy from Ningaabii'an

Migizi (Eagle)—father of Niizh Eshkanag, husband of Bizaan

Nagamokwe (One Who Sings) / Mary Song—girl from Waaban, friend of Niizh Eshkanag

Nenaginad (One Who Prevents Others)—boy from Ningaabii'an

Nenookaasi (Hummingbird)—a young girl travelling with her parents in the woods

Netaawichiged (One Who Is Skilled)—Anishinaabe father the boys meet in the woods

Niizh Eshkanag (Two Horns) / Tom Horns—son of Bizaan and Migizi, born 1878

Ogimaa Negadenimad—(Chief Who Considers Others)—chief

Ogimaa Niigaan (Chief Who Leads)—chief of Ningaabii'an

Oninge (One Who Puts Things Together)—older boy from Waaban

Zhaabiiwose (One Who Walks Through Water)—father of Giigoo, husband of Boonikiiyaashikwe

Zhingos (Weasel)—older boy from Waaban

Ziigwan (Spring)—wife of Bizhiw, mother of Esiban

Beth Demski—sister of Susan, wife of Steve

Grandma Demski—mother of Steve

Steve Demski—husband of Beth

David Poznanski—Elias's brother, Susan's husband, Roger's father

Elias Poznanski—David's brother, Helen's husband, Donald and Karen's father, Roger's uncle

Karen Poznanski—daughter of Elias and Helen, Roger's cousin

Roger Poznanski / John Bemibatood (Runner)—son of David and Susan, nephew of Elias

Susan Poznanski—Beth's sister, David's wife, Roger's mother

Nurse Boude—nurse at Poleville Infirmary

Brady—trapper

Dan—trapper

Fred—runaway hunter

Miss Jacob—seventh grade teacher at Poleville Indian School (PIS)

Jake—a white settler in the Poleville area

Mr. Knitter—PIS worker

Joe Losset—principal at PIS

Mike Murphy—maintenance worker at PIS

Mrs. Murphy—cook at PIS

Dr. Norton—doctor in Poleville

Mrs. Norton—the doctor's wife

Paul—a white settler in the Poleville area

Emma Pierce—nurse at the Poleville Indian School (PIS)

Miss Purge—matron in the boys' dorm at PIS

Bill Stacy—family friend of the Poznanskis

Steve—runaway hunter

Historical Notes for Teachers

This story takes place between the spring of 1891, when school ends for the summer, and the fall of 1892, when school is about to begin again. Below are some events that relate to the story or are mentioned by the characters.

7000 BC—First human infections of tuberculosis, also known as consumption and the White Plague.

AD 1346—1353—The Black Plague, also known as the Black Death, or the Bubonic plague, was the most fatal pandemic on record and was spread between countries by fleas.

1800s—The author occasionally uses names of his own ancestors who lived in Anishinaabe communities that are now White Earth and Fond du Lac reservations. Both Zhaabiiwose and Boonikiiyaashikwe are actual relatives in Peter Razor's family.

1862—Dakota Conflict, also known as the Sioux Uprising, began at the Lower Sioux Agency along the Minnesota River.

1870s—Fishing families from the Kaszuby region on the Baltic seacoast began to settle on Jones Island in Milwaukee Bay of Lake Michigan. The islanders harvested two thousand tons in a good year, a mixed catch of trout, whitefish, perch, chubs, and sturgeon until the 1920s, when the city of Milwaukee took the land for harbor facilities and a sewage-treatment plant.[*]

1891—On March 3, 1891, Congress authorized the Commissioner of Indian Affairs to require Native children to attend boarding schools.

---

[*] John Gurda, "Introduction," *Milwaukee Polonia*, University of Wisconsin—Milwaukee Libraries, https://uwm.edu/mkepolonia/introduction/.